THE McELDERRY BOOK OF
AESOP'S FABLES

To Molly, her book, and her mum's, too.
—M. M.

For Rupert
—E. C. C.

Margaret K. McElderry Books
An imprint of Simon & Schuster Children's Publishing Division
1230 Avenue of the Americas, New York, New York 10020
Text copyright © 2004 by Michael Morpurgo
Illustrations copyright © 2004 by Emma Chichester Clark
First published in Great Britain in 2004 by Orchard Books, London,
as *The Orchard Book of Aesop's Fables*
First U.S. edition, 2005
The text for this book is set in Stempel Schneidler.
The illustrations are rendered in watercolors.
Manufactured in China
10 9
CIP data for this book is available from the Library of Congress.
ISBN 978-1-4169-0290-4

0 4 14 HCB

THE McELDERRY BOOK OF
Aesop's Fables

MICHAEL MORPURGO

Illustrations by EMMA CHICHESTER CLARK

Margaret K. McElderry Books   NEW YORK   LONDON   TORONTO   SYDNEY

CONTENTS

FOR MR. AESOP FROM MR. MORPURGO, A THANK-YOU

THERE WAS ONCE A LION who never hunted anymore because he was too old and too tired; who didn't roar anymore because he was too sad. So he spent all day and every day in his cave, feeling very old and very hungry. All the animals who passed by would stop and tease him. "Who's roaring now?" they'd chant.

One morning he woke up and saw a young man sitting and reading a book at the mouth of his cave.

"What are you reading?" asked Lion.

"Some stories," replied the young man. "I've just written a story about you, about an old lion who won't leave his cave because he feels he's too old. He feels he's not what he was, a bit slow, a bit stupid."

"What happens to him?" asked Lion.

"One day he meets a young man called Aesop, a storyteller, who comes to his cave and reads him all of the fables he has

6

written. And the lion loves the stories so much he wants to read them again himself."

"What happens next?" asked Lion.

"That's up to you," said Aesop. And leaving Lion the book, Aesop went on his way.

Sitting at the mouth of his cave the next morning, Lion roared and roared so loud that all the animals heard and came running to the cave at once.

"My friends," said Lion, "come into my cave and I will read you the best stories ever written." And they did. All the animals marveled at Lion and how clever he was.

This lion may be old and slow, *they thought,* but this lion is not stupid.

Story after story he read, and after each one he explained the moral of the story. All afternoon, all evening, all night he read, so that one by one the animals dropped off to sleep. By morning he'd finished all of Aesop's fables, and he'd also eaten up all of his sleeping listeners, too.

A STORY IS AS GOOD AS A FEAST.
BUT WATCH OUT YOU DON'T GO TO SLEEP!

THE LION
AND THE MOUSE

ONE HOT AFTERNOON, Lion lay snoozing happily in the shade of a tree. Suddenly he felt something running over his nose. He opened one eye and saw it was a tiny mouse. Furious at being woken, he waited his moment—then he flashed out his great paw and caught Mouse by the tail.

"Oh, please," squeaked Mouse, "I didn't mean to wake you. Let me go, please. I'll pay you back one day, I promise."

Lion roared with laughter, "You repay me? A little tiddly thing like you! How could such a puny creature be of any use to a king of the beasts like me?"

"Please, great King," cried Mouse, "don't eat me." Lion yawned and thought about it. He was too sleepy.

"Oh well. If you insist. After all, you wouldn't make much of a meal, would you? Off you go, and be careful whose nose you walk on in the future."

It was not long after that Mouse and Lion met again. This is how it happened. Lion had gone off hunting at dusk. He was stalking through the trees, following a herd of zebra, when he happened to spring a hunter's trap. A great net came down on him and held him fast. He roared and raged, but in spite of all his great strength, he could not break free. His roaring echoed through the forest so that everyone heard him and everyone knew that Lion was in trouble.

Mouse heard him too, and he was a mouse of his word. Off he went, as fast as his little legs would carry him, to see if he could help. It wasn't long before he came across Lion still caught up in the net, still roaring and raging. "Don't worry," said Mouse. "I'll soon have you out of that." And he began to gnaw at the net ropes one by one, until at last Lion could break free.

"There you are," said Mouse. "I told you I'd pay you back, didn't I?"

"A little tiddly thing like you helping out a king of the beasts like me," Lion replied. "Who'd have thought it possible?"

"Everything is possible," said Mouse. "Good-bye, Lion." And off he scampered, away into the long grass.

KINDNESS IS MORE IMPORTANT
THAN STRENGTH.

THE HARE
AND THE TORTOISE

ONE DAY IN MARCH, after a morning of carefree cavorting and capering with her friends on the hillside, Hare was haring her way home along a path when she came across Tortoise. Tortoise was going the same way but slowly, very slowly, as tortoises do. Hare stopped to tease him, "Can't you go a little faster? I mean, how do you ever arrive?"

"Oh, I arrive," said Tortoise very politely. "I always arrive—and sooner rather than later. Maybe sooner than you imagine."

"True," said Fox, who was passing by. "I'm telling you, as tortoises go, this is a very speedy tortoise."

"Speedy tortoise!" scoffed Hare. "No such thing."

"Listen, Hare," said Tortoise, losing his patience a little. "I get where I want fast enough, thank you. I'll prove it if you like. How about a race? You and me. The first one to the river is the winner."

Hare leaped with laughter (keeping her distance from Fox, of course). "A race! You and me? No problem. I'll beat you easy-peasy. You won't see me for dust. You set us off, Fox. I'm ready." And Fox agreed.

"Ready, steady, go!" Fox called out. And off they went, Hare as fast as the wind, and Tortoise . . . well, Tortoise as slow as a tortoise.

But Hare raced away and was very soon out of sight. So when she next looked behind her, Tortoise was nowhere to be seen. Hare thought to herself, *There's no point in showing off if no one's watching. I'll just lie down here in the sun and have a nap and wait until Tortoise comes. No worries.* And before she knew it, she was very fast asleep.

Meanwhile, Tortoise just kept plodding on, slowly, steadily, until at last he came to where Hare lay sleeping on the grass. And he thought to himself with a smile, *Hare looks tired out with all that running, poor old thing. Best not to wake her.*

On Tortoise went, slowly, steadily, up the hills and down the dales toward the river.

Just then a fly landed on Hare's nose. She woke with a start and at once remembered the race. She hared over the fields as fast as she could go. But it was too late. By the time she reached the riverbank, Tortoise was already drinking. "What kept you, Hare?" he asked. But Hare walked off in a huff, far too angry with herself to reply. And Fox laughed himself silly all the way home.

SPEED ISN'T EVERYTHING.
THERE ARE OTHER WAYS OF WINNING.

THE DOG
AND HIS BONE

A DOG WAS WAITING outside the butcher's shop one day, as he often did, looking as hangdog and sad as he could. As usual the butcher soon saw him, took pity on him, and threw him a bone. Off the dog trotted, happy as could be, his tail wagging as he went, thinking of where he would bury the bone and how good it would taste after a week or two.

As he neared his home, he had to cross a little footbridge over a stream. He was padding across when he stopped to look down at the water because he was rather thirsty.

He was trying to work out how he could keep hold of the bone in his mouth and have a drink at the same time, when he noticed another dog gazing back up at him out of the water—a bigger dog who had a much bigger bone in his mouth than he had.

That's not fair, he thought. *His bone's bigger than*

mine, and I want it. With that he jumped into the river and made a grab for the other dog's bone. But to do that, he had to drop his own first.

Only then, as he saw his bone sinking to the bottom of the river, did he realize the mistake he had made, how silly he had been. There had been no other dog, no other bone—only his own reflection in the water.

He clambered out of the river, shook himself dry, and walked off home, his tail between his legs, feeling very stupid and very annoyed with himself.

ENOUGH IS AS GOOD AS A FEAST.
DON'T BE GREEDY.

THE CROW AND THE JUG

IT WAS BONE-DRY IN THE COUNTRYSIDE. There had been no rain for weeks on end now. For all the animals and birds it had been a terrible time. To find even a drop of water to drink was almost impossible for them.

But the crow, being the cleverest of birds, always managed to find just enough water to keep himself alive.

One morning, as he flew over a cottage, he saw a jug standing nearby. The crow knew, of course, that jugs were for water, and as he flew down, he could smell the water inside. He landed and hopped closer to have a look.

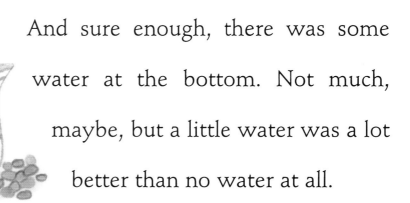

And sure enough, there was some water at the bottom. Not much, maybe, but a little water was a lot better than no water at all.

The crow stuck his head into the jug to drink; but his beak, long though it was, would not reach far enough down, no matter how hard he pushed. He tried and he tried, but it was no good. However, he knew that one way or another he had to drink that water. He stood there by the jug, wondering what he was going to do. Then he saw pebbles lying on the ground nearby, and that gave him a brilliant idea.

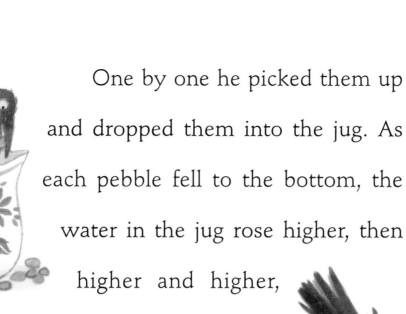

One by one he picked them up and dropped them into the jug. As each pebble fell to the bottom, the water in the jug rose higher, then higher and higher, until the crow had dropped so many pebbles in that the water was overflowing. Now he could drink and drink his fill. *What a clever crow,* he thought as he drank. *What a clever crow.*

WHERE THERE'S A WILL, THERE'S A WAY.
BUT IT HELPS IF YOU USE YOUR BRAIN.

BELLING THE CAT

SOMETHING HAD TO BE DONE. The farm cat, with his sharp eyes and his sharp claws, had killed off so many mice that those who were left held a crisis meeting to see what, if anything, could be done to stop him.

They were all very upset, of course. "Kill him!" they cried. "Squash him!" "Pull out his claws!"

Finally the chief mouse, who was the oldest mouse too, had had enough. He called the meeting to order. "Fellow mice, let us be sensible. *We* can't kill him, or squash him, or pull out his claws," he said.

"He's too strong, too big, too cunning. Wherever we go, he's always waiting to pounce—that's our problem. Now, if we knew where he was, then he couldn't creep up on us like he does and surprise us."

But try as they did, none of the mice could come up with a plan that would really work . . . until one bright, young mouse had a great idea. "Why don't we . . ." he began, "why don't we wait till the cat's fast asleep? Then we could sneak up on him and tie a bell round his neck. That way we'll always hear him coming and we can run off before he catches us. Am I brilliant or what?"

"Yes!" they all cried. "Brilliant!"

"That mouse is a genius!"

"Let's do it! Let's do it!"

When they had all calmed down a little, the chief mouse said, "That sounds like a fine plan, but there's just one little thing that worries me. Which of you will put the bell around the cat's neck?"

At this there was a long silence, as everyone looked at everyone else. "Pity," said the chief mouse. "We'll have to think again, won't we?"

SAYING SOMETHING SHOULD BE DONE
IS ONE THING. DOING IT IS
OFTEN ALTOGETHER MORE DIFFICULT.

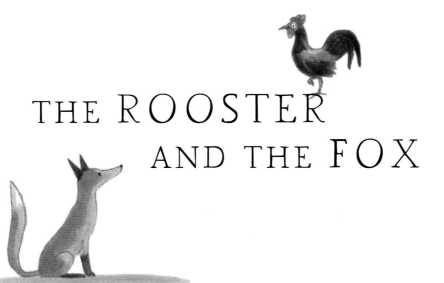

THE ROOSTER
AND THE FOX

IT WAS A LOVELY SUMMER'S EVENING with the setting sun glowing gold in the west. For the rooster it was time to roost. So he flew up into his roosting tree, alongside his hens, and crowed at the sunset as he always did. It was his way of saying, "Good night, my hens. Sleep well. Don't worry. I'm here to look after you."

He was just about to tuck his head under his wing and go to sleep, when he noticed a fox trotting through the grass below him. The fox lifted his nose and saw the rooster and his hens. He licked his lips.

"Have you heard the good news, friend?" said the fox.

"What good news?" replied the rooster, a little suspicious.

"It's peace. It's peace at last. All the animals have agreed never to chase each other or eat each other again. We can all be friends. Isn't that wonderful?"

"If you say so," said the rooster, but he was even more suspicious now.

"It's the happiest day of my life," the fox went on. "I want to hug everyone. Come down, why don't you? Let's celebrate our new friendship."

The rooster thought for a while. "If what you say is true," he said, "then it's the happiest day of my life too, and . . ." He stretched his neck and looked into the distance. "I can't be sure," he went on, "but I think I see a couple of dogs coming this way, hard on your scent. They must have heard the good news too."

In an instant the fox was off and running.

"What's up?" the rooster crowed after him. "I thought us animals were all friends now."

"Maybe," replied the fox. "Or maybe they haven't heard about it. I'm not going to hang around to find out." And he was gone, through the hedge and away.

The hens clucked and preened themselves. "How clever you are!" they cried.

"Yes I am, my hens," said the rooster. "Cleverer than that crafty old fox, anyway." And he tucked his head under his wing and slept as the last of the sun left the sky.

DON'T BELIEVE EVERYTHING YOU HEAR,
EVEN IF YOU WANT TO BELIEVE IT.

THE TRAVELERS
AND THE BEAR

ONE SUMMER EVENING LATE, two travelers, an older one and a younger one, were walking through a forest. All of a sudden they heard below them a great crashing and a terrible roaring.

A huge black bear came lumbering out of the forest. One look was enough. They both ran for their lives. But the bear was running faster than they were. He was catching up to them all the time.

"Hide!" cried the older traveler. "We must find somewhere to hide."

But they were out of the forest by now and there was nowhere to hide. Suddenly the younger traveler saw his chance of escape, a single tree by the side of the road. "I'm climbing that tree," he cried.

Quick as a flash, he shimmied up the tree to safety. But there was no time for his friend to climb up after him, and the bear was coming closer and closer and closer. . . .

Then the older one had a sudden idea. He remembered

hearing once that a bear is not interested in eating dead bodies. He would pretend to be dead! He lay down on the path and stayed quite still, not even breathing.

From the safety of his tree the younger traveler looked on in horror as the bear pawed his friend's stiff body and sniffed and snuffled at his head.

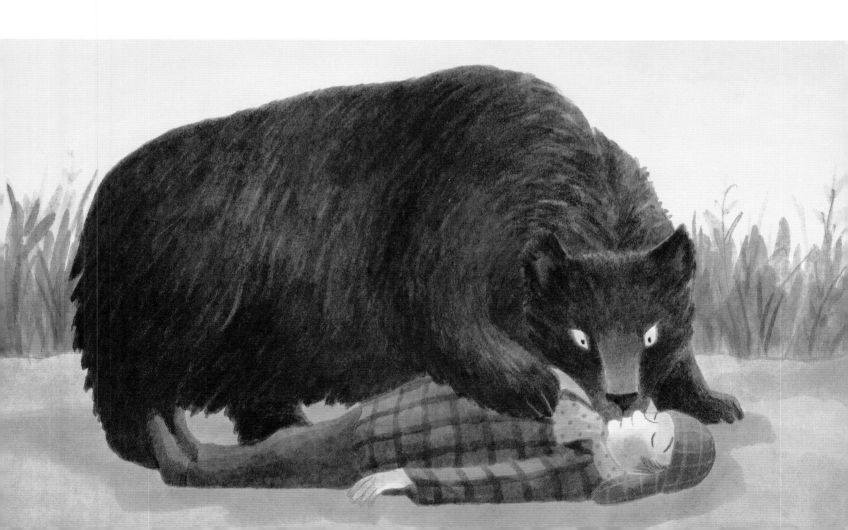

After a while the bear had had enough. He gave him one last lick on his ear and his neck and then just walked off. The younger traveler waited for a while to be sure that the bear wasn't coming back, then climbed down the tree and ran to his friend.

"Are you all right?" he cried.

"Fine," said his friend, sitting up.

"I thought you were done for, I really did," said the younger traveler.

"Me too," replied the older one.

"It was funny," said the younger traveler, helping his friend to his feet, "but when the bear was sniffing you, it looked almost as if he were whispering to you."

"He was," replied the older traveler. "He told me I should pick my friends better. That anyone who saves himself first and then abandons you to your fate can't be much of a friend."

FAIRWEATHER FRIENDS
AREN'T WORTH HAVING.

THE WIND
AND THE SUN

THE WIND AND THE SUN were always squabbling.
"I can outshine you," said Sun.

"I can outblow you," said Wind. Then a shepherd
passed by, wrapped up against the cold in a great cloak.

"All right," said Sun, "let's settle this once and for
all. Whichever of us can somehow part this shepherd
from his cloak is the stronger. Agreed?"

"Easy," said Wind. "Watch this." He took a deep
breath and blew with all his might. The shepherd felt
his cloak whipping about him and just pulled it tighter.

The more Wind blew, the tighter the shepherd clung on to his cloak because he wanted to keep warm and did not want to lose it. No matter how hard Wind blew, he could not part the shepherd from his cloak.

"My turn," said Sun. "Watch this." And with that she shone down on the shepherd with all her might. Feeling the sudden warmth, the shepherd loosened his cloak. As he walked on, he became hotter and hotter under the burning sun. "I can't go on in this heat," he said. So he threw his cloak aside and sat down in the shade of a spreading oak tree.

"Well?" said Sun, smiling.

"Poof!" snorted Wind.

"Phew!" said the shepherd. "It's a glorious summer's day!"

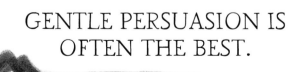
GENTLE PERSUASION IS
OFTEN THE BEST.

THE LION
AND THE FOX

THERE ONCE LIVED A VERY OLD LION, so old that his teeth and claws were worn down and blunt with age, and so slow he could no longer chase his prey. So he worked out a cunning plan. Instead of hunting his prey as he had before, he would invite his prey to come to him.

This is how he did it.

He told all the animals who passed by his cave that he was sick and likely to die soon, and he'd just like someone to talk to. Several of them, the most foolish, came to visit him, believing themselves to be quite safe.

And of course, he gobbled them up.

One day a fox came along, a wily fox. He kept a
safe distance from the cave. "I heard you were sick,"
he said. "What's the matter?"

"Come a little closer," said the lion, "and I'll tell you.
I'm so weak these days I can only talk in a whisper."

But the fox was not stupid. "I think I'll stay where I am," he said. "You see, I've noticed that there are dozens of footprints going into your cave, and strangely enough there are none coming out. I wonder why that is?"

LEARN THE IMPORTANT LESSONS OF LIFE
FROM THE MISTAKES OF OTHERS.

THE GOOSE
THAT LAID THE GOLDEN EGG

THERE WAS ONCE A YOUNG FARMER who had only one dream—he wanted to get as rich as he could, as quickly as he could. One morning he went out as usual to fetch an egg from his goose for breakfast. He reached in under her warm, soft feathers and found, as he had hoped, one huge egg. But when he looked at it, he was amazed.

This was no ordinary white goose egg. It was

gold and shining in the sun, and it was so

heavy he almost dropped it. It

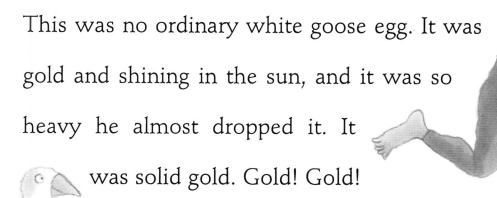

was solid gold. Gold! Gold!

The young farmer could not

believe his luck. His dream had come

true. Every day his wonderful goose

laid another golden egg, and every day he became

richer. But the young farmer was a man in a hurry. For

him, one golden goose egg a day was not

enough. *I'm getting rich,* he thought,

but I'm not getting rich

quickly enough. All

she can lay me is one

golden egg a day.

"I know what I'll do. I'll kill her," said the young farmer suddenly. "There's bound to be dozens of golden eggs inside her. That way I'll get really rich, and quickly, too."

So he took his goose by the neck and killed her. And what did he discover? There wasn't a single golden egg inside her, not one. "What have I done?" he cried. "Now she is dead and won't lay me any more golden eggs. I am ruined! Ruined! Ruined!"

BE HAPPY WITH WHAT YOU'VE GOT,
AND LOOK AFTER IT.

THE RAT AND THE ELEPHANT

THERE ONCE WAS A LITTLE RAT who was very proud of himself. To be honest, he did not have that much to be proud of at all, because he was a rat—and we all know what rats are like.

Anyway, one day this proud little rat was scurrying along from one farm to another, looking for more grain to steal, when he saw a huge procession coming up the road. There were trumpets sounding, drums beating, cymbals clashing. The rat knew very well who this must be.

It was the king and all his retinue of courtiers. He could see the king now, riding high on a huge elephant. The elephant was adorned with glowing gold and glittering jewels. And with the king, high in his royal howdah, were the king's dog and the king's cat. Dozens of people stood at the roadside in awe of the sumptuous beauty of the king's elephant, gasping in admiration as he passed by.

As the rat came closer, no one in the crowd even noticed he was there, so entranced were they by the magnificence and splendor of the king's elephant. The rat was most upset. If there was one thing he hated, it was being ignored. His pride was hurt.

"Nincompoops!" he cried. "You're a bunch of ignorant nincompoops. What is the matter with you?

Is it because the king's elephant is so big and lumpy and clumsy that you admire him so? Or is it because of his plodding feet, or his weepy eyes, or his wrinkly old hide? Look at me! I've got four legs like him, haven't I, two ears, two eyes? So I'm just as important as he is, aren't I? Look at *me!*"

Just then the king's cat did look at him. And he did

not like rats, not one bit. He sprang down off the howdah and was after the rat, chasing him along the ditch until . . . Well, I won't tell you what happened. You'll just have to imagine it. One thing's for sure though—the proud little rat found out he was *not* quite as important as he thought he was.

THINKING YOURSELF IMPORTANT
IS NOT THE SAME THING
AS BEING IMPORTANT.

THE HERON
AND THE FISH

ONE DAY A HERON was out fishing in his favorite stretch of river. He stood there still as a statue, his long, sharp bill ready to stab a tasty fish. All around his legs the fish swarmed, not even noticing him. The heron waited and waited.

"These fish aren't big enough for me," he said. "I'll wait until a big one comes along." So he waited and waited, and still there were plenty of fish—but always too small. *I don't want a snack.*

I want a proper meal, thought the heron. So he waited even longer.

Suddenly all the fish left the shallows and moved away, out into the deep water in the middle of the river. Now there were no fish for the heron to catch, not even small ones.

"Drat!" he said to himself. "I shouldn't have waited so long." And all he had for his breakfast was snail—a tiny green snail.

TAKE WHAT COMES TO YOU.
DON'T BE PICKY.

THE DOG
IN THE MANGER

THERE ONCE WAS A LAZY, OLD FARM DOG who loved to sleep. And his favorite place to sleep was in the cow barn, in a manger full of soft hay. One evening he was snoozing away happily in the manger when the cows came in. They'd been working all day out in the fields, pulling the plow, and were very tired and hungry.

"Do you mind?" they said quite politely. "But you're lying on our hay. We're rather hungry and we'd very much like to eat it."

"I don't care how hungry you are," barked the dog. "I'm not moving." And he snarled and growled at them so fiercely that they dared not come closer.

"Look," said one of the cows, "you eat meat, don't you? This is hay. We eat hay and we're hungry."

Just then the farmer came in. "You stupid mutt, you!" he cried, and he drove the dog out of the barn, out into the cold, just to teach him a lesson.

IF IT'S NO USE TO YOU,
THEN LET SOMEONE ELSE HAVE IT.

THE MILLER, HIS SON, AND THE DONKEY

ONE MORNING AN OLD MILLER and his son set out for market. With them went their donkey, which they were hoping to sell that day. They went along slowly, driving the donkey instead of riding her, because the miller and his son knew they'd have a much better chance of selling her if she didn't look too tired.

But as they went on their way, they met up with some friends, who laughed at them as they went by. "Will you look at that? Why are you walking when one of you could perfectly well ride? How stupid can you get?"

The miller was a proud man and did not like to be laughed at.

"All right," he told his son, "you ride and I'll walk."

So his son climbed up on the donkey, and off they went again.

They hadn't gone far when they came upon some travelers resting by the side of the road. "Will you look at that!" they cried. "A young man like you riding, while your poor, old father walks. Disgraceful! Have you no respect? Get down, young fellow, and let the old man ride."

The miller hated arguments of any kind. "Good idea," he said. "Get down, son, and let me ride."

And so they went on their way to market.

As they neared town, they passed by some women washing clothes in a stream. "Will you look at that!" they cried. "That poor boy has to walk while that old fellow has a nice, easy ride. Shame on you, old man.

You should let him ride up with you."

"If you say so," sighed the miller, not wanting to upset them. "Up you get, son. We'll ride together."

So now as they came into town, they were both riding together on the donkey, who was looking rather tired and fed up by this time.

The moment the market traders saw them coming,

they ran out to protest. "Will you look at that!" they cried. "You should be ashamed of yourselves, loading up a poor old donkey like that. She's tired out, poor old thing. Both of you look pretty strong and fit. Instead of just sitting there, weighing her down, you should get off and carry her."

"I hadn't thought of that," said the miller. "We'll give it a try."

They tied the donkey's feet to a pole, hoisted her up, and off they went, carrying the donkey between them, slung on the pole. When the townsfolk saw them, they laughed and guffawed and jeered.

The donkey did not like being carried at all, and she didn't like being laughed at either. So she began to struggle and kick and bray. "Hee-haw! Hee-haw!" She kicked so hard the pole snapped and the ropes broke. Once free and back on her feet, she ran off into the crowd and escaped.

No matter how hard the old miller and his son looked

for the donkey, they never found her again. So in the

end they went back home feeling very stupid, for they

had lost their donkey as well as their dignity.

IF YOU TRY TO PLEASE EVERYONE,
YOU END UP PLEASING NO ONE.

THE OAK TREE
AND THE RIVER REEDS

THERE ONCE STOOD A GIANT OAK TREE, its great branches shading the silver river beneath it. Along the river's edge was a bank of reeds. Whenever the wind blew, the reeds hung their heads and sang a sad song. The giant oak tree felt sorry for them.

"I am so lucky," he said. "When the wind blows, I just rustle my leaves and sing a happy tune. I know no storm could ever bend me as it bends you."

Just then the reeds began to tremble. A storm was coming in from the north. By nightfall the storm had become a raging hurricane. The great oak was not afraid. He stood strong against it. Below, the reeds were bent almost to the ground. Soon the ground was soaked with rain, and the roots of the great oak tree began to loosen. His leaves became wet and heavy. Still he did not bend. Then there was one mighty gust of wind. Up came the roots and over went the great oak tree, crashing down into the river.

When the storm had passed, the reeds were still there singing their sad song—a lament for the great oak tree, who lay like a fallen warrior, his battle lost.

OBSTINACY MAY LOOK LIKE STRENGTH.
IT RARELY IS.

THE FOX AND THE CROW

Out hunting one morning, Fox lifted his nose in the air and smelled something he liked, something he liked a lot. "Cheese," he said, and licked his lips. And off he went, following where his nose led him.

Suddenly he saw just what he was looking for. There was Crow sitting on the branch of an old oak tree, and in her beak was a great chunk of cheese.

Delicious, thought Fox, his mouth watering. *And just perfect for my breakfast. But how do I get it?* And then he had an idea.

"Good morning, Crow," he said. "You beautiful, gorgeous creature."

But Crow wasn't that stupid. She knew what Fox was up to. She wouldn't say a word. She would keep her cheese clamped securely in her beak. She knew the game.

Fox just sat there gazing up at her. "I have never in all my life set eyes on such a bird as you. Beside you, a peacock looks like a sparrow. You are indeed a bird of paradise. The gloss of your feathers, your delicate head, your charming eyes, your pretty little feet. Perfect in every detail. A veritable wonder of creation."

Crow was listening to this from high on her branch and loving every word she was hearing.

"Though I wonder," Fox said. "Can any creature be that wonderful? If you could sing beautifully too, then you would indeed be the queen of all the birds. But . . ." he went on, "it's too much to hope for. Not even you could be that perfect."

Oh no? thought Crow. *I'll show you, Fox. I'll show you how beautifully I can sing. Listen to this.* And she opened her beak to sing.

Crows can't sing, of course, but they can caw and they can croak. As she cawed and she croaked, the cheese fell out of her beak and down, straight into Fox's waiting mouth. Fox caught it and swallowed it up at once.

Licking his lips afterward, Fox smiled upward at Crow, who was hopping up and down on her branch in fury. "Cool it, Crow," Fox said. "Ugly you can't help. But how did you get to be that stupid?" And off he trotted to look for another breakfast, because for a fox two breakfasts are always better than one.

LOOK OUT FOR FLATTERERS.
THEY MAY MAKE YOU FEEL GOOD, BUT
THEY'LL TAKE EVERYTHING YOU'VE GOT.

THE WOLF
AND THE DONKEY

A DONKEY WAS GRAZING AWAY HAPPILY by the edge of a wood one day, when she saw a wolf skulking through the trees like a shadow. It was too late to run away; the donkey knew that. She knew that she would have to use her wits if she wanted to save herself. So as she grazed, she began to limp, hobbling along and pretending that she was in the most dreadful pain.

The wolf was in no hurry and, being the inquisitive type, he wanted to know what the matter was. "How very kind of you to ask," replied the donkey.

"I've got this blackthorn in my hoof and I can't get it out. You wouldn't get it out, would you? I'd be most obliged. I know you're going to kill me, and I really wouldn't want you to choke on it when you eat me up."

"That's thoughtful of you," said the wolf. "Tell you what. You lift up your hoof and I'll pull it out. No trouble." And the wolf came close and lay down right behind the donkey's back feet. The donkey lifted her hoof and then lashed out behind herself, sending the wolf flying.

Before the wolf could get up again, the donkey had made her escape and was nowhere to be seen.

"What a nitwit I am," said the wolf, nursing his bruises. "What was I thinking? I'm not a doctor—I'm a hunter. And in the future I'd better remember it."

STICK TO WHAT YOU KNOW,
AND BE TRUE TO YOURSELF.

THE SHEEP
AND THE PIG

ONE DAY AS THE SHEEP WERE GRAZING contentedly in their meadow, a pig wandered in and began to graze with them. The shepherd, half-asleep nearby, suddenly heard a great grunting and a snuffling and a snorting. *I like a nice piece of pork,* he thought. *I'll take you off to the butcher's shop. But first I've got to catch you.* Quick as you like, he was on his feet and chasing after the pig. The poor pig gave him a bit of a runaround, but in the end the shepherd cornered her and grabbed her. Then, tucking the pig under his arm, he set off toward the town.

The pig wasn't grunting or snorting now. She was squealing and squeaking and struggling to escape. The sheep followed along after them, at first just puzzled at this noise and fuss, then quite upset by all the squealing.

"There's no need to make such a terrible din," said one of the sheep. "He's always catching us and carrying us off. We'd never make such a great hullabaloo. You are a crybaby."

"Crybaby?" cried the pig, still squealing, still kicking. "Hullabaloo? Listen, maybe when he catches you, he doesn't hurt you. After all, when he catches you, all he wants is the wool off your back. With me it's a little different if you think about it. He wants my pork—he wants my bacon. So I've plenty to squeal about, haven't I?"

BEING BRAVE WHEN THERE'S NO DANGER
IS NOT BEING BRAVE AT ALL.

THE PEACOCK
AND THE CRANE

THERE ONCE WAS A PEACOCK who thought of little else but his own beauty. Whenever the sun shone, the peacock would spread his wonderful tail feathers and strut about the place, simply showing himself off.

One day a crane landed nearby to hunt for frogs. The peacock strutted back and forth and screeched at the crane to look at him—but the crane was far too busy hunting frogs. The peacock became angrier and angrier.

"Hey, Crane! Take a look at me. Did you ever see anything so beautiful?"

The crane ignored him and just went on with his hunting. This made the peacock really mad.

"What's it like to be so ugly, Crane?" he cried. "To have a beak too big for your head, to be all lanky and spindly, and to have such dull gray feathers."

At this moment the crane caught a frog, swallowed it, and at once flew off, circling above the peacock. "Who cares what I look like?" he called. "At least I can fly. You can't!" And away he flew, leaving the peacock feeling very silly indeed.

JUST LOOKING GOOD
GETS YOU NOWHERE.

THE TOWN MOUSE
AND THE COUNTRY MOUSE

TOWN MOUSE DECIDED ONE DAY that he would visit his cousin who lived way out in the countryside. Country Mouse greeted him warmly and sat him down to a great feast of corn and hazelnuts and berries. "Help yourself," she said. "You've come a long way and must be very hungry."

Town Mouse didn't much like this plain country food. But he did not want to upset Country Mouse, so he nibbled a little bit here and a little bit there and said how nice it was.

After lunch Country Mouse proudly showed Town Mouse over the fields and woods around her home. Town Mouse  thought it very dull and ordinary. But he did not say so. Instead he talked all the while about how much fun it was to live in the town, how exciting it was, and how you could eat any food you wanted. As he talked, Country Mouse listened, thinking to herself how wonderful it must be to live in the town.

All night long as they slept in her snug little nest in the hedgerow, Country Mouse dreamed of life in the big town.

Next morning, Town Mouse was still bragging about how much better it was to live in the town. "You should come home with me," he said. "I'll show you things you never even dreamed of." But Country Mouse *had* dreamed of them, and she wanted to find out if her dreams were true. "I'll come," she said. And off they went to town that very day.

At first it was even better than how Country Mouse had dreamed. Town Mouse clearly lived in great style, exactly as he had said.

When they arrived at Town Mouse's house, lunch had just finished and there were plenty of leftovers on the table—lots of scrumptious cheese and yummy cakes and succulent jellies. "Help yourself," said Town Mouse.

Country Mouse thought she had come to Mouse Heaven. "This is the life for me," she said.

But just as she said this, the house cat sprang up onto the table and came skittering after them. In and out of the dishes they went, the cat close behind. "Follow me!" cried Town Mouse as they ran for their lives. And they only just made it too, darting down the tablecloth and running helter-skelter across the carpet toward the mouse house in the baseboard.

It was some time before even Town Mouse dared to venture out of the hole again. Still, Country Mouse did not want to leave. She was terrified. "It'll be fine now," said Town Mouse. "The cat's gone. Don't worry." So Country Mouse followed Town Mouse across the carpet, hoping against hope that he was right, that the cat would not be waiting to pounce on them again.

The cat didn't come back . . . but the dog did. He came bounding after them, hackles up, barking his head off, sending them both scampering back to their hole for safety.

He frightened them both so much that neither dared to come out again until the following morning.

"That's it," said Country Mouse, "I'm off. You may have all the goodies a mouse could ever want in your town house, but I'm going back to the country for the quiet life."

BETTER TO BE HAPPY WITH
WHAT YOU NEED THAN RISK
EVERYTHING FOR MORE.

THE WOLF AND THE SHEPHERD'S SON

THE SHEPHERD thought his son was old enough now to guard sheep all by himself. So one morning he sent his son off with the flock into the hills. "What if a wolf comes along?" the boy asked.

"Just give us a shout," his father replied, "and we'll come and frighten him off."

Day after day the shepherd's son watched over his father's sheep. The days were hot and long. Nothing ever seemed to happen, and the boy became very

bored and fed up. So he thought he'd make something happen—just for fun.

Leaving his sheep, he ran over the hill, waving his arms and shouting as loud as he could, "Wolf! Wolf!"

Just as he had hoped, all the villagers, his father among them, stopped everything they were doing and

came running with their sticks to drive away the wolf.

But of course, as they soon discovered, there *was* no wolf.

"Fooled you! Fooled you!" laughed the shepherd's son. But neither his father nor the villagers thought it was funny at all.

Some days later, the shepherd's son played the same trick again.

"Wolf! Wolf!" he cried at the top of his voice, and again all the villagers came running. "Fooled you! Fooled you!" he laughed. But no one else was laughing, and his father was very angry indeed.

The next day, as the shepherd's son sat watching his sheep, he really did see a wolf slinking toward the sheep through the long grass. He leaped to his feet at once and ran over the hill, shouting as loud as he could, "Wolf! Wolf!"

But neither his father nor the villagers came, because none of them believed him, not this time.

"He tricked us once, he tricked us twice," his father said. "He'll not trick us a third time. There is no wolf. He's just playing games."

"Help, Father, please help!" cried the shepherd's son as the wolf came slinking closer. "There really *is* a wolf!" But no one would listen to him.

Meanwhile, the wolf attacked the flock and killed all the sheep he could—and the shepherd's son, too.

NO ONE BELIEVES A LIAR,
EVEN WHEN HE IS TELLING THE TRUTH.

Talent Management

Strategies for Success from Six Leading Companies

Talent Management

Strategies for Success from Six Leading Companies

Larry Israelite, Editor

ASTD Press is an internationally renowned source of insightful and practical information on workplace learning and performance topics, including training basics, evaluation and return-on-investment, instructional systems development, e-learning, leadership, and career development.

Ordering information: Books published by ASTD Press can be purchased by visiting ASTD's website at store.astd.org or by calling 800.628.2783 or 703.683.8100.

Library of Congress Control Number: 2009920427

ISBN-10: 1-56286-677-X
ISBN-13: 978-1-56286-677-8

ASTD Press Editorial Staff:
Director: Dean Smith
Editorial Manager: Jacqueline Edlund-Braun
Senior Associate Editor: Tora Estep
Editorial Assistant: Victoria DeVaux
Copyeditor: Alfred Imhoff
Indexer: April Davis
Proofreader: Kris Patenaude
Interior Design and Production: PerfecType, Nashville, TN
Cover Design: Ana Ilieva Foreman
Printed by United Book Press, Inc., Baltimore, Maryland

Contents

Preface and Acknowledgments

It was with some trepidation that I invited people to contribute to this book, because the track record of companies that have been held out as exemplars of best management practices is not what one might like it to be. The challenge, of course, is that times change—as do the economy, technology, natural resources, and the public's taste. What was popular one year may be less so the next. What once worked may not work as well now. And finally, what the employees of one generation may have wanted from their employers is, arguably, different from what those who follow them want. So, I suppose, it is not all that surprising that the results of a search for excellence or an analysis of what it takes to move from good to great might differ from decade to decade, if not year to year.

Yet the good news is that I am making no claims whatsoever that what is presented here represents "best practices in talent management." That would be presumptuous at best and, based on the history of this sort of thing, potentially dangerous. Rather, the authors who have generously contributed chapters to this book describe those talent management practices that have worked for them in their organizations. No one is claiming that what worked for them will work for you—though all who have contributed, I expect, believe that their firm's talent management practices do contain some universal truths about how to manage talent so that its value is maximized. But all such things are local. The talent management practices described here comprise a combination of philosophies, tools, processes, and systems that have resulted in tangible benefits for those who have used them—more capable managers, a deeper bench, increased employee engagement, and, one hopes, better business results. So we know that, at some level, they work. The trick is to figure out how and why.

Given this book's subject, one could reasonably expect that each chapter would be roughly the same, with the major difference being the business context in which the talent is being managed. After all, how much different could talent management practices be from company to company? The answer to this question, as you will see, is that these practices do have some common names, but how they are used from organization to organization can differ quite a bit.

These differences among how the six companies that are profiled in this book manage their talent is what I hope will make the book interesting for you. Some of the companies are large, and some are smaller; most are in business to make a profit (and proud of it), but one is not. From an industry perspective, they cover high technology, food services, health care, consumer products, and financial services. Some have specific internal organizations that focus on talent management, and others do not. Today, all these companies are considered successful, though, as we know all too well, success can be fleeting. But in its own way, each firm has decided that a comprehensive approach to managing talent is a worthwhile endeavor. And in all cases, they would claim that some portion of their success can be attributed to the investments they have made in it.

In addition to giving the stories of practitioners, I have attempted to provide some context for the talent management story. In chapters written by an analyst, an experienced observer, and the CEO of a software company, you will find the opportunity to look at talent management challenges from a variety of perspectives. This is not to say that one is better than the other—just perhaps a little different.

So have a look, be open to new ideas, think about some things you haven't thought about before, find some tool or technique that might be helpful to you, or just enjoy your reading. I hope you will find something useful in these pages and that something you read here might enable you to make your way through the maze of talent management with a little less resistance and fewer wrong turns. If this book helps you to do that, then we will have created something of value—and that, in the end, is all we could hope for.

Finally, I had a very interesting experience as I was doing my job as editor of this volume. As I read through the first drafts of each chapter, I forgot my role. I ceased being the editor and instead became an eager reader, trying to figure out how I could take the talent management practices each author describes and apply them to my work at the Liberty Mutual Group. I learned a great deal during the editing process, and I can say with absolute certainty that I plan to steal shamelessly from what I have read. I hope you have the same experience.

As much as we editors want to believe that we are the stars of the show, deep in our hearts, we know the truth. So I would be remiss if I did not recognize and thank the people who made this project possible:

- The nine talent management professionals who gave generously of their knowledge, expertise, experience, and time as their chapters moved through the various stages of development and production. I am truly grateful to them for their contributions and greatly admire the work they do each and every day.

- Everyone at the Liberty Mutual Group who chose to make the management of talent such an important part of the company's business strategy and who gave me an entirely new perspective on what it means to manage talent well.

- ASTD, for giving me the opportunity to embark on this journey.

- And, of course, to Wendy and the boys, who know how I feel and, I hope, understand how much of what I am I owe to them.

Larry Israelite
November 2009

Thinking about Talent

Larry Israelite, Vice President of Human Resource Development, Liberty Mutual Group

What's in this chapter?

- ◆ The struggle to define talent management
- ◆ The ingredients for an effective talent management strategy
- ◆ How to get the most from this book—an overview

◆ ◆ ◆

This chapter is being written in early 2009, which is, by most accounts, at the end of the beginning of what many consider to be the most significant economic downturn since the Great Depression. According to the U.S. Bureau of Labor Statistics, the number of unemployed people was 13.7 million in April 2009, with the unemployment rate hovering around 8.9 percent. Over the past 12 months, the number of unemployed has increased by 6.0 million, and the unemployment rate has risen by 3.9 percentage points. Many people don't have jobs, and those who do often go to work wondering if that will be the case tomorrow or the next week or month.

It isn't just the possibility of unemployment that has many of us distressed. The value of our homes has tanked, the stock market is at its lowest level in more than 20 years, the value of our 401(k) accounts is down (I am being kind), and the overall economic outlook is grim, at best. But, of course, work still remains to be done, so if there was ever a time when a clear focus on the management of talent was absolutely critical to our collective success, this might be it.

The question, or questions, that one might logically ask are

- ♦ What is talent management, and why do people keep talking about it?
- ♦ When we use the term "talent" in this context, who (or what) are we talking about?
- ♦ Other than the day-to-day direction that a manager gives to his or her employees, what actually happens when talent is managed?

There could be other questions, but most of what you will read here will be limited to providing a range of answers to these. And because 10 different people contributed to the effort, a range of answers is exactly what you will get. This chapter first provides the volume editor's point of view on these issues and then a description of the rest of the chapters.

What Is Talent Management?

The one thing that most people can agree on about talent management in the workplace is that little can be agreed upon and that this doesn't really matter all that much. For the most part, all talent management is local. What I mean is that talent management practices vary widely from company to company (and even within the same company). This isn't necessarily a bad thing, because companies, and divisions within companies, have different strategies, philosophies, and goals, all of which influence how their employees are managed. And of course, what works in one place may not work in another. So differences are not necessarily a bad thing. For the purposes of this book, however, a common definition of talent management might be helpful.

ASTD and the Institute for Corporate Productivity conducted and published a research study titled *Talent Management Practices and Opportunities* (ASTD 2008), whose goal is "to discover how talent management is currently being used by a diverse range of organizations and to discern the best practices of an effective talent management program." The study is a comprehensive look at talent management practices, based on the responses to a series of in-depth questions answered by more than 500 people from a wide variety of companies. The study used this definition of talent management:

> A holistic approach to optimizing human capital, which enables an organization to drive short- and long-term results by building culture, engagement, capability, and capacity through integrated talent acquisition, development, and deployment processes that are aligned to business goals.

At the risk of biting that hand that feeds me (ASTD is also the publisher of this book), I must say that I find this definition to be a little complex. To me, a simpler definition of talent management is "the collection of things companies do that help employees do the best they can each and every day in support of their own and the company's goals and objectives." You might ask why the definition even matters, and that would be a fair question. The answer is simple, and it gets to what I call "Larry's First Rule of Talent Management," which is that talent management does not belong to, nor is it the sole domain of, human resources (HR) departments. Talent management belongs to "the people." As a result, a good definition of talent management has to be written in language that everyday people might use so that is has meaning for them.

Find a friend, and have that person read you the definition of talent management from ASTD that I quoted above. Have your friend read it loudly, and with feeling.

Who do you imagine might actually say something like this definition? Would it be a customer service representative, or a software engineer, or a nurse, or the person who takes your order at a fast food restaurant? I don't think so. These words would be spoken by a vice president of HR or a director of talent management. And though both these people are part of the talent management equation, they are not the most important part. Simply put, talent management must belong to everyone, at all levels of an organization, whatever their salaries, titles, education, or work.

In fairness to ASTD and the Institute for Corporate Productivity, they were conducting research, and their target audience was, I suspect, HR professionals. As a result, the definition they created was completely appropriate. But HR professionals, like people from most other technical disciplines, have a tendency to use language that is hard for others to decipher, and I believe that the more we use language and concepts like these when dealing with talent management, the less successful we are likely to be. I am not saying that the alternate definition I provided above is better—it just works for me. What I am saying is that you should create a definition of talent management that works in your organization and that can be easily understood by everyone you expect to be involved with it or affected by it. (For more on the changing understanding of talent management, see the sidebar.)

Who Is the Talent?

Answering the question "Who is the talent?" seems easy—or is it? The ASTD study asked respondents to identify the employee groups on which they focused their talent management activities. The results, which are shown in table 1-1, are quite interesting and, in my view, somewhat distressing. Less than 20 percent indicated that they focus talent management activities on all employees. Slightly more than 30 percent focus on skilled workers, and just under 40 percent focus on professionals. As you can see, senior executives and high-potential talent were the big winners. The key question is whether or not the results shown in table 1-1 are the desired state or just a snapshot of what might be thought of as the unfortunate current state.

The issue of who constitutes the talent in our organizations leads to "Larry's Second Rule of Talent Management": All full- and part-time employees who are assigned and held accountable for doing work are part of an organization's talent (on a good day, one might even consider including contractors and consultants). Based on this definition, talent

Talent Management in Transition

As this book, and especially this chapter, make clear, the practice of talent management is in a state of flux and uncertainty. Many business leaders have come to realize that they have no greater problem than leveraging knowledge workers. And though many are keen to solve this problem, few approaches fit well with the uncertainty of today's work environment.

ASTD's research on talent management, done with the Institute for Corporate Productivity in early 2009, showed little agreement among companies on how to define talent management, what practices it should comprise, and which employees it should target. If the research was a clear picture of anything, it was of the struggle that companies face in maximizing their talent by using traditional approaches in the midst of constant change (ASTD 2009a).

When firms had the luxury of making five-year plans, talent management usually meant an orderly process of succession planning and executive development. But today, when it can be fatal for companies to remain static, they are seeking new and better ways to harness all their talent to the engines of change.

It's clear that the skills and abilities of many kinds of employees—not just executives—contribute to successful performance. It's clear that a range of practices for finding, developing, and keeping talent exists in most organizations but the practices are rarely integrated or linked to overall strategies. And it is clear that in many firms, high-level direction of talent management is a job no one really owns.

The original ASTD definition of talent management—written in 2008 for a research study—is complex and doesn't roll easily off the tongue. But it was a starting point for encouraging a comprehensive, strategic approach to managing talent that would not fall into the silos that have hampered success in the past. It was meant to encourage learning professionals in particular to take a leadership role in challenging conventional approaches to building organizational capability.

Since publishing the white paper *The New Face of Talent Management: Making Sure Your Employees Really Are Your Most Important Asset* in 2009, ASTD has been taking its own advice, continuing to revise and test the definition of talent management. For a summary of this white paper, including the definition and a corresponding model, see the appendix to this book (ASTD 2009b).

ASTD's definition of talent management, like the activity itself, is a work in progress. We hope that organizations can change, adapt, refine, and apply it to fit their unique situations.

—Pat Galagan, executive editor, ASTD

Table 1-1. The Focus of Talent Management Activities

Employee Group	Percentage[a]
Senior executives	60.0
High-potential talent	58.1
Employees in "pivotal" roles	47.8
Professionals	37.9
All managers	33.9
Skilled employees	31.1
All employees	18.1

[a]The percentages represent the number of respondents to a recent study who selected one of the top two options (high or very high) when asked to what extent these employee groups were the focus of talent management activities.

Source: ASTD (2009a).

should not be defined on the basis or grade, salary, education, or any other demographic that might distinguish one person from another. In the same way that the definition of talent management should make sense and have meaning to all employees, the same employees should be included in some way in the development and implementation of a talent management strategy.

A reasonable, reflexive response to this notion would be to express outrage—"How can he expect us to do talent management with or for everyone [the next section addresses what 'doing talent management' actually means]? We don't have the time or the resources!" I would understand this response. I am not suggesting, nor do I believe, that it is reasonable to expect all talent management practices to be used with all employees. But what might be reasonable is to have at least some practices that are used consistently with everyone across the organization. Yet by restricting the definition of talent to include only high-ranking, highly paid employees, we exclude a significant majority of our employees, and, as a result, we may miss significant pools of talent at lower levels of the organization. Somehow this doesn't seem like a desirable outcome.

What Are Talent Management Activities and Practices?

The answer to the question "What are talent management activities or practices?" is a function of how one answers the question asked in the previous section—"Who is the talent?" Because the more narrow the talent management audience, the fewer the activities that would be viewed as talent management practices. For example, if the primary focus of talent management practices is senior managers or executives, these activities might be included:

♦ succession planning

♦ high-potential programs

♦ external executive education programs

♦ executive coaching.

Each of these makes sense, because they contribute to the identification and development of a group of employees from which future leaders will likely be selected. But would you consider performance management as a talent management activity for this group? Probably not.

However, suppose we take the more expansive view of the employees whose talent we are endeavoring to manage. In this case, the list of activities might expand to include (to name a few)

♦ onboarding

♦ new hire training

♦ performance management

♦ career development

♦ management development

♦ employee opinion survey.

As the audience expands, so too does the list of activities that constitute talent management practices.

Table 1-2 lists 20 activities identified through the ASTD study as being included in talent management programs. At least two conclusions can be drawn from the table. First, many activities or practices could

Table 1-2. Talent Management Activities

Activity	Percentage[a]
Performance management	63.7
Learning/training	61.7
Leadership development	59.1
High-potential employee development	52.8
Individual professional development	44.4
Recruitment	43.2
Engagement	40.0
Compensation and rewards	39.9
Succession planning	39.2
Retention	38.4
Organization development	37.9
Assessment	37.9
Competency management	37.0
Team development	35.5
Career planning	34.8
Critical job identification	32.7
Integrated human resources management systems	28.0
Workforce planning	27.3
Diversity initiatives	24.8
Acquisition of outsourced or contract talent	18.4

[a]The percentages represent the number of respondents to a recent study who selected one of the top two options (high or very high) when asked to what extent these employee groups were the focus of talent management activities.

Source: ASTD (2009a).

reasonably be included as part of a talent management strategy. Second, we have a long way to go before talent management practices are broadly institutionalized. Only three activities—performance management, learning/training, and leadership development—were rated highly by 60 percent of the respondents to the study. This means that the other 40 percent did not select them. Is the glass 60 percent full, or is it 40 percent empty? One could argue that the 40 percent not choosing these activities may do them but simply don't think about them as being part of a talent management program. But even if this is the case, what does it say if an organization doesn't see the connection between performance manage-ment and talent management? Would this be an organization in which talent was really valued? There is no answer, of course—but it gives one pause.

Given all this, you might guess the drift of "Larry's Third Rule of Talent Management": Anything we do to support the definitions of tal-ent management described earlier in this chapter should be viewed as a talent management activity or practice. Earlier I suggested that we should be expansive in our view of the populations whose talent we (are attempt-ing to) manage. The same is true of the practices we use to achieve this goal. Simply put, more is better than less, in almost every situation. Please remember that I am not advocating that we do everything with all audi-ences. Rather, I am saying that a talent management strategy should include something for all audiences.

The Net

In the first section of this chapter, I have tried to provide a perspective on the three key questions that are the foundation for any conversation about talent management:

1. What is it?
2. Who is it for?
3. What is included?

"Larry's Rules" were designed to offer a perspective on each of these questions. So here is "Larry's Fourth Rule of Talent Management": Feel free to disregard rules 1 through 3. Or even better, make up your own rules. If anything is true about talent management, it's that how you define it, whom you do it to (or with), and what you do to (or with) them are completely and entirely a function of the organization where you work and the beliefs and values of the executives who run it. The best you can do is develop a point of view and a strategy to support it, become incredibly good at articulating it, and work tirelessly to communicate it. And after you do all of that, work like hell to deliver everything you promised and then some. The rest of this book is intended to help make this easier for you.

Overview of This Book

There is no particular reason to read this book from end to end. There is no plot, little character development, and I am reasonably certain that the butler didn't do it. So you should feel free to look for chapters that seem like they might be helpful. What follows is a series of short descriptions of the key issues addressed in each chapter. Scanning these descriptions may provide you with the information you need to choose a reasonable path through the book. The companies that are represented are very different from one another, each author tells a different story, and you will soon see that talent management is not the same from place to place. This, however, is a good thing, because it gives you lots of choices and options. It is also important to note at the outset that chapters 3 through 8 are case studies in which talent management practitioners describe the practices they use in their companies to achieve business goals through the effective identification and deployment of talent. They are, quite appropriately, somewhat narrow in their perspective, because they are focused on what happens in individual companies.

Chapter 2: The Business of Talent Management

In chapter 2, Josh Bersin, founder of Bersin & Associates—an organization of senior analysts and consultants with extensive experience in corporate learning, e-learning, performance management, leadership development, talent management, and enterprise systems—provides a slightly broader perspective. He describes the results of his firm's research on talent management (using comprehensive surveys and in-depth interviews) and advocates for the position that talent management is a business imperative and not an HR strategy.

Chapter 3: Talent Management: Function and Transformation at Cisco—The Demands of the Global Economy

Cisco enables people to make powerful connections—whether in business, education, philanthropy, or creativity. Cisco's hardware, software, and service offerings are used to create the Internet solutions that make networks possible—providing easy access to information anywhere, at any time. Cisco was founded in 1984 by a small group of computer scientists from Stanford University. Today, with more than 67,647 employees worldwide, this tradition of innovation continues, with industry-leading products and solutions in the company's core development areas of routing and switching, as well as in advanced technologies. In chapter 3, Annmarie Neal, Cisco's vice president of talent, and Robert Kovach, director of the Center for Collaborative Leadership at Cisco, describe the role that talent management has and will continue to play in transforming Cisco's leaders as a critical element in the strategy for transforming both the organization and the business.

Chapter 4: McDonald's Talent Management and Leadership Development

McDonald's is the leading global food service retailer, with more than 30,000 local restaurants serving 52 million people in more than 100 countries each day. More than 70 percent of McDonald's restaurants worldwide are independently owned and operated by local men and women. And, among what seems like an onslaught of companies reporting declining revenue, McDonald's continues to grow in all parts of the world. In chapter 4, Neal Kulick, vice president of talent for McDonald's, describes how a corporate turnaround strategy and then a series of personal tragedies reinforced the need for an intense focus on talent, which began several years ago and continues today.

Chapter 5: Turnaround Talent Management at Avon Products

Avon, the company for women, is a leading global beauty company, with more than $10 billion in annual revenue. As the world's largest direct seller, Avon markets to women in more than 100 countries through more than 5.5 million independent Avon sales representatives. Avon's product line includes beauty products, fashion jewelry, and apparel. In chapter 5,

Marc Effron, vice president of talent, presents the Avon strategy for using a new approach to managing talent as a key lever in implementing the most radical restructuring process in the company's 122-year history.

Chapter 6: A People-Focused Organization: Development and Performance Practices at Children's Healthcare of Atlanta

For decades, the hospitals of Children's Healthcare of Atlanta have provided leading pediatric care, but now Children's Healthcare faces a mounting challenge. By 2010, the pediatric population of metropolitan Atlanta is projected to grow by a record-breaking 120,000 children—one of the fastest rates of growth of any city in the nation. As the Atlanta region's pediatric population grows, so too does the demand for health care and programs that address the leading dangers to children. Beyond the talent required to effectively deliver health care in today's environment, Children's Healthcare must prepare itself for the future. In chapter 6, Larry Mohl, vice president and chief learning officer, describes how Children's Healthcare is meeting this challenge through an integrated people strategy with comprehensive develop-and-perform practices.

Chapter 7: Talent Management beyond Boundaries at Ciena

Ciena Corporation is a leader in communication network infrastructure, associated software, and professional services. Its solutions form the foundation for many of the largest, most reliable and sophisticated service provider, enterprise, government, and research and education networks across the globe. Given Ciena's size, with about 2,000 employees, one might question whether the types of talent management activities used in larger companies are necessary or appropriate. In chapter 7, Jim Caprara, vice president, global HR development, demonstrates the value of a structured approach to talent management and the importance of thought leadership about learning for companies of all sizes.

Chapter 8: Managing Talent at the Liberty Mutual Group

The Liberty Mutual Group is a global property and casualty company that offers insurance products in more than 25 countries. Since its founding in 1912, its employees have worked hard to make the world a safer, more secure place to live and work in. In addition to its products and services, the company's safety breakthroughs, industry firsts, patents, and innovative programs have helped reduce workplace injuries, illnesses, and disabilities for millions of men and women. Liberty Mutual has had a consistent record of growth and profitability since the early 1990s. In chapter 8, Larry Israelite, vice president of human resource development, describes the critical role that comprehensive talent management practices have played in the company's ongoing success.

Chapter 9: Talent Management: The Elephant in the Room

The people who spend their days creating and implementing talent management practices must learn to deal with constant change in management, the business environment, competitive challenges, technology, and many other things that make their work complex and challenging. In chapter 9, Nigel Paine, strategic adviser on talent management, makes and effectively defends a compelling argument that changes in the nature of work itself and the capabilities, needs, and expectations of the people who do this work will require a rapid, comprehensive change in the conventional wisdom associated with talent management. He lays out a road map for building a talent-centric organization and explores the benefits that this will bring to any employee.

Chapter 10: Talent Management Software and Systems

Is it possible that our ability to manage talent, however we define it, was limited in the past by our ability to effectively integrate all the data talent management activities created? Would the availability of software make the work so much easier that the effectiveness of talent management practices would dramatically increase? In chapter 10, Adam Miller, chief executive of Cornerstone OnDemand, a company that provides on-demand, integrated learning and talent management software and services, describes the evolution of talent management software and illustrates its potential effects on talent management practices and, therefore, on management itself.

Chapter 11: Talent Management at Work

The final chapter summarizes the key talent management practices and processes described by each of the chapter authors and offers a set of recommendations for individuals and organizations who are starting to formalize talent management in their organizations.

A Final Thought

The authors of the chapters in this book tell their own stories. Although they all started out with the same set of questions, the differences in their companies and in how they think about talent took them down different paths. Although it may be difficult to be completely accurate at this point, I suspect that you already have an idea which of the six companies profiled briefly above is most like the one where you work. As a result, you might be tempted to skip around a little as you read. That would be a fine approach. However, it might be helpful to read chapter 2 next, because it does provide some context for everything that follows. After you gain a better understanding of the talent management road map, it may be easier to understand the different paths that each company has taken.

Finally, you may be tempted to skip over the chapters about companies that are nothing like your own. Yet there is much to learn from each of the chapters, and although the sequence in which you read them is not particularly important, it would be unfortunate if you missed something valuable because the company in which it happened is different from your own.

The Business of Talent Management

Josh Bersin, President and CEO, Bersin & Associates

What's in this chapter?

- The meaning of integrated talent management for today's organizations
- The elements of the High-Impact Talent Management Model
- A business-driven approach to talent management
- The four steps in developing a talent management strategy
- The governance and business ownership of talent management
- How the key elements of talent management fit together
- The importance of organizational culture

◆ ◆ ◆

In the last few years, the topic of integrated talent management has become one of the most talked-about issues in corporate human resources. As the head of a research analysis firm, I have the opportunity to talk with hundreds of companies about their definitions, implementations, and solutions for talent management. In this chapter, I share my firm's findings about the real definitions, best practices, and applications of talent management in businesses today. In particular, this chapter discusses concepts of "business-driven talent management" with the goal of convincing you that, ultimately, talent management is a business strategy, not a human resources strategy.

Defining Talent Management

Books on talent management are certainly not new. In fact, the term "talent management" has been used for many years, referring primarily to management of "the talent," meaning an organization's top people. So "talent management" used to refer to the development and succession management of these top leaders. Today, however, the term refers to what we would call an integrated approach to managing all the aspects of an organization that have to do with people. Today the term refers to all the integrated practices we use to attract, manage, develop, and compensate people.

Before we get into the processes of talent management themselves, it is important to realize that in today's organizations, "the talent" is everywhere. Organizations that used to be hierarchical no longer work this way. The traditional views of "talent" and levels of management that drive the organization have changed (figure 2-1).

In fact, in most highly effective organizations today, some of the most-valued employees (those in what one would call the "pivotal roles") are functional specialists in sales, customer service, engineering, manufacturing, research, or support. These specialists range from young new-hire employees to senior people in their 50s and 60s. Talent management practices must accommodate the fact that people with high potential go beyond those who can be promoted to management; they are also people who can take on more responsibility as individual professional contributors.

At Qualcomm, for example, one of the world's most profitable and successful technology companies, people with PhDs and patents are given some of the most important responsibilities. The company prides itself on "depth," not "breadth," in talent—because its core business is to out-innovate everyone in the mobile telecommunications market. If its

Figure 2-1. Redefining an Organization's Talent Well Beyond Its Leaders

leaders tried to manage Qualcomm with a purely hierarchical model, it would fail.

Retail organizations have similar but different challenges. Their most important employees are the high-turnover workers in their stores. Management plays a critical role in recruiting, coaching, and managing these people, but research shows that some of the most important roles in retail are not only managers but the sales specialists themselves. (The source for this finding is proprietary research by Lowe's Stores, which found that the "pivotal role" in its retail stores is the "sales lead," a nonmanagerial role.) So how can a talent management strategy ensure that young, high-turnover retail employees perform at the optimum level at all times?

The Manager's Changing Role

In addition to the flattening of organizations and the general agreement that "talent is everywhere," we also have organizations that function as networks. Nearly every employee now has a cell phone and access to email, computer, and vast intranet resources. Many employees no longer even work in the same office or city as their managers; rather, they interact and work with teams across the world. Employees can no longer just walk into the manager's office for help.

This means that many companies have a "matrix" management process, which means that employees both have managers who help them with personnel-related issues and also have a vast network of peers and project leaders with whom they work to get their work done. As a result, the belief that managing means providing one-to-one coaching and day-to-day support has changed. When we think about performance management, coaching, and development, we must consider how the process works across a network of people, not just in a hierarchy.

Consulting firms have been managed this way for years. Employees of Accenture, IBM, Deloitte, and many other accounting and consulting firms have many managers—they have "people managers," and they have "project managers." An employee's ability to work within teams and interact with many people in a variety of roles and contexts is now a core competency. In fact, Bersin & Associates' research shows that in these organizations, true performance is measured by a matrix of functional competencies (skills) and span of influence (ability to influence, lead, and collaborate among large groups); for more information, see Lamoureux (2009). Thus, we must think of talent management as the process of managing this vast array of networked resources, not just providing tools to managers.

Talent Pools, Critical Talent, or Pivotal Talent

Finally, consider the fact that an executive cannot possibly manage everyone in the same way. Some roles drive more value than others. In software firms, experienced programmers can write 10 to 100 times as much code as junior developers. In oil companies, exploration and production engineers can drive billions of dollars of market value, while refinery employees have little or no real leverage on the bottom line. In insurance companies, key roles include actuaries and customer service leaders.

As companies implement talent management strategies, they quickly realize that they must focus their energies on particular groups of people, referred to as "talent pools" or "talent segmentation." By implementing standardized talent management processes and systems, organizations can now target critical pools of talent that need attention and that can drive the greatest potential business impact.

One example of such a solution is the implementation of talent pools at one of the nation's largest health care and insurance providers. In this industry, the nursing population is a particularly pivotal talent pool; nurses are in short supply, they drive tremendous enterprise value, and their role is changing from one of service delivery to consulting on wellness. Thus, this health care firm needs special types of managerial and talent programs to make sure that it meets its overall business goals.

In this firm, the chief learning officer worked with the CEO and labor leaders to develop a new leadership program focused on the service-provider population. This program focused on providing all service-provider leaders (nurses, technicians, and other roles) with a broad range of skills. The company is using this program as a backbone infrastructure to help this critical population improve its leadership skills and transform its role from service provider into wellness consultant.

The High-Impact Talent Management Model

Bersin & Associates defines talent management as "a set of organizational processes designed to attract, manage, develop, motivate, and retain key people." The goal of a talent management program is to create a highly responsive, high-performance, sustainable organization that meets its business targets (for more information, see Bersin 2007a).

In accord with this understanding of talent management, Bersin & Associates has created a High-Impact Talent Management Model, which has four core functions (figure 2-2):

- ♦ talent acquisition, typically consisting of sourcing, recruiting, and staffing
- ♦ performance management, referring to the process of goal setting, goal alignment, coaching, manager evaluation, self-evaluation, and development planning

- ◆ succession planning and management, which includes processes like calibration and evaluation of employee potential

- ◆ leadership development.

Each of these four core people processes is both complex and highly strategic. One of the biggest changes that has occurred in the last few years is the rise of the concept of "integration." Heretofore, many large and small organizations separated these various human resource development processes among different groups and different managers. Today, they are viewed as interrelated processes that must work together.

Bersin & Associates developed this model after interviewing many hundreds of companies. Remember that although many organizations are not necessarily organized in this way (yet), these pieces fit together into a whole. Consider five key issues, as shown in figure 2-2. First, notice that competency management and learning and development (L&D) form a platform for talent management. An organization cannot develop strong recruitment, assessment, performance management, or leadership

Figure 2-2. Bersin & Associates' High-Impact Talent Management Model

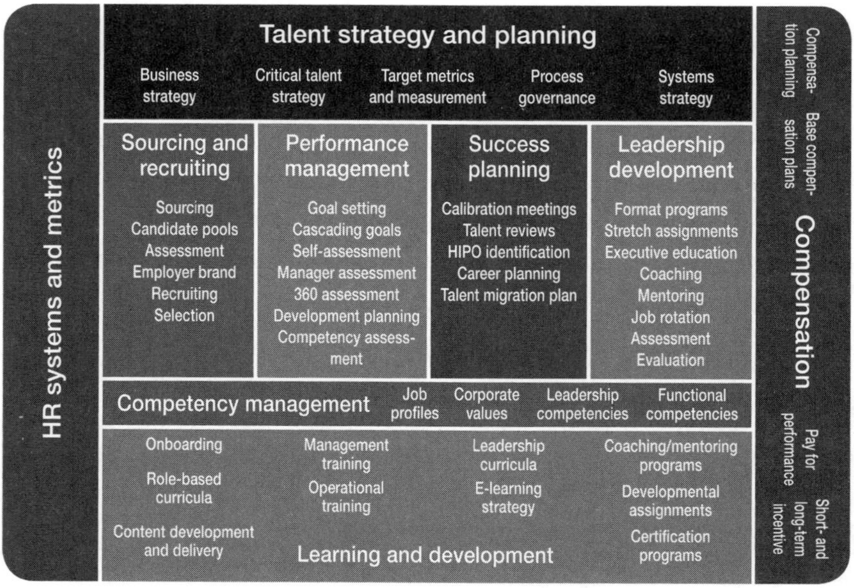

© 2008 Bersin & Associates. All rights reserved. Used with permission.

development programs without a series of competency and capability models. These models are foundational for a strong talent management program. And our research has found that competency management does not need to be detailed and highly specific; high-level competencies in each area drive 90 percent of the value.

Second, leadership development is a critical element of talent management. Although some organizations consider it a training function, our research shows otherwise: Strategic leadership development programs dovetail with total talent management strategies—they establish leadership values and competencies, they train leaders at all levels, and they establish the rules for succession management (and deciding who will become a leader). Leadership development also drives performance management, recruiting, and other coaching skills. In today's slowing economy, organizations are refocusing their leadership development programs and using them to build skills from the first-line manager up. In fact, many successful talent management leaders come from leadership development backgrounds.

Third, what role does corporate training play in a talent management strategy? Our research shows that, ultimately, the corporate training group (or corporate university) is best viewed as a partner or supporting function to the talent management team. The reason for this is that corporate training has two somewhat tangential missions. On one hand, corporate training groups must develop, manage, and steward what we call "talent-driven learning" programs. These programs, often considered career development or role-based programs, focus on building deep levels of competence across many stages of an individual's career. Leadership development is this type of program. These talent-driven programs should be incorporated into the talent management strategy, because they provide stepping stones, waypoints, and development planning anchors for all employees.

On the other hand, much of corporate training falls into a second category, which we call "performance-driven learning." These programs are shorter term, and they focus on day-to-day process changes, product rollouts, and the technical needs of the workforce. High-performing training organizations manage both types of programs together, working with line training groups in what we call a "federated" model. So, though L&D must support talent management, it must also be somewhat independent—and thus has two roles (figure 2-3).

Sourcing and recruiting, or "talent acquisition"—on the left side of the model shown in figure 2-2—is perhaps one of the most important parts of talent management, because unless the "right people" are hired, the rest of management makes no sense. Ideally, then, the sourcing, recruiting, staffing, and onboarding processes in talent acquisition should be designed and integrated with the other three areas shown in the model. Sophisticated companies (Boeing, for example) take the job roles, competencies, and proven performance measures of high performers and use this information to screen and assess candidates. In most companies, however, the staffing department is still separated from the talent management team. Though this integration is becoming more and more common, today most companies are spending their time first optimizing the areas of performance management, succession, and leadership development. Once these areas are established, they can be used for talent acquisition.

Fourth, compensation is clearly a talent management issue, but it is rarely integrated into today's talent management portfolio. Again, the reason is mostly evolutionary: "Total rewards" or compensation is quite complex and is typically associated more with finance than with talent management. However, today's focus on pay-for-performance, pay-for-contribution, incentive compensation, and other variable pay programs has forced organizations to integrate such functions into the design of the performance management process. Bersin & Associates' research shows that although compensation is clearly a critical driver to organizational performance, it actually has less impact than what people may think; in most roles, compensation is a "hygiene" factor—it must be high enough to keep people engaged, but an excessive focus on compensation does not necessarily improve performance. (Of course, some roles and industries are very compensation driven. Sales organizations are notoriously "coin operated," so their compensation structures are critical to high performance. Investment banking, real estate development, legal partnerships, and other industries also have traditionally been managed by tremendously large and complex compensation incentives. Many companies in

Figure 2-3. The Two Roles of Learning and Development

	Performance-driven learning	Talent-driven learning
Drivers:	Business performance issues in operational units and functions	Talent and leadership gaps, critical skills shortages, engagement, and culture
Goal:	Develop individual capabilities and fill performance gaps	Develop organizational capabilities driven by competencies, not performance
Examples:	Sales training, customer service training, field service certification	Multi-tier leadership development, new-hire onboarding programs
Organization:	Aligned by job within function	Aligned to all job roles in a job function
Timeline:	Months or even shorter	Multiple quarters to years
Complexity:	Functional	Enterprise- or division-wide
Integrated with:	Product launches, new service offerings, geographic expansion	Performance management, recruiting, succession planning
Challenges:	Performance consulting, program design, manager engagement	Resource allocation, program design, job alignment, manager adoption
How to measure success:	Solving business problems: sales, service, quality, turnaround	Filling and solving talent gaps (i.e., shortages, recruiting goals)

these industries actually suffer from more immature talent management processes and replace them with heavily targeted incentive compensation strategies.)

Fifth, notice the "talent strategy and planning" box at the top of figure 2-2. One of the most immature aspects of the talent management framework is the ability of organizations to actually understand the current state and plan for future talent needs. Though many companies have a good record of open head-count and hiring requirements, our research shows that fewer than 6 percent of organizations have a deep understanding of the skill and capability gaps of their entire workforce, and even fewer model these as part of their business planning process. We believe that one of the next steps in talent management will be the integration of all these processes into the business and financial planning process. In today's economy, more than 35 percent of all companies are going through some type of restructuring. Without a strong talent planning process, these programs are difficult to implement quickly and effectively.

High-performing companies integrate these processes in a very strategic and dynamic way. Consider Caterpillar, for example. The company has centralized its talent planning and management process under the umbrella of Caterpillar University. The university is now the head of talent programs for the company and has developed a program to integrate skills planning, head-count planning, and monitoring of employee engagement and performance management into the planning process of every major business unit. Lowe's, IBM, Accenture, and many other high-performing companies are going down this path. Once an organization reaches this level of maturity, talent management goes far beyond human resources (HR) and becomes truly an integrated business process.

It often takes many years to reach this level of maturity. Companies like Boeing, GE, Textron, IBM, McDonald's, and Aetna have worked hard on these processes for many years, and they now credit their ability to adapt and change to integrated talent management programs.

A Business-Driven Approach to High-Impact Talent Management

Having discussed the technical aspects and history of talent management, now let us turn to the most important issue of all: how talent management drives business impact. Why does talent management matter?

The first thing one must realize is that talent management practices, which look and feel like "HR work," really make up the underlying infrastructure for any high-performing organization. Any business, government, nonprofit, or educational venture needs the principles of strategy, alignment, accountability, feedback, leadership, management, learning, and development. These fundamental people processes can be applied in very different ways—but if an organization ignores them, it will ultimately fail.

At Bersin & Associates, our research has found that "enduring organizations"—those that survive over many years and through many business cycles—have one major thing in common: They realize that their ultimate organizational strength comes not from their technology, products, or patents but from their people, culture, and strategy. These companies use talent management to grow, restructure, change, and adapt to their markets. They use it to select the right candidates, promote the right leaders, and reward the right high performers. But this kind of high-level talk will never cost-justify a new system or a reorganization. So let's look at some specific business applications of talent management strategies.

Downsizing or Restructuring?

One of today's top business challenges is the need to downsize and restructure. Though this problem is urgent today, it is actually a continuous problem in any company. Whenever a company restructures, sells a division, or gets out of a business, some positions need to be eliminated and new ones need to be created.

With so many baby boomers starting to retire, the pool of candidates necessary for making these changes may be insufficient. Who should we let go, and who should we keep? Who would be the best people to move into newly created positions in a fast-growing business unit? Who are the people we really do not want to lose during a downsizing? How do we identify the high performers within a low-performing division or business unit? How do we identify the low performers within a high-performing business unit? Do we have clearly defined ratings and skills data to make these decisions? With an integrated talent management program, these decisions can be made quickly and with sound judgment.

Improving Performance and Engagement

Another significant challenge is finding ways to improve individual employee productivity and workplace engagement. How does one deal with such systemic issues across a broad base of employees? The solution requires a heavy focus on leadership and management development, a passion for organizational learning, the alignment of goals and a clear distinction of responsibilities, and clarity about the organization's mission. These lofty goals are difficult to implement without defining and developing the processes mentioned above. For example, at IBM, which has transformed itself from a computer manufacturer into a leading consulting firm, people are incentivized and rewarded for sharing knowledge with each other in a highly transparent way. This cultural goal drives performance and engagement and is embedded in IBM's leadership development and performance management processes.

An Aging Workforce and Impending Retirements

In some industries, there is still an impending shortage of workers. For example, Chevron, a highly profitable company with operations all over the world, expects as many as 50 percent of its key employees to become eligible for retirement in the next five years. The average tenure of a Chevron employee will soon drop from 15 to eight years. Though the slowing economy has slightly reduced the impact of this problem, the company sees a tremendous need to rapidly build its skills and leadership pipeline.

The only way to accomplish this is to identify the critical skills; develop successors; revamp career development programs; and implement new approaches to recruiting, onboarding, and employee development. Such programs are urgent if Chevron wants to continue its global growth and its rapid transition from an oil company to an integrated energy company.

Revamping or Improving Compensation Strategies

Today, as a result of the economic downturn, many companies are rethinking their compensation strategies to create more pay-for-performance elements. The goal here is to raise the level of employee performance through incentives, while keeping total compensation levels flat or even reducing them. Who should participate in these programs, and how should they be measured? What level of managerial discretion should be applied, and what are the criteria for making such decisions? Does the performance management process have the maturity and validity to support these decisions?

One well-known retailer implemented a new talent management program and found that more than $11 million in bonuses was handed out to store managers—with very little relationship to true employee performance. But once the new performance management system was put in place, this expense was reduced to $5 million, more than paying the entire cost of the system and the new processes it supported.

Improving Skill Levels and Enabling New Business Opportunities

Suppose your company is expanding into a new area (who isn't, these days?) and exiting old businesses. How well do your managers understand the ability of their people to move into the new roles and perform the new work? Do you have an overall understanding of skills gaps across the organization? An integrated talent management program should quickly provide insights into these skills and provide the L&D organization with clear direction for focusing on its audience. Even better, when major business transitions occur, the program should facilitate coaching and knowledge sharing as part of key employee performance plans.

For example, when Aetna went through its massive turnaround in the mid-2000s, the company realized that many of its acquisitions were not performing well. Once it rationalized its businesses, the CEO's first priority was to build a process to align employee skills with business needs. Over a five-year period, Aetna implemented an integrated talent management, skills assessment, performance management, and business planning approach, which built skills development right into the company's business plan. Today, every employee has a development plan targeted toward the company's strategic goals—and when a reorganization takes place, the company can quickly identify the right candidates for movement. Aetna today has become one of the most profitable insurance companies in the United States, which it credits largely to its integrated business and talent management process.

There are many other business drivers behind talent management. These include global expansion, rapid growth, and the acquisition of another company. Ultimately, these drivers will be very company dependent and will vary from year to year. But as you will see in the next section, talent management is far more than the solution to a problem—it is an underlying business competency.

The Four Steps in Implementing a Talent Management Strategy

Given the business challenges described above, what is the right way to go about building a talent management strategy? After talking with many companies, Bersin & Associates developed an integrated process and framework, which we'll explore in this section.

Remember, the viewpoint here is that talent management is not a squashing together of HR roles but something quite different: applying strategic HR disciplines to your company's business needs. Consider a simple thought: *No successful business strategy can succeed without a related talent strategy.* This is the essence of talent management: building a process infrastructure that supports business goals.

So how do you do this? Consider these four steps (figure 2-4):

1. Identify the business problem or problems to be solved.
2. Determine the business-related talent challenges.
3. Design the human resources processes.
4. Implement the new systems and processes.

Step 1: Identify the Business Problem

The first step in the development of a talent management strategy is to clearly identify the business challenges your organization faces. What are the business goals for the next 12 to 24 months? Into what new products, services, markets, or geographies will you expand? What changes in structure or customer focus will drive your organization? What major new programs, initiatives, or restructurings must you accomplish? This information should be available to you from the company's one- to two-year business plan.

Step 2: Determine the Business-Related Talent Challenges

Step 2 is, perhaps, the most important and most difficult one in developing a talent management strategy. What business-related talent challenges could prevent you from achieving the goals of this plan? What skills, capabilities, or head-count gaps could prevent you from achieving the goals outlined in Step 1?

In most companies, these questions are very difficult to answer. Only 6 percent of organizations claim to have a detailed understanding of their skills and capability gaps. Ideally, talent gaps should be readily available from line executives. In fact, mature talent management strategies will force business leaders to create talent plans as part of their annual business plans. Once you have established your core talent management strategy, you can start asking business leaders to assess capabilities against this strategy.

In most cases, talent challenges are somewhat obvious (a lack of nurses for health care providers, high turnover level in sales, low skills in manufacturing, and so on). But ideally, you need to do modeling—comparing growth plans with worker productivity plans, for example—to see where expected gaps will develop. In other cases, you will find information readily available in other HR departments: current gaps in performance, high levels of turnover, changes in workforce demographics, or low levels of engagement or commitment. This information should make up this second part of your talent plan.

Figure 2-4. The Four-Step High-Impact Talent Management Strategy

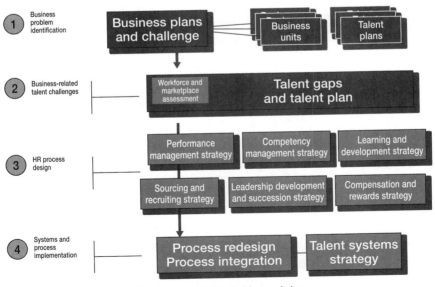

When Starbucks was expanding, for example, it carefully assessed the number of baristas and store managers required to succeed. Using established turnover rates by store location, its planning staff looked at the local geography to make sure the required labor pool was available to meet expansion needs. Sometimes this process told the company that it had to relocate key managers. Today, as Starbucks cuts back on its locations, it uses this same planning process to predict attrition and plan store closures.

When the military contractor Raytheon started planning its 10-year plan through 2015, it found a pending gap of 25,000 or more technical professionals. The combination of retirements and growth in national defense programs surfaced a tremendous undersupply of technical professionals at various locations. The ultimate solution was an integrated program of career development, relocation of work to new locations, and technical succession management, which required the development of a new technical career model, competency assessment, and implementation of talent management software.

Step 3: Design the Human Resources Processes

Step 3 in developing a talent management strategy is designing (or redesigning) the HR processes required to meet staffing and talent gaps. This is the step that many HR practitioners enjoy the most. Do you need an improved university recruiting program or a new employer brand to attract younger workers? Do you need a career model for the impending gaps in the technical pipeline? Or perhaps the process for employee evaluation should be scrapped and then re-created? We will discuss performance management later in this chapter, because it is, perhaps, one of the most central talent management processes.

In this step, you, as an HR or L&D professional, must think through your options in creative ways. In almost every case, you probably have many HR processes in place—but they may be old or ineffective. How can you improve them to meet the new talent needs? How can you further enlist line managers to help you redesign or streamline the process to gain greater acceptance and value? Many HR professionals design complex, highly sophisticated processes that are difficult or impossible to implement. Bersin & Associates' research in performance management, for example, shows that organizations that tweak their process over many years end up with simpler and simpler approaches. In most cases, a simple but highly strategic process works better than one with many steps and options.

Most HR processes depend on an underlying job competency model, career model, and set of leadership competencies. Before you rush into designing new processes, make sure these fundamental pieces are up to date, relevant, and aligned with the company's strategic direction.

Step 4: Implement the New Systems and Processes

The fourth and final step in developing a talent management strategy is implementing the new processes and systems. Many companies believe that software is their first step, and they try to start here (and most HR software vendors push this as well). The problem with this approach is that it is nearly impossible to configure, implement, and roll out talent management software without clear, strategic, well-agreed-upon processes. Remember that the best talent management strategies and programs do not necessarily rely on technology. Many of the world's best-managed companies implement world-class management and talent processes using paper-based forms and tools. Though paper is certainly not the most reusable and sharable approach, we find it is best to use technology as a tool for solving a problem, not as a tool looking for a solution.

Consider the performance management systems implementation at Teletech, one of the world's largest and most profitable call center outsourcing companies. The company had a strong culture of operations management for many years and then decided to implement a new performance management system to help corporate managers better assess skills gaps on their teams. The business case focused primarily on process automation.

The project leader, a senior HR leader at corporate headquarters, found tremendous resistance to the project because it was not anchored in a fundamental business problem or business change. In the first nine months of the performance management process, the system went through several major redesigns, and the overall implementation could take two years or more. Though we are big fans of HR software, remember that talent management software is not talent management. If you first focus on the problem, processes, and governance, systems implementation can go quickly and successfully. But failure to do so may lead to significantly different, and less pleasant, results.

The Governance of Talent Management

No HR process is more interlocked with business, leadership, IT, and HR than talent management. Remember that ultimately the "owners" of talent management are not HR but the business leaders themselves.

If you tell the organization that "talent management is coming from HR," you may undermine your entire program. The purpose of the talent management program is not for HR alone to gain information but rather to enable the business leaders, managers, and employees themselves to make better decisions. The program will clearly have many benefits for HR, but ultimately the processes and systems you implement must be "owned" by line management. This is why the proper governance of talent management processes and program plays such a critical role (figure 2-5).

Look at the elements of figure 2-5. There are many stakeholders who should be involved in the strategy, design, and implementation of the talent management program—including line business managers (at least one from each major division or geographic owner), information technology, L&D, and at least one major business executive sponsor.

Consider, for example, the talent management program at Caterpillar, a large and complex global manufacturer. Each geographic unit of Caterpillar across the world is responsible for its own profit-and-loss statement and has both the authority and responsibility to implement strategies for its local market. The company, however, takes organizational learning, individual learning, and talent management very seriously. The organization currently called Caterpillar University is responsible for global development planning and talent management processes throughout the company. This includes performance management, succession management, and development planning.

To implement global standards while enabling regional control, Caterpillar University works closely with the senior leaders of each business unit. These leaders create common talent plans as part of the annual planning process, participate in the university's executive committee, and assign senior representatives to work with the university on detailed process design. We call this a "federated" organization model—and it works very well for large organizations.

These people will be the ones who "carry the torch" for the leadership development program, the performance management process, employee development programs, and the new HR portal. They should be consulted regularly for input on program design and project timelines. Remember that talent management programs only succeed when managers adopt them, which leads us to the next topic: business ownership.

The Business Ownership of Talent Management

Who do you think really owns the talent management process—the director of talent management or the vice president of HR? Neither. Ultimately, talent management is not an HR initiative at all but is part of a business strategy. Bersin & Associates' research clearly shows that if you

Figure 2-5. The Governance of Talent Management

Enlist business leaders to create adoption, not compliance

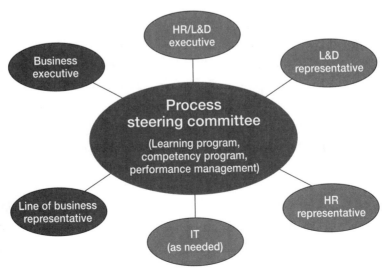

want the process to succeed, it must be owned by the business leaders in each major division of your company. Your job as an HR or L&D leader is to be the process "steward," consultant, or change agent.

Consider the information shown in figure 2-6, captured from Bersin & Associates' *Talent Management Factbook*, which distills research on more than 1,000 companies in 2008 (for more information, see O'Leonard 2008). This research asked companies to characterize their talent management programs into four possible approaches: those owned by a top executive, those owned by HR, those owned by the line of business, and those delegated fully to business managers. In figure 2-6, the percentages given show the relative improvements (or negative impact) in the area listed in the left-hand column for each of the governance models, which are listed across the top. For example, companies that delegate leadership development to individual business areas show a 22 percent reduction in business impact from the average—and those that have CEO sponsorship show a 14 percent improvement over the average.

As figure 2-6 clearly shows, top executive ownership drives higher outcomes than the other models. The reason for this is somewhat obvious: Talent management at its best should influence the behavior of every manager in the company in some way. If managers in your organization do not see the implementation of these processes as part of their jobs, you will find spotty implementation and a lack of engagement.

Consider these statistics: Although approximately 66 percent of organizations claim to have some form of corporate performance management, almost 75 percent told Bersin & Associates that their managers are undertrained or insufficiently focused on employee assessment, coaching, feedback, and development. According to anecdotal research, at least half of new managers receive little or no training in supervisory or management techniques when they take on this new role. (For more on these data, see Levensaler 2008a, 2008b.)

If line managers do not believe that performance management is a major part of their jobs, they will look at the associated process as just one more HR compliance program. And thus, though they may comply with the program, they may not commit to achieving its goals. Organizations need to structure their talent management processes so that line

Figure 2-6. The Positive or Business Negative Impact of Four Approaches Relative to Talent Governance Models

Align with the business first—all business challenges also have talent challenges

Talent governance model:	CEO or top executive owns process	HR owns and manages the process	Lines of business own, HR supports	Lines of business own independently
Leadership development	+14%	-7%	Average	-22%
Performance management	+6%	-5%	-9%	-26%
Hiring the best people	+8%	Average	-4%	-24%
Creating a performance-driven culture	+11%	-12%	+6%	+8%
Creating high levels of engagement and retention	+19%	-7%	-6%	-9%

Note: The "business impact" referred to here refers to the self-reported business results from this particular process or area. For the thousands of respondents, this data is highly differentiated and correlated.

managers and executives do their job because they see its value, and this demands top-level executive support.

The Four Key Elements of a Talent Management Strategy

As organizations implement more integrated talent management strategies, they start to see how performance management, competency management, leadership development, and corporate L&D fit together. Let us briefly examine several key issues for each of these areas.

Performance Management

In many ways, performance management is the core of talent management. As we like to remind people, performance management *is* management. This process, which is often described as the annual appraisal or "performance management process"—PMP—is understood today by organizations as establishing the foundation for much of the rest of talent management.

Ideally, performance management should be built around an organization's culture—in some organizations, there is a rigorous, competitive nature to work; in others, there is a highly collaborative, innovative approach. Bersin & Associates' research has shown that, broadly speaking, organizations fall into one of two camps: the competitive assessment approach, or the coaching and development approach. Of course, all organizations use both to a degree.

When asked to select which they believe best represents their culture, approximately 59 percent of organizations rate themselves as coaching and development related, and 41 percent focus more on the competitive assessment approach.

Our research identified seven separate practices within the defined process of employee performance management:

♦ goal setting

♦ goal alignment

♦ employee self-assessment

♦ management assessment

♦ competency analysis and discussions

♦ 360-degree or peer assessment

♦ development planning.

As HR professionals know, each of these practices is complex, demanding thought and sometimes training.

Unfortunately, the whole area of performance management is constantly changing; when we interviewed organizations to understand their practices, more than 70 percent were "changing something," and the changes tend to be widely varying. The reason for this is that, over time, performance management processes tend to start on the left of the chart (with a highly competitive process) and move toward a process focused on coaching and development, following the maturation of a business in general. When the company is small, people can be held directly accountable for results. But as the company grows, roles become more complex, and the ability to coach and develop people becomes more important. We also see a shift based on the business cycle: When companies go through tough times, their process becomes more rigorous and competitive; when they go through times of growth, they focus more on development and coaching. (For more on this data, see Levensaler 2008a, 2008b.)

Ultimately, this process is a vital foundation for talent management because it sets the rules for discussions between managers and employees, it establishes competencies and processes for evaluation, and it produces performance and potential ratings used for leadership development, compensation, and succession management.

Competency Management

Organizations struggle with competency models in many ways. Bersin & Associates' research uncovered two key findings. First, you cannot implement a sound talent management strategy without a clear understanding of your organization's core competencies, leadership competencies, and some level of role-based competencies. And second, it is not necessary to overengineer competency management at all—in fact, the process can be quite simple.

As figure 2-7 shows, there are many types of competencies: core values, effectiveness competencies, functional competencies, and leadership competencies. Ultimately, you must think about the purpose of a competency model before you build it: A leadership competency model is used for leadership assessment and development; a functional competency model is used for training associated with a particular job or business function; core values are used for performance management and coaching.

One key best practice that Bersin & Associates found in our research is that for many highly successful companies, fewer is better. Organizations like GE, American Express, IBM, and Coca-Cola, which have been evolving their performance management processes for years, simplify their competency models to eight or fewer competencies. Though many

Figure 2-7. Types of Competencies

functional competencies are useful for developing training programs, they are usually of little value in real managerial performance management and leadership development.

Our research also shows that although there are many excellent competency models and books, organizations gain the greatest benefits from competency management when they focus on identifying the unique, culture-specific competencies that drive their organization. (Bersin & Associates' research on the effective use of competency models is available at www.bersin.com.) When we looked at the in-depth competency models in place in eight major corporations in financial services, technology, retail, and manufacturing, we found that the best-performing companies in each industry had markedly different types of competency models in their performance management programs. More successful companies tended to focus on higher-level values, such as quality, communication, and leadership, while less successful organizations tended to focus on hygiene competencies like safety and operational skills (for more information, see Bersin 2007b).

We have found that companies succeed by focusing on one of four underlying business strategies: product leadership, low cost, customer intimacy, and service leadership. In each industry, high-performing companies can succeed by focusing on any of these four business strategies. For example, in the retail coffee marketplace, Peet's is a product leader, McDonald's and Dunkin Donuts are low-cost leaders, and Starbucks is the leader in customer intimacy. As you can easily imagine, the competencies required of a high performer in each of these companies may be quite different. Remember that the value of your organization's competency model is its ability to reinforce and integrate your company's unique strategy into the everyday life of every employee and manager.

Ultimately, the development of a competency model for leadership and performance management is a highly strategic part of talent management and must be done early and with a strong level of executive support.

Leadership Development

Though many organizations view leadership development as another set of L&D programs, in reality it plays a far more strategic role. As we all know, leaders make organizations succeed: They hire people, define strategies, implement programs, and set the organization's culture. Only by developing and codifying leadership can an organization grow and thrive over time.

Our research shows that organizations fall into four stages of maturity with regard to leadership development, with the relative percentage of companies at each stage shown in figure 2-8:

- strategic leadership development
- focused leadership development
- structured leadership training
- inconsistent management training.

Many talent management leaders have a background in leadership development. Without strong leadership development, it is very difficult to implement performance management, succession, and many of the other parts of a strategic talent management program. Not only does leadership development feed the rest of the program, but it is one of the most important elements of a business-driven HR organization.

As figure 2-8 illustrates, most companies still focus on leadership as a subject within management training programs. Though training for new managers and supervisors is important, these are questions to ask: What type of managers do we want? How can we reinforce our culture, principles, processes, and behaviors? Today, more and more organizations realize that to do this, there must be a strong commitment from top executives—with leaders sponsoring the program, speaking at courses, reviewing and selecting leadership candidates, and establishing program strategies.

One example of the power of leadership development is Hewlett-Packard's dramatic turnaround. When Mark Hurd, the new CEO, started at the company in 2004, he found a highly innovative organization that had lost its ability to focus, execute, and hold itself accountable. He brought a new managerial focus on execution, growth, and profitability. These three principles were developed and driven across all levels of executives using a powerful new leadership development program. We at Bersin & Associates believe that all strong talent management strategies must focus heavily on the principles and practices of leadership development.

Figure 2-8. The Four Stages of Leadership Development

Strategic leadership development 7%
Championed by executives, talent management integration

Focused leadership development 14%
Culture setting, future focused, developing organization

Structured leadership training 29%
Core competencies, well-defined curriculum, developing individuals

Inconsistent management training 34%
Content available, no development process, benefit to employees

No management or leadership training 16%

The Role of Learning and Development

The final element of talent management is the role of corporate L&D. The concepts of integrated talent management have entered the marketplace at the same time many companies are trying to rationalize and consolidate their L&D spending. Thus, one of the big questions companies face is whether or not corporate L&D should be part of the talent management organization.

The right answer is "kind of." Ultimately, corporate or departmental L&D organizations have two roles: the implementation of what we call performance-driven learning (programs that deal with new products, processes, and systems) and talent-driven learning (programs that develop deep levels of skills across an entire range of responsibilities in a role). A product rollout would be a performance-driven learning program, and leadership development or sales training would be a talent-driven learning program.

Our research shows that the L&D team must balance its resources so that it doesn't go 100 percent in either direction. If it focuses too heavily on performance-driven learning, it does not have the time or resources to focus on key talent development programs—and if it focuses too heavily on talent-driven learning, this could lead the organization to build separate, disconnected functional training groups.

In the end, Bersin & Associates has found that L&D is a critical foundational or supporting element of talent management. Organizationally, it is often best for L&D to report to a chief learning officer or director of training and then partner with the vice president of talent management. Organizations that move the L&D team under the talent management leader must make sure that L&D investments are not overly focused on talent programs. In this type of organization (Caterpillar is a good example), the talent management leader must take on a broader and higher-level role, in which all learning and development activities are seen as necessary and valuable.

One important factor to consider in the design and implementation of an L&D strategy to support talent management is that career development programs are highly strategic and important parts of today's talent management processes.

Figure 2-9 shows the business value (measured on the left) of a talent management program for more than 1,000 organizations, relative to the organization's fundamental model for career development. On the far left-hand side of the figure are organizations that implement the "manage your own career" approach. These companies expect employees to find their next jobs, plot their career strategies, and create their own development plans. As we move to the right, we have organizations where the manager takes on this responsibility. In these companies, managers are given tools, models, and coaching on how to help employees plan their careers and create development plans. On the far right, we see organizations that try to do this at the business unit or enterprise level.

As the data show, the impact goes from negative on the left to positive on the right, with the greatest value (or slope of the curve) at the managerial level. What this is telling us is perhaps obvious: Career or professional development must be focused at the managerial level or higher. If we expect people to find the right jobs or develop the right skills to achieve individual and organizational goals, we must create models and programs that enable managers and business units to drive career development activities.

One senior vice president of HR at a global defense and aerospace contractor said this: "We used to have the 'pinball' model of career development. People bounced around from job to job—some of them bounced out of the machine, and we just kept pumping more balls into the machine. The problem is that many of our best people went out the bottom and, due to impending retirements and demographic changes, we have fewer and fewer technical professionals available to shoot into the machine. We need a more 'deterministic' model to moving people into the right roles to help us grow."

Once an organization realizes that career development is part of its business strategy, the work to build these programs and models will fall upon L&D.

The Importance of the Organizational Culture

As more and more organizations seek to understand how talent management can be used most strategically, one of the most important dimensions to consider is culture. As many researchers have found (Schein 2004; Cameron and Quinn 2005), organizational culture both creates

Figure 2-9. The Higher Value of a Centralized Approach to Career Development Programs

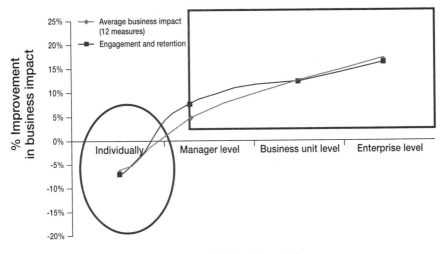

and reinforces behavior. Many of the processes and programs that make up a talent management strategy (particularly leadership development and performance management, but also training) must be highly customized and adapted to align with an organization's culture.

As Edgar Schein (2004) states in his research, people in companies do not "see the culture" any more than fish "see" the water in which they swim. Culture defines the underlying assumptions and beliefs that make an organization work.

If your company has a highly competitive environment that thrives on concepts like market leadership, competitive analysis, and growth at any cost (similar to GE), your talent management program must reflect and reinforce this culture. In these kinds of companies, talent management focuses on building organizational and process savvy, and on moving people around from role to role.

However, if your organization succeeds through deep levels of innovation, creativity, and product excellence (Qualcomm and Apple come to mind), your talent management program must reflect this culture and focus on building deep levels of skill, collaboration, and communication of technical excellence—focusing on a more "vertical" or "function-specific" talent management strategy.

And if your organization has a culture of a client intimacy or service (IBM comes to mind), your talent management program may focus on helping people build customer-focused teams, industry expertise, and contacts, and creating an "open listening," customer-centric set of people processes.

Recognition of and respect for an organization's culture is a critical element in a talent management strategy, because any program or process that does not fit into and reinforce this culture becomes underused, poorly regarded, or undervalued.

The Bottom Line

Today's integrated talent management strategies are an important and exciting way to help HR and L&D professionals add value to their organizations. As an HR or learning leader, you must remember that your job in talent management has two parts: On one hand, you are a highly specialized HR and L&D expert—armed with expertise in talent programs, processes, and systems—with a focus on consulting, process design, communications, and change management. On the other hand, you must become a business leader. You must engage with business managers to help configure, customize, tailor, and refine talent management strategies so that they reflect your organization's business strategies and culture. In this latter role, you have the opportunity to reshape the company and the way it does business.

One of the biggest challenges for all HR and L&D leaders is to stay aligned, relevant, and valued by the business. HR has a legacy of jargon, best practices, and traditions that many businesspeople neither understand nor care about all that much. Talent management, if executed with the principles outlined here, will give you a real seat at the table and enable you to add value to your organization in a highly strategic way.

Talent Management: Function and Transformation at Cisco—The Demands of the Global Economy

Annmarie Neal, Vice President of Talent, and Robert Kovach, Director of the Center for Collaborative Leadership

What's in this chapter?

♦ How Cisco built a strong talent management foundation

♦ The three pillars of strategic success

♦ What Cisco has learned from its efforts

♦ ♦ ♦

Even before the economic chaos that hit the global markets late in 2008, the world's business environment was marked by turbulence, complexity, and relentless speed. Never before has the world been so flat, so networked, or so interdependent. Competition comes from every corner in a real-time, on-demand environment that defies convention and shuns complacency. The capabilities and accessibility of emerging technologies are driving a frenzied pace of change in global economic, political, and market trends. At the same time, knowledge, power, and productive capability are more dispersed than at any other time in our history. This complex, decentralized business environment is creating a demand for new operating models and a new approach to leadership.

The Demands on the Talent Market

Even as the world gets flatter and spins faster, there is a perfect storm converging on talent, as four business- and talent-related factors converge:

- First, economists predict that in the next three to five years, we will essentially run out of talent. Our demand for globally minded talent will exceed the supply as baby boomers retire and future generations enter the workforce.

- Second, for the first time in the history of the workforce, four generations will coexist in the workplace, with very different organizational and psychological needs from their employers. Socially, this will create incredible changes for how to best attract and motivate talent, as well as how we manage and lead our organizations.

- Third, as organizations expand operations globally, our opportunities to leverage the world as our talent market increase 10-fold. Organizations are excited about and, simultaneously, worried about where to strategically locate organizational competencies and the talent to support their global operations.

- Fourth, as customers and partners from developing countries increase in strength and size, they will increasingly demand to see leadership teams that reflect their own customers and markets. And with a new generation of U.S.-educated, multilingual leaders coming out of Brazil, Russia, India, China, and Europe, U.S. companies will find ambitious, bright international counterparts that will not only lead their competitors but also provide competition for positions within their own companies.

In sum, there has never been a more exciting or challenging time to be a talent management professional.

The Demands of a New Cisco

Cisco Systems is a $40 billion company headquartered in San Jose. With more than 68,000 employees, it does business in 83 countries across 23 time zones. And since the boom of Internet 2.0, it has been experiencing global growth at double-digit rates. With such growth rates, Cisco expects to be a $50 billion company in the next three to five years.

Cisco's evolution will largely depend on Cisco 3.0, a global business initiative aimed at bringing the firm closer to its customers. At a time of increased market pressures and fierce competition, it believes that the key competitive advantage is an intimate and solutions-focused relationship with its customers. Delivering the leadership capability necessary to realize this new vision is talent management's core challenge.

Cisco is a 24-year-old company that grew up largely through acquisitions, with more than 135 to date. As such, its culture tends to be quite entrepreneurial and innovative. It is the largest functionally aligned technology organization, with the one profit-and-loss statement held by the CEO. Its executive leadership team comprises a seasoned group of executives who have been at the helm for the better part of the last 13 years. Most of those who led it through its incredible growth of the 1990s and 2000s remain in executive roles today. All its leaders are now expected to lead in an entirely new and fundamentally different way.

A Wall Street darling, Cisco grew very quickly and has been extremely successful as a product company. Historically, its growth has been built through execution against a single business model and delivered to an information technology customer. Today, it is operating as a solutions-based company, managing a large portfolio of products and services that need to work together. This is all delivered in a consultative manner to a different customer: a higher-level business executive. In this new environment, what is being delivered, how it's delivered, and to whom it's being delivered have all changed. This new consultative model requires leaders who are people-oriented consultants adept at anticipating the future. This new customer model requires leaders to create vertical depth and to understand the dynamics of their customers' businesses better than the customers themselves understand them.

As Cisco enters into new markets and provides new services, one of its first changes has been to its soft structure and management practices. As noted above, it is the largest, functionally organized technology company in existence. To keep itself agile and close to the market, it operates with cross-enterprise boards and councils designed to bring leaders and experts from around the globe together on key business priorities. This soft structure requires leaders to operate in a new way, collaboratively, and in the service of the whole, rather than in the service of their respective functions. Competition for power and resources has now been replaced by shared responsibility for success.

Best in the World; Best for the World: The CEO's Vision for Business Transformation

Cisco's network is capable of "changing the way that people work, live, play and learn." As described in the firm's 2008 Annual Report, its progressive networking technologies "give employees remote, highly secure access to customers, resources and the network so they can connect and collaborate from places—and get more done." Technology creates the network that enables the new processes that are capable of changing business processes and organizational culture. For the Cisco 3.0 strategic transformation to be successful, the firm can't just tell the world that the network is the center of innovation; it must show the world by modeling what that looks like. It must be capable of changing its processes and culture. That is why its CEO's vision is both internally and externally focused: "Best in the world; best for the world."

Transforming Leaders to Transform Cisco: Foundational Goals
To deliver on this transformation, Cisco's talent management organization knew that its leaders would all have to lead collaboratively and

anticipate the future in ways that created closer, more consultative customer and employee relationships. The foundational vision of our work became: Transform leaders to transform Cisco.

To build our leadership agenda, we began where all talent programs should: by making sure that every component we created aligned directly with the organization's strategic goals and vision for transformation. We knew that to develop successful Cisco 3.0 executives, we would need a comprehensive talent program that would

- Elevate the importance of the human dimension of the business. Leaders need to lead people, not just develop, sell, or service technology.

- Evolve the leadership. We have some of the best and brightest leaders in the high-technology sector. We need to prepare them for the challenges to lead with a global general management skill set. Our senior leaders either have been or could be CEOs in other companies. It is important that they leverage the successes they've had and build upon them to lead Cisco's future.

- Help successful people "unlearn" some of what had made them successful in the past. To change how leadership worked in Cisco, we needed to demonstrate to executives that they could be even more successful by shifting their attention to learning skills that would make them successful in the future.

- Mature the talent management/leadership development processes. Cisco had many good processes in place, but they had been created for a different time in the company's history. Processes needed to evolve to meet the demands of a transforming global enterprise.

We also knew that to truly deliver a program that met these goals and was truly transformative, we had to build nothing less than a center of excellence; a center capable of bringing Cisco the same kind of recognition for our leadership engine that we get for the way we build and deliver customer solutions—one that has produced sustainable, competitive differentiation in the marketplace that is linked directly to the management and leadership systems we have built.

From Foundations to Framework: Building the Right Solution

So how did all these lofty goals translate into what talent management is (and is not) at Cisco? *Talent management* is the discipline of managing the leadership capital of the corporation to ensure that the best leadership talent is deployed to the most significant strategic priorities with the capability needed to execute strategy for speed and scale. To accomplish this mission, our primary challenge was to engage the business leaders in a way that they had never been engaged—to provoke them in ways that they had never been provoked and to partner with them in ways that enabled them to safely explore their individual leadership styles and capabilities. Our goal was to transform our leadership development and talent management practices in a similar fashion to how Cisco was transforming its business and management practices. Table 3-1 illustrates our vision, strategy, and execution plan.

This was the first question we had to answer: How does a talent management organization help very successful executives change, midcareer? We answered this question by establishing a few basic but unconventional principles that we knew would set the right direction for our overall strategy:

◆ *We would operate as practitioners first and then as administrators.* A small team of specialist practitioners trained and experienced to deliver this work from a management consulting and organizational psychology perspective forms the core of our executive development team. We would deliver high-impact core consulting as internal providers, while outsourcing nonstrategic context work to external providers.

◆ *We would adopt a portfolio management approach focused on business impact.* Similarly to how financial planners manage investment portfolios, we set out to manage executive assets as talent portfolios. In doing so, we took a holistic approach to assessing and evaluating our talent in terms of investments. Talent managers are asset managers and, as such, are each assigned a portfolio of leaders based on geography or function. Every talent manager intimately knows the executives in his or her portfolio inside and out; the talent managers know the executives'

Table 3-1. Cisco's Plan for Vision, Strategy, and Execution

Vision	Strategy
• Strengthen and deepen Cisco's portfolio of leaders so they can manage in a complex and global environment. • Build a leadership development core competency for sustained business growth and profitability. • Establish Cisco as the employer of choice for the world's best leaders.	• Start at the top: Build a mindset; lead by example. • Take an architectural approach: Create a leadership development track that spans career paths from ICs to C-level. • Track the health of the portfolio: Measure and monitor Cisco's leadership capability and bench strength to ensure "ready now" status. • Accelerate change: Target innovative learning methodologies to accelerate Cisco's collaborative leadership engine (i.e., boards, councils, and working groups). • Establish a capstone brand: Build brand recognition for Cisco's leadership and management thought leadership to increase competitive differentiation.
	Execution • C-LEAD socialization to become synonymous with Cisco culture • One-look, cross-functional processes for talent review, executive advancement, and talent portfolio management • Succession planning for C-Suite positions • Executive assessment and development planning • Innovative learning methodologies to accelerate collaborative leadership • Targeted solutions and practices for high potential and new leaders • Organizational transformation practice to accelerate company and functional change management

Source: Center for Collaborative Leadership, Cisco.

strengths, their development needs, and their career aspirations. Though these talent managers administer standard talent management processes, their primary role is to act as asset managers for their designated business geography or function. Toward this end, they not only provide consultation on individual leadership issues but also step back and provide insights on broad organizational dynamics that help guide the development that truly creates a significant return on investment of their talent portfolio. Talent managers will regularly ask themselves a series of questions: How are my talent assets performing? Where are my liabilities and vulnerabilities, and how do I need to manage (short term and long term) for them? Where do I need to rebalance my assets to gain greater performance in the portfolio? Are there specific assets that need to be added to the portfolio to strengthen long-term performance? Strong financial planners understand their assets under management extremely well. So do our talent management professionals.

♦ *We would customize our delivery of solutions.* Because we were dealing with seasoned, successful executives, we knew that we would not be successful if we took a transactional approach. A customized approach is critical not only to understanding each executive on an individual level but also to creating different conversations about leadership. One-to-one relationships help build the foundational trust that is necessary to do the work at the level it needs to be done.

♦ *We would never sacrifice quality.* Although sometimes it is easier for talent organizations to accept simpler, shorter-term solutions, the team made the commitment that we would never sacrifice quality to make the work easier. We knew that to create an integrated program that was truly aligned to our CEO's vision, we would have to work harder and deliver greater quality than the system had even known was possible. Beyond transactional support, we were committed to creating customized solutions that addressed specific business needs.

♦ *We would leverage Cisco's technology to scale our impact.* By leveraging visual networking technologies like Telepresence, we connect global executives with executive development professionals to provide personal, face-to-face consultations. Our executive development team brings a variety of nationalities, backgrounds, and perspectives to their work. The faculty engagements and psychological assessments that this team delivers are made possible by the efficiencies these technologies afford us. These approaches deliberately model a use of the network that is at the center of the innovation Cisco delivers to its global customer base.

Changing the Rules of the Game: Three Pillars of Strategic Success

Because Cisco was changing the rules of the game in the marketplace, we knew we had to change the rules of the game internally. Only an aggressive and out-of-the-box strategy had a chance of delivering the desired results. We decided on a few key transformational processes, organized as three pillars, that focused deliberately on executive audiences. We knew we couldn't just tell people to change; we had to give them each their own reason and their own path.

Pillar One: Defining Collaborative Leadership with the C-LEAD Model

To effectively transform our leadership paradigm, the Cisco talent team, in partnership with the firm's business units, needed to define what kind of leadership behaviors were necessary for Cisco to achieve its aggressive growth goals. To do so, we leveraged collaborative technology to engage 200 leaders around the globe in the creation of the competency model. This collaborative approach increased engagement and the rate of adoption, and it stands in contrast to the more traditional approach of having leadership models created by external consultants and rolled out by human resources.

Finally, after having benchmarked the work against industry best practices and other large corporations, we were left with a highly customized, strategically aligned model that was developed by the business and for the business and was enabled by human resources. Though some of the model was consistent with current thinking about successful business leadership, three components unique to the Cisco challenge emerged: collaborate, accelerate, and disrupt—which led to our C-LEAD model, the first pillar of strategic success.

The Cisco C-LEAD model, shown in table 3-2, establishes five leadership themes and 12 competencies, each designed to answer an integral question:

- *Collaborate:* Does the leader work across traditional boundaries to achieve success on behalf of the customer and the enterprise?

- *Learn:* Is the leader building individual as well as team skills to succeed in a complex, dynamic environment?

- *Execute:* Is the leader engaging others in the work and empowering the team to achieve exceptional results?

- *Accelerate:* Is the leader building bold strategies for the future as well as the organizational capability needed to achieve these strategies?

- *Disrupt:* Does the leader promote innovation and manage change in support of Cisco's strategy?

C-LEAD, which is now being embedded in all of Cisco's leadership and people practices, creates a common language and a clear definition of the organization's leadership expectations and aspirations. When a leadership paradigm is well articulated, even employees deep within the organization will be better informed regarding the right questions to ask and the best direction to take. And in C-LEAD, the push to collaborate and disrupt bookend the model, providing the right emphasis on how leadership at Cisco is different, by definition.

Before moving to the second pillar, let's consider how Cisco evaluates its leadership portfolio in light of C-LEAD requirements. C-LEAD

Table 3-2. C-LEAD Competency Definitions

	Theme Definition		Competency Definition
C	*Connecting with customers, partners, suppliers, and colleagues across functions as well as geographies to achieve significant results.*	Working across boundaries	Involving customers, partners, suppliers, and groups from across the enterprise to develop strategy and maximize results.
		Engaging others	Motivating others to align with and execute against the organization's objectives.
		Earning trust	Earning the confidence of others through open communication and respectful behavior.
L	*Building Cisco's capabilities by continuing to develop own and others' skills.*	Developing self	Continuing to develop the leadership and technical/functional capabilities needed to achieve results for Cisco.
		Developing others	Helping others develop the capabilities needed for individual career growth and effective leadership at Cisco.
E	*Delivering exceptional results by building commitment to the business and enabling teams to succeed.*	Demonstrating passion	Communicating personal commitment to Cisco's vision and success in the global marketplace.
		Empowering teams	Providing the direction, support, and authority teams need to achieve significant results.
		Achieving results	Translating strategy into clear operating plans and promoting operational excellence in the delivery of results.
A	*Developing bold strategies and the organization's capability to achieve its objectives.*	Shaping strategy	Developing a bold strategy for the business that is based on input from multiple sources and promotes short-term as well as long-term success.
		Building capability	Building an exceptional portfolio of talent to lead and execute against Cisco's business strategy.
D	*Promoting change and innovation to support Cisco's strategy and set Cisco apart in the global marketplace.*	Promoting innovation	Creating an environment that encourages innovation in support of Cisco's business strategy.
		Leading change	Initiates and effectively guides the organization through change.

defines a common standard for leadership at Cisco. To gauge leadership performance against these core competencies, we have designed two signature processes that have elevated our talent management approach and business impact.

The first process is the *one-look leadership review*. The key question in leadership and succession management is this: Do the leadership capabilities of our portfolio of senior executives meet current and future business needs? Cisco's leadership review process was designed two years ago to formally and thoroughly answer this question. Annually, the talent management team goes through the process of calibrating executive talent and completing depth chart planning, a holistic and comprehensive look at senior talent by function and across the organization.

This review process changes the game because talent management is placed squarely in the context of systemic business planning; talent is projected directly against current and future requirements, and the direct result of the leadership review is a series of talent management action plans that intend to close identified gaps. Cisco's process is by design administratively simple but consultatively rich. The impact of this process comes not from the completion of the templates but instead from facilitating a robust dialogue about people and organizational issues and opportunities. By compiling these functional reviews for Cisco's board, we help keep talent at the center of strategic conversations.

The second process is *executive nomination*. This process helps answer the question: Are we promoting the best leaders who are most capable of leading Cisco through transformation? Traditionally, executives would be promoted for past performance or significant operational results. We have elevated the executive nomination process to make sure that several factors are considered, including the scope of the proposed role, the formally assessed capability of the leader (against C-LEAD), and the business relevance of the role. The nomination committee conducts these executive nomination reviews quarterly, leveraging customized executive assessments prepared by our small team of highly qualified internal executive development consultants.

Pillar Two: Executive and Leadership Development

The foundational Cisco Leadership Series was developed in an effort to retain high-potential industry talent during the "dot-bust" downturn. It includes management education offerings that provide the educational component of our talent development approach. Each program provides education on a different aspect of management.

Although we believe strongly in the role of this educational foundation, we recognize that Cisco's transformation requires a significantly different and more customized approach to developing each of our executives—the second pillar of strategic success. Educational products like the Cisco Leadership Series only provide one piece of a much more comprehensive, solutions-based approach to developing global executive talent. To round out our educational offerings, we developed two game-changing processes.

The first is the *customized executive assessment process*. The first step in this process is a customized, qualitative 360-degree evaluation of executives against the expectations that our C-LEAD model enunciates. Ultimately, the process assesses the potential and capability they have against the impact that they wish to create on the future. All our assessments employ some of the most rigorous assessment techniques on the market and use either internal assessors or a small, select group of external assessors who are prepared to make a longer-term commitment to Cisco's success. Several objectives drive this process:

- ♦ Helping smart, successful people learn how to lead "differently"—which could mean under different market conditions, with different business model demands, in new or different markets, and/or with more advanced products and solutions. Successful leaders need to unlearn certain behaviors that made them successful earlier in their careers to assimilate new leadership behaviors that are relevant to their current and future leadership challenges.

- ♦ Putting honesty and edge into the leadership system. Creating specific, goal-oriented individual leadership development plans adds significant transparency to the development process.

♦ Building consigliere relationships with senior executives. Trusted advisers counterbalance the "loneliness at the top" dynamic that executives often experience by creating a confidential sounding board for working through key business decisions.

♦ Connecting and networking Cisco's leadership system. Building an ecosystem of leaders who operate in different ways broadens perspectives and adds an additional support component to the process. This builds the power of the executive human network.

The individual development plans produced as a result of these customized assessments purposefully leverage the organization itself to develop executives, based on the experiences and exposures they each need. These plans are not built to mitigate areas of opportunity uncovered in past performance but to help create skills that will be required against a projection of Cisco's future needs.

The second process involves the *Action Learning Forum (ALF)*. In ALF, these directed development plans are implemented in a real-time, real-world approach that sets our action learning approach apart from most. C-LEAD provides important guidance that informs Cisco's collaborative leadership development approach, but it only provides the foundation. The customized executive assessment process adds another layer by creating strategic development plans using the C-LEAD model as one important measurement. Experiential programs provide the creative environment for competencies and opportunities to bloom fully into proven capabilities.

ALF was launched in 2007 and is now a signature development initiative for executives. The forum provides high-potential leaders with opportunities to accelerate the development of their general management and collaborative leadership skills by working on projects of high strategic importance to Cisco. ALF provides the most effective means of developing executives at this level because it combines top-notch business school teaching with real work on meaningful projects that creates measurable business results. Simulations are not part of the program.

Each ALF project is created when the business uncovers a significant strategic opportunity that needs to be addressed. ALF provides both the methodology and the capability to address the strategic opportunity by incorporating three important development components:

♦ A customized executive assessment against the C-LEAD competency model that identifies key strengths and development needs for the leaders involved.

♦ Cross-organizational collaborative assignments that bring together senior leaders from around the globe to solve significant strategic problems for the corporation.

♦ Exposure to a senior executive governance board that reviews business proposals, provides real-time feedback, and makes investment decisions.

Rather than being a one-time educational event, ALF intends to drive actual sustainable, transformational change for both the organization and the individual leader. Each forum comprises 40 to 60 leaders with the potential to ascend into Cisco's most critical (or linchpin) positions. These participants are then divided into cross-functional global teams that are charged with both competing and collaborating with each other to design strategy solutions for "disruptive innovation" business models for Cisco. Over a six- to 12-week period, an ALF cohort will produce on average six comprehensive business plans that each result in $1 billion in business opportunity for the company. To date, Cisco has benefited from more than $25 billion of well-researched business plans as a result of ALF.

Pillar Three: Organizational Transformation

Once we have established our consultative relationships with executives and helped each of them create a transformational body of work, it's time to tie it all into something even bigger. Ultimately, we aim to leverage our consultants to support the transformational work of the executives we serve. But each piece of work we do to enable an executive to be transformed must feed into the whole. Our aim is not individual transformation but organizational transformation achieved as a collective result of all of our individual, regional, and functional efforts. To do this, we must operate within the common framework that the first two pillars of strategic success express. Those pillars, built on the foundation of strategic alignment and cemented with the work that our small band of experts applies across the globe, can only provide structural security when joined by the third pillar: the transformation of Cisco as an organization, accomplished by talent management consulting performed at the organizational level.

Measurement: The Impact

As with many aspects of Cisco's talent management program, we take a nontraditional approach to measurement. Historically, talent programs have looked for validation in measurements that are hard (if not impossible) to correlate to business impact. For example, being able to recite what percentage of your executives has been through a particular educational program gives no insight into the readiness of your talent to face tomorrow's business challenges. Nor do "theoretical" projections about the impact of executive education on stock price or company profitability allow for a brutally honest discussion to take place regarding which development practices are *both* developing the people and affecting the business. That is why we aren't nearly as concerned with those kinds of measurement as we are with alignment, accountability, and impact.

Ultimately, our success will be measured by the success of Cisco's leadership transformation. To build these capabilities, we have defined the next generation of leadership with our C-LEAD model. We have leveraged our key processes to identify, deploy, and develop leaders against this model through our executive assessment, leadership review, executive nomination, and action learning programs. We are enabling Cisco's business transformation from command and control (traditional vertical leadership) to collaboration (horizontal leadership) by creating customized development plans and partnerships with our executives. Perhaps most important, we have infused everything we do with transparency so that our goals are always explicit and that our leadership team clearly understands the "who, what, where, when, and why" behind our processes and programs.

In Cisco's Center for Collaborative Leadership, we spend most of our time focused on strategies for solving unique business problems faced by Cisco. By spending most of our time on the business side and defining who we are and what we do strictly in terms of the top priorities of the business, we are accomplishing our objective, which organically leads to business impact. Our formula could be expressed like this:

business strategy + the highest quality assessment and development planning + tailored people and organizational consulting solutions = guaranteed business impact.

Specific successes can be impossible to measure, but if the business is performing holistically, success is hard to miss.

The Role of Cisco's Executives in Talent Management

In three important and distinct ways, we at Cisco formally and deliberately engage our leadership to keep them interested, involved, and informed about the direction of our talent management efforts. We don't perform executive development for them; we do it in partnership with them. We know that the executives are experts at running a successful business and that our talent management professionals are experts in how adults learn, develop, and grow over time. This collaboration between experts, with mutual respect, allows for true synergy. And it keeps talent management's strategic vision right where it belongs: at the forefront of executives' daily business decisions. These are three ways in which we engage our leadership:

♦ *The advisory committee for Cisco's Center for Collaborative Leadership:* The center receives guidance from an advisory committee of executives from across the organization. This guidance provides the firm's next generation of leaders with an opportunity for direct input into its executive and leadership agenda. The advisory committee is made up of 10 up-and-coming senior executives. They are all leaders who are passionate about Cisco's future and who sit in senior roles, through which they have the credibility and power to effect the necessary changes to our people and organization strategies and systems. Additionally, the advisory committee has one external member to keep our thinking relevant and progressive. Our current external member is a leading expert in the areas of innovation, strategy, and organizational transformation.

♦ *The Executive Nominations Committee:* The executive vice presidents who sit on this committee are accountable for the governance and process that guide executive nomination and top talent strategy. The talent management staff meets with these executives quarterly to discuss issues related to the executive talent portfolio.

♦ *Leaders as teachers:* Cisco's entire executive learning program is topic specific and oriented toward practical action. Although we use external faculty for various components of our program, we recognize the value that top leaders can provide by focusing on the real-life challenges of working at Cisco. Those leaders who teach are chosen selectively and are recognized role models of the leadership behaviors necessary for success in the future.

What We Have Learned

It is stating the obvious and has been talked about for years, but talent managers must align talent management to business strategy. Talent management must start with business strategy and, when executed well, become a key lever of strategy execution and organizational success. We think often about how we can effectively leverage our full suite of talent management services in support of the development of a strong and strategically aligned organizational culture. How can we lead our organization through comprehensive cultural change? It requires starting with a strong definition of what our culture needs to be and then systematically hiring, developing, and rewarding the executive talent necessary to achieve what has been defined.

Actively Managing Change

The real strategy effort involves not so much aligning our work with our business strategy as assessing the organization's readiness to embrace the work that the strategy demands and predicting the psychological and organizational resistance inherent in the process. Leaders make difficult business decisions every day, yet they often become paralyzed when they need to make difficult people decisions. We expect resistance, we welcome it, we predict how it will show up, and we appreciate that working through it productively is a core part of our talent management process. Organizational and cultural change begins with individual change. Moving individuals successfully through change is labor intensive and requires psychological awareness, stamina, and endurance. We believe that managing change proactively will prevent us from the need to address issues later when resistance can build up and derail our initiatives.

We remind ourselves regularly that, by definition, effective, high-impact talent management will both challenge and change the organization's culture. To be the best talent management executives that we can be for Cisco, we commit to doing our work in highly purposeful and strategic ways. During our collective years of experience, we've observed that success and failure are relative to the organization's culture. The unconscious dynamics of a corporation's culture are powerful and at work to sustain homeostasis. The forces that attempt to keep the organization at a steady state are always greater than the forces that attempt to drive change. Thus, anything that threatens the current state of balance will be viewed with suspicion. Talent management processes and tools affect the lives and careers of executives. When done well, they also influence the many financial and positional rewards that come with career acceleration and demotions. Good talent management work will disrupt and even threaten the incumbent power infrastructure. We work hard to keep aware of, diagnose, and navigate through these dynamics. Sometimes we feel impotent in the face of these dynamics, but we consider this a good sign that organizational resistance is at its peak and that desired change is well under way.

All major organizational changes are threatening. We appreciate that by setting out to change Cisco's culture, we will threaten a group of incumbent leaders who may be insecure regarding their long-term position or who are more committed to the past than they are to the future (we call these legacy leaders). Thus, we can't stress enough the importance of paying attention to this dynamic as you are setting your organization's talent management agenda. If your leaders are not ready to accept a new generation of talented, empowered leaders, then don't help develop them. You will only threaten those leaders in power today while frustrating those who are emerging. And, sadly, you will just grow your talent, only to send them out to your competitors armed with more information and skills. If you fail to recognize that there are leaders who are afraid of the success of strong talent management, your agenda will be at risk.

It is essential to be insightful and predictive about threatened leadership. Leaders become threatened for a whole host of reasons, all of which revolve around some fear of failure. Leaders may feel out of control, out of balance, overshadowed, or shown up. Even worse, they may feel that their power is being challenged or completely taken away. In our collective years as corporate psychologists, we have never heard of a leader who set out in the morning to come to work and fail. Yet many set out unconsciously protecting themselves from the threats of failure. When your talent management initiatives bump up against these fears, they will likely create mostly unconscious reactions in leaders of protection—my position, my patch of responsibility, my power—and survival. For this reason, we pay as much attention to building organizational confidence in those who are at risk of acting out as we do to building organizational capability in the next generation of leaders. That is why individually tailored consultation is central to Cisco's approach.

You Can't Do It Alone

Collaboration among talent management, human resources, and company leadership is essential to achieving the desired success. To effectively compete in this war for talent, everyone must be unified and aligned toward common goals. There is the same familiar rallying cry here, but it still applies: Talent management professionals, human resources professionals, and business leaders must work together to identify needs and build strategies to address these needs. At Cisco, where we seek to inspire collaborative leadership, settling for anything less undermines our own reputation and contradicts our overarching strategy.

Be the Change You Want to See in Your Organization

To effectively manage change, we must be change resilient ourselves. We, too, have to unlearn those behaviors that made us successful in the past. As our businesses become more flat, more global, and more complex, our talent management approaches must become more adaptive and relevant to an ever-changing business environment. We must constantly change our mindsets to keep ourselves relevant, vital, and on edge—looking forward to what is next, not looking backward at what was. Create collaborative relationships across your team, with human resources, and with your other business partners so that you can model the leadership traits you seek to develop in others.

Focus on Quality over Quantity

Cisco leverages its technology to maximize the productivity of our most highly experienced and educated talent management professionals. Using a customized approach is not the most cost-effective method, but it is the most effective for getting desired results. We constantly choose quality and business impact over breadth and numbers. By being innovative in how we use technology, we've been able to increase our reach across our internal leadership market while reducing costs of delivery by approximately 33 percent.

Be a Practitioner First, Then an Administrator

We made the choice to be more than just administrators of talent management processes and products. We constantly assess where the right point of balance is along the practitioner-administrator continuum for our company, both now and in the future. As practitioners, we made the decision that we must be thought leaders and not order takers. We've adopted a mantra on the team to "meet clients where they are at *and* show them a different way of thinking and operating." We try to show that we understand the current mindset they are operating from and show them both the advantages and compromises within that mindset. To take this position, we had to be sure that we had a common point of view of what good work would look like vis-à-vis the business strategy. We actively push the organization, knowing and fully accepting that we would rather be fired for doing the right work well than keep our jobs for doing the wrong work adequately.

It's Not about the Process

The best talent managers rely on and leverage their organizational development skills every day. Because we strategically chose a practitioner model on which to execute our approach, our talent team diagnoses, strategizes, and operates every minute of every day with a product tool kit second to their consulting tool kit. We view our work as being less about designing processes and programs and more about assessing organization readiness and preparing leaders for change. Our best talent management work is strong organization development work. This makes perfect sense, given the coming challenges of how to manage cultural change. We know that we need to operate well within our culture, while at the same time utilizing our consultancy skills to challenge cultural assumptions and call attention to cultural obstacles and barriers. It is a tight rope to walk.

Understandably, it is easy for us as talent managers to see a talent problem and solve it by building a tool or launching a process. Too often in our profession, the tendency is to conduct a best practices study to learn what others are doing and then cherry-pick the best ideas and implement them as if they were designed and customized for our company. We all borrow ideas from other organizations, and we should. However, we've learned that our best solutions come when we step back and apply these ideas in the context of our organization's business challenges, culture, leadership, and, most important, readiness to absorb the change.

Can You Really Measure What Matters?

A subtheme within this overarching theme of tools and accountability is the pressure to measure that which, in fact, may not be measurable.

Measuring impact is a challenge, because there is a logical tension between the need to measure to show business relevance and the need to appreciate that, given the long-term nature of the work (and the fact that so many confounding variables and exogenous factors are at play), the attainment of pure measurement is more a fantasy than a reality. For this reason, we suggest measuring return-on-expectations rather than return-on-investment. This perspective helps us collect data and tell our story in a way that is unique to each audience: our board of directors, our CEO, our executive team, and our human resources partners. If we begin by trying to understand each group's expectations and then build our talent management strategy specifically on the goal of creating business impact, the pressure to produce incremental, less-productive measurement can be reduced.

Summing Up

The complexity of moving from theory to reality comes from the contrary forces at work in most organizations. Just because the business strategy demands it doesn't mean the organization will embrace, execute, or sustain good talent management. It is important to gain visible executive sponsorship and to continually position the talent management agenda at the forefront of the business planning process and the CEO/board agenda. Don't be distracted by ideals; focus on what is achievable. Assess your own skills as talent managers, and start with a plan for managing change—a focus on what you know your culture can absorb and on what is achievable. Don't ever believe that one size fits all or that a best practice will necessarily be the best one for your situation. We do operate in a complex world, yet talent management systems are typically created by members of one culture to manage members of the same culture. Tools and processes must never take the place of human interaction, quality must never suffer for expediency, and measurement must always focus on business impact, not on activities.

The economic crisis of 2008 reminds us that the future is unwritten and in some ways unknowable. A quick scan of the news indicates that the level of turbulence in our economic and political environment probably won't abate. And in talent management, we are trying to predict winners in a race with no finish line. An old adage about business planning goes, "When times are good, have a simple plan; when times are complex, have a very simple plan." So our philosophy of talent management is simply stated but, like most things, more difficult to actually achieve: Know your business and what it's trying to achieve, know your leaders and what they want and need, and remember that you are affecting many people's lives and possibly their livelihoods with your talent consultation, tools, and processes. For this reason, we take our responsibility as talent management executives very seriously.

So . . . Simple? Yes. Easy to achieve? No. High impact and rewarding? Definitely!

McDonald's Talent Management and Leadership Development

Neal Kulick, Vice President, Global Talent Management (Retired as of July 2009)

What's in this chapter?

♦ How talent management is structured at McDonald's

♦ A step-by-step explanation of how McDonald's built its talent management capability

♦ The impact of the talent management approach on McDonald's

McDonald's Corporation is a $23-billion-plus global business with more than 31,000 restaurants in 118 countries serving more than 55 million customers each day. Founded by Ray Kroc in 1955, at the tender age of 54, McDonald's has been in business for more than 53 years. It has had a long track record of outstanding and steady growth and, since going public in 1965, has provided outstanding total returns to its shareholders. McDonald's more recent history, specifically from 2000 to 2009, has been particularly interesting for several reasons, each of which is explained below.

For the first time in its history, the business declared a loss (for the fourth quarter of 2002). In spite of significant growth in new restaurants and huge investments in capital to support this growth, the business was not earning sufficient returns on investments. Additionally, it was clear that restaurant operations, the hallmark of McDonald's success, were suffering and that quality, speed, and cleanliness performance had slipped. Our customers noticed, and they told us about it.

McDonald's stock price hit a low of below $13 per share in March 2003, and in December of that year the board of directors made the decision to replace the CEO. His replacement, James Cantalupo, 60 at the time of his appointment, had recently retired from the company after a long career in finance and international operations. Appointed as his COO was another long-time McDonald's executive, Charlie Bell, who started as a McDonald's "crew" member in Australia and progressed rapidly in the business. Charlie was only 43 when appointed as COO. The board charged Cantalupo and Bell with "righting the ship"—getting McDonald's back on track and turned around.

In 2003, they, along with other key business leaders, crafted a turnaround strategy that is still in place—labeled McDonald's "Plan to Win." This global strategy, which has been adopted in every market, essentially laid out five areas of focus—known as the "five Ps"—and standards for each:

- people
- product
- place
- price
- promotion.

Each market, working under this common Plan to Win framework, was able to customize and localize its specific approach, as long as the market remained within the framework. This governance philosophy was labeled freedom within a consistent framework, and it, too, is still in place today as McDonald's overall governance philosophy.

McDonald's went from its historical focus of building new restaurants as the primary growth strategy to getting better, not bigger. The growth of new restaurants was scaled back almost completely so that the overwhelming focus could be on improving the existing 30,000-plus restaurants already in the system. The other growth strategy of acquiring new brands to scale (including Boston Market, Chipotle, Pret à Manger, Donato's Pizza, and the like) was also reversed, because it was determined that these new brands would take too long to scale in a meaningful way and, more important, they were a distraction to the management team and others in the system. The bottom line was that the focus was back on McDonald's restaurants to grow revenue significantly with better quality, service, speed, cleanliness, value, and new products.

Tragedy struck McDonald's in 2004 in a way that few other companies have known or likely will experience. The first tragedy occurred in April 2004, at McDonald's owner-operator convention in Orlando. Early in the morning of the first day of the convention—which was attended by more than 15,000 owner operators, employees, and suppliers—Jim Cantalupo suddenly died of a heart attack in his hotel room, only a few hours before he was scheduled to give the opening keynote speech. Needless to say, this postponed the opening session on Monday morning, and the board of directors had an emergency meeting to appoint Charlie Bell as the new CEO. The convention went carefully forward with Bell and other key executives leading with remarkable skill and sensitivity, moving on in a way that enabled everyone to express their emotions with regard to the tragedy and support one another, but still go forward with the most important business at hand.

The tragedies would not end with the loss of Cantalupo. Shortly after Bell returned to Chicago the week following the convention, he was diagnosed with colon cancer. He battled the cancer valiantly but had to resign in December 2004 and died in January 2005. The board named Jim Skinner, a former "crew kid" with more than 30 years of service, who had progressed to his then-current role of vice chairman, as the new CEO.

Skinner wasted no time in establishing his priorities and communicating them to both the board and to his entire leadership team. He launched his CEO agenda with three priorities. One of these was talent management and leadership development. It was clear that the tragedies suffered by McDonald's, with the loss of two CEOs to illness within a 12-month period, influenced his priorities, for the importance of having a deep internal pipeline, and maintaining it going forward, was never clearer to him or the board. McDonald's received a great deal of positive press for its ability to have a deep pool of executive talent ready and able to step up to the CEO role in a short time. After all, Skinner was McDonald's fourth CEO in a 24-month period. And there have been only seven CEOs in McDonald's entire history.

As of this writing, in December 2008, McDonald's has had an incredible run of success. The company has experienced 68 consecutive months of positive comparable sales (that is, improvement in sales for a particular month relative to the previous year's same month). This is the longest positive run in McDonald's history, and the stock price hit an all-time high in September 2008. It has been one of the few stocks in the Standard & Poor's 500 that has managed to maintain its value during the economic crises of 2008–2009. In 2008, McDonald's served 58 million customers a day!

Expanding Talent Management to the Leadership Level

McDonald's has had a long history of focusing on its people and on talent. Most of this history, until recently, has focused on the talent in the restaurants (crew and management). With more than 1.5 million employees wearing a McDonald's uniform worldwide, people have been and always will be at the center of McDonald's success. Ensuring that all restaurant staff are properly trained and motivated is key. To accomplish this, Hamburger University was established in 1961 as the training center for all restaurant and supervisory staff employees. HU, as it is known, is based in Oak Brook, Illinois, at Corporate Headquarters, but it has seven regional branches throughout the world. Approximately 5,000 students attend HU each year, and since its inception there have been more than 75,000 graduates.

McDonald's focus on talent management was reassessed in 2000 by the then-chairman/CEO, Jack Greenberg, who realized that the business was struggling in the marketplace and was concerned that there was not enough focus on developing McDonald's leadership talent. He believed that the time had come to put much more emphasis on developing leaders at McDonald's and wanted to form a new organization to focus on both succession planning and leadership development. This new organization was funded and established in July 2001 and charged with building a succession planning and leadership capability to ensure that McDonald's would have a high-performing leadership team in place both "today and into the future."

Figure 4-1 shows the message map that was developed to communicate this new organization's overall goal of talent management (center) and the three subgoals. Figure 4-2 describes the four major process areas that the organization has in focus.

Taken together, these four areas—along with compensation/benefits, which remains as a separate organization but is within human resources (HR)—define what is now called talent management at McDon-

Figure 4-1. The Goal of Talent Management

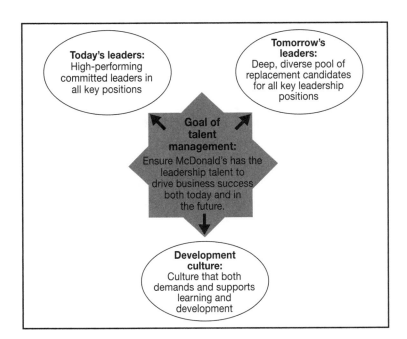

Figure 4-2. The Scope of Talent Management

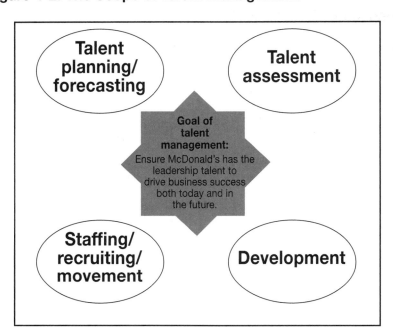

ald's. Building a capability and capacity for these four key areas has been the focus of the organization since its inception in 2001.

What follows are some details about how this capability was built and what has been accomplished. We'll also look at initiatives that fell short and at what could have been done differently and, presumably, better. This chronology occurred, as stated previously, across the tenure of four different CEOs in this short seven-year time frame.

Step 1: The Starting Point—Fixing the Performance Management System

Until 2000, McDonald's performance management system seemed to work well. At least it was making a lot of people happy in that the distribution of ratings, especially among the top leadership team (top 200), was significantly skewed to the positive. The ratings for 2000, using the five-point scale in use at the time, are shown in table 4-1. At this time, the business was performing extremely poorly, and the stock price was

Table 4-1. Ratings for McDonald's Performance Management System, 2000

Rating	Percent Receiving the Rating
Exceptional	60
Outstanding	38
Good	2
Needs improvement	0
Unsatisfactory	0

declining steadily. A total of 38 percent of these officers were rated as "ready now" for advancement, and another 60 percent were rated as "ready future."

Without differentiating between individuals on performance and potential, there was no way to install a succession planning process at McDonald's. Therefore, it was decided that it was time to change the culture at McDonald's from one of "entitlement" to one of "earning." One aspect of this change was to fix the performance management system. These significant changes were made and implemented, effective in 2002:

- ◆ Moved from five to three rating categories, with new rating labels.
- ◆ Established target rating distributions of 20 percent in the highest category, 70 percent in the middle category, and 10 percent in the lowest category, as a way of reducing rating inflation.
- ◆ Added demonstrated competencies to the evaluation criteria, in addition to simply assessing performance against goals, so that ratings were based not only on what was accomplished but also on how it was accomplished.
- ◆ Established calibration roundtables for performance and potential assessment.
- ◆ Aligned compensation systems to ensure that pay differentiation matched performance differentiation.

The decision was made to introduce the new performance management system at the officer level so that the top 200 leaders would personally experience the new process before it was implemented with their teams. As expected, the first year resulted in a lot of anguish in that a high percentage of officers received performance ratings in the middle category (significant performance). This was the first time in many, if not most, of their careers that they had been rated less than outstanding or excellent! Fortunately, the shock wore off in time for the new system to be implemented globally over the next few years. The new performance management system resulted in clearly differentiated ratings, as illustrated in figure 4-3.

There were several "lessons learned" related to changing the performance management system:

◆ You can't do talent management unless there is a performance management system in place that clearly differentiates both performance and potential.

Figure 4-3. Performance Rating Guidelines

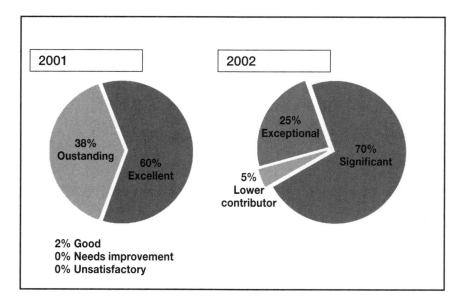

- You don't move to the 20/70/10 distribution guideline without upsetting people, but the good news is that they will get used to it!

- Aligning compensation is critical.

- Starting implementation at the top will help get support for full implementation (misery loves company).

Step 2: Establishing a Talent Management Plan Process and Review

In 2002, once McDonald's had a performance management system that clearly differentiated on performance and potential, we could begin to assess the depth and diversity of our talent pipeline with much greater confidence. To accomplish this, a Talent Plan template was developed as a guide for every major business unit (area of the world) and every major country to utilize. This template laid out what was expected in the Talent Plan and provided samples and illustrations to support it.

The key elements of the Talent Plan were

- forecast of leadership requirements tied to the business strategy for that business unit

- assessment of the performance and advancement potential of each member of the current leadership team

- identification of backups and feeder pools for all key leadership positions

- if replacement gaps existed, an action plan to close the gap

- diversity analysis and an action plan, with the general rule that diversity improvement should occur year over year

- a retention strategy for top talent

- a leadership development strategy for the business unit and individual development plans for key talent.

Talent Plan reviews were established at the senior management level on an annual basis. The CEO met with each of those reporting directly to him in the April–May time frame to review and discuss his or her talent plans in detail. Similarly, senior leaders reporting to the

COO also had their plans reviewed. HR's leadership was present during these reviews, but the meetings were led by the senior leader, not the HR leader.

These Talent Plan reviews were meant to be iterative and based on discussion. The goal was for senior managers to report on the strengths of their leadership teams today and the depth and diversity of their leadership pipeline. During these sessions, many critical issues were discussed with the CEO and/or COO, who provided their viewpoints and insights.

To ensure that this planning process was tied to meaningful metrics, five key goals were established, although it was not expected that all these goals would be met in the initial years. The goals were as follows:

- A total of 95 percent of the current leadership team would meet or exceed their performance objectives.
- A total of 100 percent of lower performers would be on improvement plans, with dates to either "improve or remove" them from their roles.
- A total of 90 percent of the key leadership positions would have adequate succession candidates, including at least one ready now and one ready future candidate.
- There would be 95-percent retention of the top talent, including both the highest performers and high potentials.
- There would be written development plans for all those with high potential.

The first time these plans were completed and reviews took place, the results and metrics were not encouraging:

- More than 50 percent of the key leadership positions lacked adequate backups.
- There was a clear need to improve diversity, especially gender diversity.

Based upon these findings, it was clear that McDonald's needed to take steps to accelerate the development of the feeder pool to build up the depth and diversity of the next generation of leaders. This would be the next step in the evolution of McDonald's talent management capability.

McDonald's learned these lessons from the establishment of this Talent Plan process:

- The first iterations of a Talent Plan will be a bit disappointing—it takes a few years before the plans reflect sufficient quality and detail.

- There is a need to reinforce the strong linkage required between the business strategy and the Talent Plan, because this linkage may not be made as naturally as one might expect.

- It is important to establish a disciplined follow-up process to the plans so that commitments that are made within the plans are tracked and leaders are held accountable.

- It is useful to start at the top of the organization and then work your way down through all levels.

- Goals and metrics are important, but be careful not to put so much emphasis on them that you may encourage managers to "stretch the truth." (Example: If a metric is the percentage of leadership positions for which there are strong backup candidates, there might be a tendency to list names of individuals as backups who are really not as strong as required.)

Step 3: Designing Accelerated Development Processes to Build the Depth and Diversity of Feeder Pools

With the goal of increasing the depth and diversity of the replacement pools for McDonald's top 200 leadership positions, an accelerated development program was designed and piloted in 2003. The program was titled the Leadership @ McDonald's Program (LAMP). The program was global, with 24 high-potential directors/senior directors assessed as having the potential to assume a "top 200" position within the next three or four years. Participants came from Europe, Asia and the Pacific, the Middle East, Latin America, and the United States, with a wide variety of functional backgrounds. From a diversity standpoint, there were

40 percent women and 39 percent minority participants representing 11 countries.

Candidates for LAMP were nominated by the senior leader of their respective organization and screened and admitted into the program by the CEO. Criteria were provided to guide the nomination process, including the goal to nominate a diverse group of candidates so that we could achieve our goal of building up the diversity of our feeder pool. That said, no specific numerical targets were set for diversity. Fortunately, and to the credit of the senior leaders who nominated candidates, our first class was extremely diverse.

The goals of LAMP were to

- ♦ broaden participants' understanding of our business, from a global and cross-cultural perspective
- ♦ enhance leadership skills, with a special focus on those skills and perspectives required of a more senior leader, both today and into the future
- ♦ build relationships and a strong network among the participants
- ♦ provide exposure to business issues and best practices outside McDonald's
- ♦ reinforce the commitment to continuous learning and self-development
- ♦ provide senior leaders with the opportunity to get to know the participants better via active participation and dialogue during the sessions
- ♦ provide special recognition for participants via their being nominated to participate in LAMP, hence building their level of organizational engagement.

LAMP participants went through a personal orientation with a member of the Talent Management Team. The purpose of the orientation was to provide each participant with a realistic picture of the program, including the time commitment. Given that LAMP participants were expected to continue their normal work assignments during the duration of the program, LAMP was a significant overlay on their already busy schedules. It was expected that their participation would take approximately 25 to 30 percent of their time.

LAMP was primarily designed using McDonald's internal resources, but there was a strong partnership with an outside consultant/facilitator who worked shoulder to shoulder with the internal staff both to design and execute the program. The combination of internal and external thought leadership proved to be outstanding, as the program design was unique for McDonald's, reflecting outside thinking and experiences, but also relevant and appropriate to the company's culture.

The key elements of LAMP included

♦ a nine-month program with six classroom sessions of three to four days each

♦ a third-party assessment and a 360-degree (boss, peer, direct report) survey feedback

♦ detailed personal development plans based on the results of the assessment and feedback

♦ executive dialogues at every session

♦ coaching, both by the program facilitators and by peers

♦ leadership modules, focused on enabling program participants to step up to greater leadership roles

♦ a university experience, comprising two weeks at the Thunderbird School of Global Management, as part of a consortium with other major companies

♦ an action learning project

♦ a presentation to the senior leadership team.

The initial LAMP pilot was extremely successful. The feedback from participants was outstanding, and follow-up with their managers indicated both increased capabilities and extremely strong commitment to their own continuous development. Many LAMP participants took the lessons they learned from the program and applied them on the job, including doing a much better job coaching and developing their own direct reports.

One measure of the success of LAMP was the fact that the area of the world (AOW) presidents for Asia and the Pacific, the Middle East and Africa, and the president for Europe asked the Talent Management Team at Corporate Headquarters if they would do a "LAMP-like" program just for their AOW. They felt that their need to build their own feeder pools was so great that they needed to give more of their people a LAMP experience than would be possible if the program was done only on a global basis with a fixed number of participants. By doing a similar program in their own AOW, they could accelerate the development of 15 to 20 people with high potential rather than the three to five if the program remained global.

When both AOW presidents offered to totally fund their program, the Talent Management Team was excited to partner with their HR leaders to build and deliver such a program. In 2004, three separate accelerated development programs were in place: the European Leadership Development Program (ELDP); the Asian Leadership Development Program (ALDP); the Middle Eastern and African Leadership Development Program; and LAMP Americas, which now focused on the United States, Latin America, Canada, and the corporate office.

If we fast-forward to 2009, here are some statistics related to these three programs:

♦ Since 2003, there have been four LAMP sessions, three ELDP sessions, and three ALDP sessions, with a total of 200 graduates.

♦ Women made up 42 percent of the participants in all programs, and 36 percent of the participants have been from minority groups (counting only participants from the United States, where minority group definition is tracked).

♦ Participants have represented 45 different countries.

♦ A total of 37 percent of the graduates of all programs have been promoted.

By most standards, these statistics demonstrate that these accelerated development programs, implemented in response to significant gaps in the replacement pools for McDonald's top 200 positions, have successfully filled those gaps. Further evidence of this fact is that McDonald's now has moved the number of key leadership positions for which we have strong backups from 50 percent to more than 80 percent in the five-year period since these programs were first piloted.

The LAMP efforts have a strong pull and a strong brand within McDonald's. Graduates of the LAMPs, once they are promoted, are anxious to identify potential leaders they can send to these programs, and it is considered high recognition to be selected to participate.

Several important lessons have been learned as a result of designing and delivering accelerated development programs to grow top leaders:

♦ Start small, with a pilot, and establish a brand.

♦ The length of the program matters. Having the program conducted over a several-month period (in this case, eight to nine months) provides much more sustained attention to development not possible when a program is "one or two weeks and done."

♦ Action learning projects have to be chosen carefully and have to have strong sponsors. Also, the projects need to scaled correctly and be relevant to leadership.

♦ Programs in different areas of the world need to be shaped and customized accordingly. This can be done while still keeping the core elements of the program intact.

♦ Be careful not to put too much focus on those with high potential, thus making other managers feel that they are not valued.

Step 4: The Launch of the McDonald's Leadership Institute

In 2006, a few years after McDonald's began delivering accelerated programs in three areas of the world, it was decided that it was important to address the development needs of the entire leadership population, both those with high potential and others. For this reason, and because McDonald's wanted to send a clear and loud signal that leadership development was one of its highest priorities, the decision was made to launch the McDonald's Leadership Institute. The institute would not have "bricks and mortar" but would be a virtual center for providing development resources to leaders from middle management to senior officers. The institute would house all the accelerated development programs and develop additional programs, such as

♦ transition programs for newly promoted directors and officers

♦ core programs (two- to three-day workshops) on key leadership and business topics that would be aligned with both the competencies expected of leaders and the direction of the business

♦ an Online Development Resource Center containing development- and career-related resources supporting personal development that could be accessed from anywhere in the world

♦ leadership dialogues on timely topics through which senior leaders could meet face to face with employees, and often with external thought leaders, to discuss key topics relevant to the business.

Figure 4-4 shows the scope of the resources contained within the Leadership Institute, which change frequently in response to business needs.

The institute launched a new initiative in 2006, the McDonald's Global Leadership Development Program (GLDP), that focused on accelerating the development of some of the highest-potential officers. The program was completely funded from the CEO's budget, which sent a loud message regarding Jim Skinner's support for leadership development. The GLDP was a truly global effort built using a combination of internal expertise and external thought leaders. The GLDP faculty comprised a combination of external speakers/facilitators and senior leaders. Several members of the McDonald's Board of Directors also participated.

The program design focused on

♦ knowing the market and the customer

♦ executing to deliver results

♦ leading innovation

Figure 4-4. Scope of Resources for the McDonald's Leadership Institute

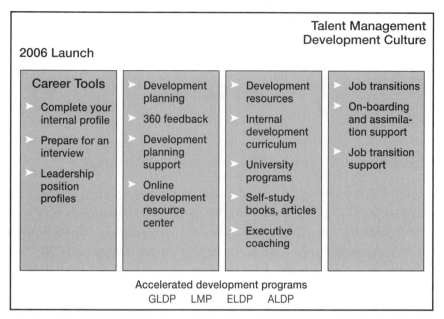

- paying attention to ethics and values
- enhancing self-awareness and driving for continuous personal development.

The initial 20 program participants came from all over the world to attend the three-week course (made up of three one-week sessions spread over five months in both U.S. and non-U.S. locations). There was a great deal of "stretch" built into the program that forced participants to think beyond McDonald's in a broader, more strategic way than they were accustomed to doing. Several members of the 2006 class have been promoted as of this date. The GLDP's second course of study took place in 2008, and plans are for the program to run every other year to to ensure that its high standards are maintained.

The McDonald's Leadership Institute continues to grow, and its brand has become increasingly prominent within the company. The institute and HU have a strong partnership and are collaborating on several major initiatives to ensure that their focus and curriculum are totally aligned from crew training through officer development. The vision and end goal is for every McDonald's employee to understand the leadership and technical requirements for every role at every organizational level and to know how to access the development support needed to meet these requirements. Though there is still a great deal to be accomplished, significant progress has been made, and there is a strong commitment to "stay the course" until the vision has been achieved.

The Impact of Talent Management Initiatives

It is clear that talent management initiatives have made a significant contribution to McDonald's, thanks to the efforts of many. There is now a strong discipline for talent management processes, and solid metrics to measure success are being tracked on a yearly basis. Let's look at three of these metrics. The first metric is the strength and diversity of the current leadership team, which includes

- the annual performance rating distribution
- the percentage of leaders assessed as having advancement potential
- the percentage of lower performers on improvement plans ("improve or remove")
- year-over-year changes in diversity.

The second metric is the depth and diversity of feeder pools, which includes

- the percentage of key leadership positions for which there are at least two backups identified (year-over-year improvement)
- the diversity of feeder pool candidates.

The third metric is the retention of top performers and those with high potential, which includes the percentage of those rated exceptional (top 20 percent) and leaders with advancement potential who are retained each year.

Progress has been made on all these metrics, and, for most, we are at levels of performance that are within our target levels. (For confidentiality reasons, the data on actual results cannot be shared.)

The commitment level of our CEO and our senior leadership team has been strong and has been sustained for several years. Senior leaders are modeling behaviors that demonstrate their commitment to talent management and leadership development. CEO Jim Skinner credits the focus on talent management and leadership development as one of the, if not the most, important factors accounting for the company's financial and market performance.

McDonald's has been receiving much recognition for its talent management efforts in the external community. In 2006, it was ranked by *Fortune* magazine and Hewitt Associates as one of the top companies for leaders. In 2009, it was also recognized as a top company for leaders by *Chief Executive Magazine* and Hay Associates.

Overall, though McDonald's is extremely pleased with the progress it has made in the talent management arena, it is also recognizes that there is much more to do. Three areas where progress needs to be made are

- forging a stronger linkage between talent planning and strategic planning—this is occurring, but the rate needs to increase
- making better use of planned job moves to accelerate development—finding creative ways of overcoming the barriers imposed by mobility restrictions and work/life balance issues
- improving overall execution.

Conclusion

McDonald's has taken a carefully planned approach to building its talent management and leadership development capabilities since 2001. It started by fixing its performance management system, the foundation for any and all talent management initiatives. It progressed steadily and was bolstered by strong support from its senior leadership team. Some of this support was generated or "awakened" by the untimely and tragic deaths of two CEOs in little more than a year, which made talent management and succession painfully real for McDonald's—and they have been real ever since. The metrics that have been tracked over the last several years attest to the fact that there is now a strong leadership team in place at McDonald's and a strong pipeline of internal leadership talent ready to replace them. The performance of the business reflects this strength.

Chapter 5

Turnaround Talent Management at Avon Products

Marc Effron, Vice President, Talent Management

What's in this chapter?

- ♦ How Avon faced down a talent management challenge
- ♦ How to build a new talent management system
- ♦ The results of successful change

In early 2006, Avon Products, a global consumer products company focused on the economic empowerment of women around the world, began the most radical restructuring process in its long history. Driving this effort was the belief that Avon could sustain its historically strong financial performance while building the foundation for a larger, more globally integrated organization. The proposed changes would affect every aspect of the organization and would demand an approach to finding, building, and engaging talent that differed from anything tried before.

Chapter 5

A Success-Driven Challenge

Avon Products is a 122-year-old company founded by David H. McConnell—a door-to-door bookseller who distributed free samples of perfume as an incentive to his customers. He soon discovered that customers were more interested in samples of his rose oil perfumes than in his books and so, in 1886, he founded the California Perfume Company. Renamed Avon Products in 1939, the organization steadily grew to become a leader in the direct selling of cosmetics, fragrances, and skin care products.

By 2005, Avon was an $8 billion company that had achieved a 10 percent cumulative annual growth rate (CAGR) in revenue and a 25 percent CAGR in operating profit from 2000 through 2004. A global company, Avon operated in more than 40 countries and received more than 70 percent of its earnings from outside the United States. By all typical financial metrics, it was a very successful company.

However, as the company entered 2006, it found itself challenged by flattening revenues and declining operating profits. Though the situation had many contributing causes, one underlying issue was that the company had grown faster than portions of its infrastructure and talent could support. As with many growing organizations, the structures, processes, and people that were right for a $5 billion company weren't necessarily a good fit a $10 billion company.

The Turnaround

Faced with these challenges, Avon's executive team launched a fundamental restructuring of the organization in January 2006. Some of the larger changes announced included

- *Moving from a regional to a matrix structure:* Geographic regions that had operated with significant latitude were now matrixed into select global business functions, primarily marketing and supply chain.

- *Delayering:* A systematic, six-month process was started to take the organization from 15 layers of management to eight, including a compensation and benefit reduction of up to 25 percent.

- *Significant investment in executive talent:* Of the 14 people report-ing directly to the CEO, six were replaced externally from 2004 to 2006, including the CFO, head of North America, head of Latin America, and the leaders of human resources (HR), marketing, and strategy. Five others were put in new roles.

- *New capabilities were created:* A major effort to source brand management, marketing analytics, and supply chain capabili-ties was launched, which brought hundreds of new leaders into Avon.

The Talent Challenge

As the turnaround was launched, numerous gaps existed in both the tal-ent Avon had and its ability to identify and grow its talent. Though some of these gaps were due to missing or poorly functioning talent processes, an underlying weakness seemed to be the overall approach to managing talent and the talent practices supporting it.

After reviewing Avon's existing talent practices, members of the tal-ent management (TM) group identified six overriding weaknesses that hurt their effectiveness. Specifically, they found that existing talent prac-tices were

- *Opaque:* Neither managers nor associates knew how existing talent practices (that is, performance management, succession planning) worked or what they were intended to do. To the average employee, these processes were a black box.

- *Egalitarian:* Though the Avon culture reinforced the belief that every associate should be well treated, this value was being misinterpreted as requiring every associate to be treated in the same way. High performers weren't enjoying a fundamentally different work experience, and low performers weren't being managed effectively.

- *Complex:* The performance management form was 10 pages long, and the succession planning process required a full-time employee just to manage the data and assemble thick black binders of information for twice yearly reviews. Complexity existed without commensurate value, and the effectiveness rate of the talent practices was low.

- *Episodic:* Employee surveys, talent reviews, development planning, and succession planning, when done at all, were done at a frequency determined by individual managers around the world.

- *Emotional:* Decisions on talent movement, promotions, and other key talent activities were often influenced as much by personal knowledge and emotion as by objective facts.

- *Meaningless:* No talent practice had "teeth." HR couldn't answer the most basic question a manager might ask about talent practices: "What will happen to me if I don't do this?"

A New Model

Avon's TM group found itself in a difficult situation. Fundamental changes were needed in every talent practice, and the practices had to be changed and implemented in time to support the company's turnaround. This meant that the practices had to be quick to build, easy to use, and, most of all, effective immediately.

Taking our guidance from the Top Companies for Leaders study (Effron, Greenslade, and Salob 2005) and the philosophies of Marshall Goldsmith (2006), we decided to build our talent practices with two key guiding principles:

- *Execute on the "what":* The Top Companies for Leaders study found that simple, well-executed talent practices dominated at companies that consistently produced great earnings and great leaders. We similarly believed that fundamental talent practices (that is, performance management or succession planning) would deliver the expected results if they were consistently and flawlessly executed. We decided to build talent practices that were easy to implement and a talent management structure that would ensure that the practices were consistently and flawlessly implemented.

♦ *Differentiate on "how"*: Though disciplined execution could create a strong foundation for success, the six adjectives that described Avon's current processes were largely responsible for their failure. We realized how we executed our talent management practices mattered as much as the practices themselves. We drew inspiration from Goldsmith's revolutionary re-creation of the executive coaching process. He had taken a staid, academic/therapy model for improving leaders and turned it into a simple but powerful process that has been proven effective in changing leaders' behaviors.

With these two guiding principles in place, we began a complete transformation of Avon's talent practices.

From Opaque to Transparent

One of the most simple and powerful changes was to bring as much transparency as possible to every talent practice. TM redesigned existing practices and created new ones, using total transparency as the starting point. Transparency was only removed when confidentiality concerns outweighed the benefits of sharing information. The change in Avon's 360-degree assessment process was a telling example.

The Avon 360-Degree Assessment

Avon's 360-degree assessment process was hardly a model of transparency when the turnaround began. When the new TM leader arrived at Avon, he asked for copies of each vice president's (VP's) 360-degree assessment, with the goal of better understanding any common behavioral strengths and weaknesses. He was told by the 360-degree administrator in his group that he was not allowed to see them. The TM leader explained that he did not intend to take any action based on what he learned but simply wanted to learn more about his clients. He was again told "no"—that confidentiality prevented their disclosure.

Although the administrator was correct in withholding the information (the participants had been promised 100 percent confidentiality), the fact that the most critical behavioral information about top leaders was not visible to the TM leader (or anyone else) had to change. A new, much simpler 360-degree program was designed and implemented that explicitly stated that proper managerial and leadership behaviors were critical for a leader's success at Avon. Citing that level of importance, the disclosure to all participants and respondents stated that the 360-degree information could be shown to the participant's manager, HR leader, regional talent leader, and anyone else whom Avon's senior HR team decided was critical to the participant's development. It also stated that the behavioral information could be considered when making decisions about talent moves, including promotions and project assignments.

Helping to make this transition to transparency easier, the new 360-degree assessment and report differed from typical tools and borrowed heavily from the "feedforward" principles of Goldsmith (2006). Feedforward is a technique to accomplish behavior change by providing specific examples of behaviors desired in the future. This differs from traditional feedback techniques, which focus on rating the quality of a manager's previous behaviors. The new 360-degree assessment identified the exact behaviors 360-degree respondents wanted to see more of, or less of, in the manager going forward. Without the potential stigma of having others see you rated as a "bad" manager, the issue of openly sharing 360-degree findings quickly evaporated.

Broad-Based Transparency

Transparency was woven into every talent process or program in a variety of ways. Examples include

> ◆ *Career development plans:* To provide associates with more transparency about how to succeed at Avon, the HR team developed "the Deal"—shown in figure 5-1—which was a simple description of what was required to have a successful career at Avon and the parts the associate and Avon needed to play. The Deal made clear that every associate had to deliver results, display proper leadership behaviors, know our unique business, and take advantage of development experiences if he or she hoped to move forward in the organization.

Figure 5-1. The Avon "Deal"

Working Together to Help You Create a Great Career at Avon

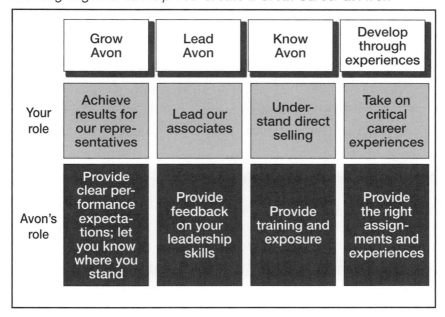

	Grow Avon	Lead Avon	Know Avon	Develop through experiences
Your role	Achieve results for our representatives	Lead our associates	Understand direct selling	Take on critical career experiences
Avon's role	Provide clear performance expectations; let you know where you stand	Provide feedback on your leadership skills	Provide training and exposure	Provide the right assignments and experiences

◆ *Development courses:* Avon acknowledged the unspoken but obvious fact about participating in leadership or functional training courses—of course, you're being observed! We believed it was important for participants to understand that we were investing in their future and that monitoring that investment was critical. The larger investment that we made, the more explicitly we made the disclosure. For our Accelerated Development Process (a two-year, high-potential development process offered to the top 10 percent of VPs), we let them know that they were now "on Broadway." The lights would be hotter, and the critics would be less forgiving. Executive committee members often sponsored these courses and observed throughout each class. The quality of leaders' participation, how they interacted with their fellow participants, and even any unusual interactions (a member screaming at the hotel staff during an off-site meeting, for example) were data points that were considered during talent reviews.

♦ *Performance reviews:* Switching from a three-point scale to a five-point scale provided additional clarity to participants about their actual progress, as did clarifying the scale definitions. Associates were informed about what performance conversations their manager should be having with them and when. The recommended distribution of ratings across the scale was widely communicated. As part of our talent review process, managers were asked to share our assessment of a leader's future potential with them him or her after the meetings.

From Complex to Simple

One of the most important changes made in Avon's talent practices was the radical simplification of every process. We believed that traditional talent processes would work (that is, grow better talent, faster) if they were effectively executed. However, we understood from our experience and a plethora of research that most talent practices were complex—without that complexity adding any significant value. This level of complexity caused managers to avoid using those tools, so talent wasn't grown at the pace or quality that companies required.

We committed ourselves to radically simplifying every talent process and ensuring that any complexity in these processes was balanced by an equal amount of value (as perceived by managers). Making this work was easier than we had anticipated. As the TM team designed each process, we would start with a blank sheet of paper and an open mind. We would set aside our hard-earned knowledge about the "right" way to design these processes and instead ask ourselves these questions:

♦ What is the fundamental business benefit that this talent process is trying to achieve?

♦ What is the simplest possible path to achieving this benefit?

♦ Can we add value to the process that would make it easier for managers to make smarter people decisions?

Using just these three questions, it was amazing how many steps and bells and whistles fell away from the existing processes. In fact, we were able to simplify most processes to a one-page form or report, which caused us to label our approach "one-page talent management." The two examples that follow provide helpful illustrations.

Performance Management

Aligning associates with the turnaround goals of the business and ensuring that they were fairly evaluated was at the foundation of the business turnaround. As we entered the turnaround, the company had a complex 10-page performance management form with understandably low participation rates. Many associates had not had a performance review in three, four, or even five years. It would have been impossible to align associates with the vital few turnaround goals using that tool and process.

We stated that the fundamental business benefit of performance goals and reviews is that they aligned associates with business goals and caused associates to work toward these goals with the expectation of fair rewards.

It seemed obvious that the easiest way of achieving the business goal was simply to have managers tell their associates what their goals were. It was straightforward, and the value to managers outweighed any complexity. After taking this small step forward, we advanced at the same pace, taking incrementally small steps forward in the design process. At each step, we would ask ourselves: Does this step add more value to managers than it does complexity? As long as it did, we added the additional design element. When the complexity/value curve started to level, as shown in figure 5-2, we carefully weighed adding any additional elements. And when we couldn't justify that adding another unit of complexity would add another unit of value, we stopped.

What went away as the design process progressed? Just a few examples would include

- goal labels (highly valued, star performer, and so on), which added no value (in fact, blurred transparency!) but did add complexity

- individual rating of goals, which implied a false precision in the benefit of each goal and encouraged associates to game the system

Figure 5-2. The Complexity/Value Curve

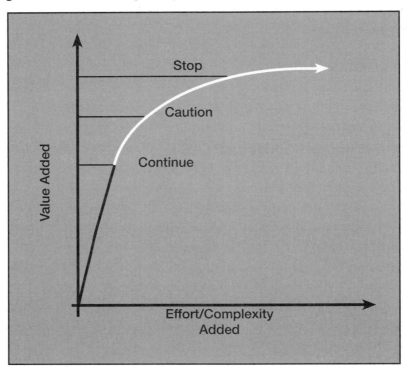

♦ behavioral ratings, which were replaced with a focus on behaviors that would help achieve the current goals.

The output was a one-page form with spaces for listing the goal and the metric and recording the outcome. A maximum of four goals was allowed. Two behaviors that supported achievement of the current goal could be listed but were not formally rated. As a result, participation reached nearly 100 percent, and line managers actually thanked the talent team for creating a simple performance management process!

The Engagement Survey

When the turnaround began, there was no global process for understanding or acting on associate engagement issues. Select regions or departments made efforts of varying effectiveness, but there was no integrated focus on consistent measurement and improving engagement. In designing the engagement survey process, we applied the same three questions.

The first question concerned the business benefit. We accepted the substantial research that showed a correlation (and some that showed causation) between increasing engagement and increasing various business metrics. In addition, we felt the ability to measure managers' effectiveness across engagement levels and changes would provide an opportunity for driving accountability for this issue. As with performance management, we knew that managers would use this tool if we could make it simple and, ideally, if we could show that it would allow them to more effectively manage their teams.

The second question concerned the simple path. Two goals were established for simplicity. One goal was to understand as much of what drove engagement as possible while asking the least number of questions. The second goal was to write the questions as simply as possible, so that if managers needed to improve the score on a question, their options for action would be relatively obvious.

The final version of the survey had 45 questions that explained 68 percent of the variance in engagement. The questions were quite simple, which had some value in itself, but the true value was multiplied 10-fold by the actions described below.

The third question concerned adding additional value. We were confident that if managers took the "right" actions to improve their engagement results, not only would the next year's scores increase but the business would also benefit from the incremental improvement. The challenge was to determine and simply communicate to the manager what the "right" actions were. Working with our external survey provider, we developed a statistical model that became the engine to produce these answers. The model allowed us to understand the power of each engagement dimension (that is, immediate manager, empowerment, senior management) to increase engagement and to express this power in an easy-to-understand statement.

For example, we could determine that the relationship between the immediate manager dimension and overall engagement was 2:1. This meant that for every two percentage points a manager could increase his or her immediate manager dimension score, that manager's overall engagement result would increase by one percentage point. Even better, this model allowed us to tell every manager receiving a report which particular three or four questions were the key drivers of engagement for his or her group.

No longer would managers mistakenly look at the top 10 or bottom 10 questions to guess at which issues needed attention. We could tell them exactly where to focus their efforts. The list of these questions allowed managers to understand their survey results by reading just one page.

From Egalitarian to Differentiated

A critical step in supporting Avon's turnaround was determining the quality of talent we had across the business—an outcome made much easier with transparent processes and conversations. Once we understood our talent inventory, we made a broad and explicit shift to differentiate our investment in talent. Though we would still invest in the development of every associate, we would more effectively match this level of investment with the expected return. We also differentiated leaders' experiences to ensure that our highest-potential leaders were engaged, challenged, and tied to our company.

We made the shift to differentiation in a number of ways. Let's look at three.

Communication to Leadership Teams

At the start of the turnaround process, presentations were made to each of the regional leadership teams to explain the shift in talent philosophy. The presentations helped to emphasize that we were serious about differentiation and allowed us to be relatively specific about what that meant and how we planned to apply it. We used a traditional "nine-box" grid that mapped performance over time and potential to illustrate the differences. The specific areas on which we differentiated included

- compensation targets
- development investments

♦ eligibility for participation in high-potential programs, global moves, and assignments to special projects.

Showing the differentiation on our new performance-and-potential matrix also let leaders know that accurately assessing talent on this tool was critical to our making the right talent investments.

A Few Big Bets

A key aspect of our philosophy was that we believed in placing a "few big bets" on a small number of leaders. This approach was informed by the research showing the vastly superior performance of the top five or 10 percent of a specific population and by the belief that flawless execution of well-known, high-potential development tactics would rapidly accelerate development (Hunter, Schmidt, and Judiesch 1990; Jones 1986). With limited funds to spend, we needed to make a decision about which talent bets would truly pay off.

Our monetary investment in our highest potential leaders was five to 10 times what we would invest in an average performer. This investment would include training, coaching, and incentive compensation, but we also invested the highly valuable time of our CEO, executive team, and board members. Our highest-potential leaders would often have an audience with these executives on a regular basis.

Tools and Processes

Our new talent review and performance review processes also emphasized our differentiation philosophy. Our new five-point performance scale came with a recommended distribution that assumed 15 percent of our managers would fail to meet some of their goals during the year. We believed that if goals were set at an appropriately challenging level, this was a reasonable expectation. As a consequence, we saw marginal performers—those who typically could have limped along for years with an average rating—receive the appropriate attention to either improve their performance or move them out of the business.

Our performance and potential grid (3 x 3) also had recommended distributions, but we found over time that the grid definitions better served our differentiation goals. After initially rating managers as having higher potential (the ability to move a certain number of levels over a certain period of time), their managers saw that the movement they predicted didn't occur, and those with more potential to move became a smaller, more differentiated group. We also asked managers to "stack rank" box six, which contained average performers who were not likely to move upward within the next 24 months. This process helped to differentiate "solid average" performers from those who were probably below average and possibly blocking the career movement of others.

From Episodic to Disciplined

As with many companies, Avon had plenty of well-intentioned but busy managers. Processes like talent reviews, which were administratively complex and difficult to understand, were not going to inspire the typical manager to reorder his or her priority list. By greatly simplifying these processes, we had removed one barrier to effectiveness, but we hadn't actually moved the process forward. We still needed to build organizational discipline around the execution of these simple new processes. We did that in a number of ways. Let's look at three.

Consistent Global Tools and Processes

Many parts of the organization had created their own tools for activities like performance management or individual development. The corporate talent management function was not empowered to push for global consistency, and consequently there was no common approach to build Avon's talent. This changed with a shift to global consistency that was championed by the senior vice president for HR.

Although all talent practices would now be designed by the corporate TM group, each still had to be vetted with the HR leaders of each geographic region and functional discipline. As a final part of the design process, adjustments were made to tools and processes to ensure that they met needs around the world.

Adding Talent Management Structure Globally

We created the role of regional talent management leader, a manager- or director-level role with responsibility for the local implementation of global processes. Five of these roles were created—one in each key geographic region—and the improved process discipline can be credited to them and their HR leaders. Regular contacts between regional leaders and the corporate TM group helped ensure great dialogue and consistent improvements in the processes.

A Committed CEO

Avon's CEO, Andrea Jung, showed herself to be a tremendous supporter of effective talent processes. Both through her role modeling (that is, conducting performance reviews and setting clear goals for her team) and instilling process discipline (she held semi-annual talent review meetings with each person reporting directly to her and an executive committee talent calibration meeting twice each year), she signaled that these processes were important to her and had value for the organization.

This new level of discipline was an incredibly strong lever in our ability to assess and develop our talent. By executing these talent processes every six months, we were able to drive transparency for talent issues on a regular basis and instill accountability to take action on issues before the next cycle.

From Emotional to Factual

Avon had always been a company with genuine, heartfelt concern for its associates and an organization where strong relationships were built over a lifetime of employment. As the organization grew, a leader's personal knowledge of associates' performance or development needs often served as a key factor in determining talent movement. Though, in many cases, a leader's individual knowledge was relatively accurate, it's likely that a more calibrated point of view or additional quantitative facts may have allowed for richer discussions and more confidence in decision making.

The TM team worked to inject more fact-based decision making into talent discussions. Some of those facts were qualitative and others were quantitative, but as a whole they enabled a more complete discussion of an individual's performance and potential.

Qualitative Facts Added

Additional qualitative facts were found in activities ranging from talent reviews to leadership and functional courses. In talent reviews, calibration discussions were added at each level so that individual managers could justify individual potential ratings to their peers. Those ratings might also be reviewed once again at the next level. Regional talent management leaders would facilitate many of the meetings to help leaders have complete and honest discussions, helping to ensure that the qualitative data were accurate.

Additional qualitative data were also added from a leader's participation in leadership or functional development programs. Senior line managers would sponsor these programs, frequently attending the entire one-, two-, or three-week process. As mentioned above, these managers would then bring rich observations to the talent discussions about an individual's performance in these classes—on projects, with their team, and so on.

Quantitative Facts Added

Two of the new tools discussed above—the 360-degree assessment and the engagement survey—provided quantitative facts that helped Avon assess talent. Progress toward engagement goals or individual behavior improvement (or the lack of it) was often a key indicator of readiness for additional development and responsibility.

From Meaningless to Consequential

Injecting managerial accountability for talent practices was a key factor in managers' effectiveness. Before Avon's turnaround, there was no accountability for these practices, and some managers took personal responsibility for implementing them while others did very little. In creating the new talent practices, we tried to inject accountability into each one, answering the critical question "Why should I do this?" For instance:

♦ *Monetary accountability:* Varying a leader's pay for successfully or unsuccessfully managing talent is a dream of many HR and compensation leaders. We chose to use this lever in a targeted way when we applied it to engagement survey improvement. The executive team believed that the survey provided a strong enough measure of a manager's focus on people issues that managers could be held accountable for improving it. The executive committee established year-over-year improvement in engagement scores as a goal in every VP's performance plan.

♦ *Associate-led accountability:* To encourage the timely completion of the performance management process steps, we empowered associates to hold their managers accountable. A memo was sent to every associate at the beginning of each year informing them of the specific action steps and corresponding dates their managers should be taking to set goals. A similar note was sent for midyear and year-end reviews. The note asked associates to let their local HR leaders know if these steps weren't occurring.

♦ *CEO-led accountability:* Every six months, each executive team member would meet with the CEO to present his or her talent review. Actions promised at the last meeting were reviewed, and progress was noted. Leaders knew that promises were being tracked and reviewed and that progress would need to be shown at the subsequent meetings.

Though accountability was applied in many different ways, the common outcome was that leaders understood that focusing on talent during the turnaround (and after) mattered and that they were responsible for getting this done.

The progress that was made on talent issues was helped by the various factors discussed above, from a committed CEO and senior vice president for HR to the urgency of a turnaround to the dramatic change in talent practices. But it would not have been possible without the desire of Avon's managers to do the right thing. We started with a culture that valued every associate, and we channeled this positive spirit using sound processes and unflinching discipline. We didn't delude ourselves into thinking that these talent changes would have been possible without the power of Avon's culture.

The Results of a Talent Turnaround

At the beginning of this chapter, I described the six weaknesses in Avon's talent practices. Over the initial turnaround period (12 to 18 months), we moved these processes:

- *From opaque to transparent:* Leaders now know what's required to be successful, how we'll help them get there, how we'll measure success, and the consequences of higher and lower performance. They know their performance rating, and our feelings about their potential to advance.

- *From egalitarian to differentiated:* We actively differentiated levels of Avon's talent and provided each level with the appropriate experience. Our highest-potential leaders understand how we feel about them, and they see a commensurate investment. Our lower-performing leaders get the attention they need.

- *From complex to simple:* Managers now do the right thing for their associates, both because we've lowered the barriers we'd previously built and because we've helped them with value-added tools and information.

- *From episodic to disciplined:* Processes now happen on schedule and consistently around the world.

- *From emotional to factual:* Talent decisions are made with an additional layer of qualitative and quantitative information drawn from many different leaders' experiences.

- *From meaningless to consequential:* Leaders know that they must build talent the Avon way for both their short- and long-term success.

Measuring the Talent Turnaround's Success

The specific talent practices we targeted have seen significant improvements in effectiveness. Ratings of immediate managers (including items like clear goal setting, frequent feedback, and development planning) have increased up to 17 percent, with directors and vice presidents giving their immediate managers nearly a 90-percent approval rating. The ratings of people effectiveness (which captures many HR and talent practices) have increased up to 16 percent, including strong gains on questions related to dealing appropriately with low performers and holding leaders accountable for their results.

More transparency has allowed faster movement of talent into key markets. Simpler processes have allowed us to accelerate the development of leaders. And holding leaders accountable for their behavior has improved the work experience for associates around the world.

Though these changes were hard-fought and we believe created much more effective processes, a more important set of metrics exists. Avon has achieved all of its expense-savings goals since the start of the turnaround and has recently reinforced its commitments to even greater expense reductions. Even with this lower cost base and 10 percent fewer associates, Avon has grown from revenues of $8 billion in 2005 to nearly $11 billion in projected 2009 revenues while delivering strong single-digit earnings growth.

We can't say with certainty that our new talent practices have contributed to either these cost savings or our revenue increases. We are confident, however, that the talent practices now in place will deliver better leaders, faster, to help Avon meet its business goals.

Note: The views expressed by the author are his own and do not necessarily represent those of Avon Products.

A People-Focused Organization: Development and Performance Practices at Children's Healthcare of Atlanta

Larry Mohl, Vice President and Chief Learning Officer

What's in this chapter?

- How to implement a people-centered strategy
- How to move toward a successful develop-and-perform strategy
- How to design a comprehensive measurement system

Try an exercise in imagining. Think about your company. Now imagine that you know exactly what talent you need, now and in the future, to meet your company's strategic objectives. Imagine you know what mix of hiring, development, and internal movement is required and makes economic sense. For the talent you need to hire, imagine that you know where to find, and how to attract, the best of the best. As candidates apply for your openings, imagine that your selection process confidently and automatically moves the most promising people forward, based on a deep understanding of what makes a successful employee. Then, once you've hired all these talented people, imagine that they understand where the company has been and where it is going. New employees are welcomed into their new roles, easily find a network of trusted colleagues, and quickly add value to the organization.

Imagine that managers in your company fully understand the link between their employees' engagement and their results. Your managers know the specific engagement needs of their teams and are taking action to fulfill those needs. You never, ever lose someone from your organization due to factors that could be addressed by that person's manager. Imagine that everyone in your company has an honest understanding of his or her talents, strengths, and development areas. Now imagine that managers and employees are in an active partnership to achieve excellence. Managers are crystal clear about expectations and how each person contributes to departmental and company success. They are skilled at providing frequent feedback and actionable coaching.

Imagine that, when leadership positions become available, you fill them quickly with just the right mix of internal and external talent. Your internal leadership pipeline is robust, and your comprehensive process identifies and develops leaders at all levels. You have leaders ready for the future before it arrives. Now, imagine that your leaders take ownership of filling the pipeline with their leadership talent. Leaders actively develop their leaders and so on throughout your management hierarchy. Hiring managers are willing to take risks on internal talent because they are confident that they can provide the coaching required to develop someone in a role.

Imagine that all the information needed to make more proactive and leveraged talent decisions is at the fingertips of employees, managers, and the human resources (HR) team. Do you need to know the correlation between new employees' performance and their school of origin? Click here. Instead of wrestling with data, you are making new connections and asking questions you didn't even know you needed to ask. You are past the stage of proving that investments in people pay off through improved company performance. Instead, you are busy optimizing your portfolio of people investments to gain the highest return.

Imagine this were all true—today. As the song says, "What a wonderful world it would be." At Children's Healthcare of Atlanta, we like to dream big, and big dreams are needed to accomplish our important vision and mission.

Children's Healthcare at a Glance

Children's Healthcare of Atlanta has become one of the top pediatric hospital systems in the country, operating three hospitals, 14 neighborhood locations, and the Marcus Autism Center. Our organization has 7,500 employees, 1,400 physician partners, and 20,000 volunteers. Research and teaching partnerships with Emory and Morehouse Universities as well as the Georgia Institute of Technology enable the organization to fulfill its mission of enhancing the lives of children through excellence in patient care, research, and education. In 2008, we cared for more than half a million children.

Strategically, the key issues facing Children's Healthcare are multifaceted. Over the past 10 years, the population of the Atlanta metropolitan area has exploded, and with it the resulting need for pediatric medical services. Children's Healthcare has responded with the largest hospital building expansion in the history of Georgia. In the last four years alone, we have grown from 300 beds and 5,500 employees to 525 beds and 7,500 employees. Most estimates predict that the pediatric population growth trend will level off to some degree but continue to climb.

Although rapid growth is generally positive, it also brings challenges. Local and national shortages of pediatric medical professionals make it difficult to keep pace with expanding staffing needs. Nationally, Georgia ranks low on standard child wellness indicators that are based on health and economic status factors. In addition, 50 percent of children in Georgia are either uninsured or insured through state government programs. The result is that more than 50 percent of the children Children's Healthcare serves are enrolled in insurance programs that do not reimburse the hospital for the full cost of services. Though the organization must respond to more complex medical needs, increasing costs and uncertain reimbursement, our top priority remains clear: Children's Healthcare strives to deliver the highest levels of quality and patient safety.

These challenges are, now and for the foreseeable future, the reality for Children's Healthcare. They define the type of talent we look for and how we equip our workforce to be successful. We are grounded by our senior leadership's conscious decision to build a culture recognizing that health care delivery is, at its core, all about people—their passion, their expertise, their productivity, and their pride.

The People Strategy of Children's Healthcare

To continue to address the challenges we face and, at the same time, deliver on our strategic plan, Children's Healthcare has developed a comprehensive framework that operationalizes our focus on people, which we call our People Strategy. This strategy describes the vision of who we want to be as an employer. It translates organizational goals and strategies into the specific people goals and strategies we pursue.

The thinking behind the People Strategy of Children's Healthcare is the work of a dedicated and talented group of HR leaders led by Linda Matzigkeit, senior vice president of HR. Linda's drive to create a truly strategic HR function that plays an important role in the organization's success drew many of us to Children's Healthcare. Deploying an integrated People Strategy requires an integrated HR team. Under Linda's leadership, we have built trusting relationships and put the needs of our employees and patient families ahead of our own function.

The People Strategy of Children's Healthcare addresses employee, manager, and organization perspectives. Our employees want to know how they can best utilize their skills and abilities. They want to grow and contribute to the organization's mission. Our managers want to know how they can best utilize their precious time and energy to find, engage, develop, and retain their talent. At the organizational level, we must set overall direction and specific annual targets in the key areas we use to measure success. We must invest in areas that have the greatest leverage, balancing local and organization-wide needs. We must integrate and orchestrate talent actions in a way that creates a coherent experience that is uniquely Children's Healthcare. We must have an architecture that is stable enough to be repeatable and dynamic enough to flex with changing needs.

The execution of our People Strategy is owned by the entire organization in partnership with our HR team. The organization's leadership makes it a priority to attract, engage, retain, and develop employees. They establish goals and invest in developing the capabilities of their people. The HR team provides thought leadership and innovative programs, as well as analysis and counsel, on a wide variety of organizational issues. In addition, we are employee advocates and strive for operational simplicity in all we do.

An organizing framework for many of the components of our People Strategy is shown in figure 6-1. Ultimately, everything we do supports the strategic plan of Children's Healthcare. The actions we take in our

Figure 6-1. Organizing Framework for the People Strategy of Children's Healthcare

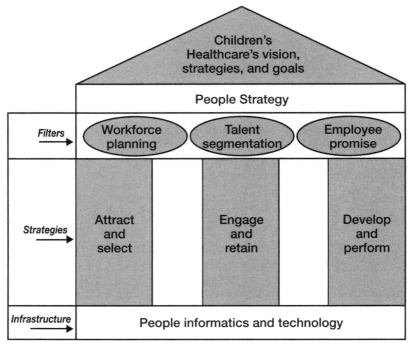

People Strategy are based on a deep understanding of our unique culture and the type of talent that excels in our organization.

We are proud of the results our People Strategy has yielded. We have been fortunate to perform at industry benchmark levels on most of our key measures. A sample of specific organizational results is displayed in table 6-1.

Perhaps one of our most exciting accomplishments was to be the first pediatric hospital system in *Fortune* magazine's 100 best places to work in America. This distinction is owned by the entire organization and is one that we have been honored to receive for four consecutive years.

This chapter covers several aspects of our People Strategy. First, I briefly touch on our system of filters that work to guide our strategies and approaches. The bulk of the discussion then focuses on the practices in our Develop-and-Perform Strategy. As part of this strategy, I explore our approach to leadership development and performance management. Finally, I highlight several key aspects of the technology infrastructure we are currently implementing.

Filters That Guide

One of the key planning efforts Children's Healthcare undertakes uses the simple idea of supply and demand. In most markets, the goal is to match

Table 6-1. System Results and Trends for the People Strategy of Children's Healthcare

Scorecard Item	2008 Results (percent)	Trend (percent)
System retention	90.5	Up from 83.4 in 2002
Nursing retention	90.7	Up from 85.3 in 2002
System vacancy	2.5	Down from 4.9 in 2002
Nursing vacancy	2.9	Down from 6.6 in 2002
Employee engagement	88.0	Up from 86 in 2006
Internal leadership hiring	64.6	Up from 40 in 2005

Source: Data from Children's Healthcare of Atlanta.

supply to demand in a way that creates a return-on-investment. In talent markets, we must understand first what talent is needed over different time horizons. We must then meet the need with a smart mix of hiring, development, and retention actions. Our workforce plan is designed to create projections of demand based on the Children's Healthcare strategy. Then, using retention and other assumptions, estimates of supply are created and talent gaps are identified. Our resulting workforce plan thus forms an important filter that guides the overall mix of the external and internal talent we will require to execute our strategic plan.

Although all people may be created equal, strategic and operational priorities call for different investments in different segments of the Children's Healthcare population. As a result, goals and strategies change from segment to segment. In traditional market segmentation, the idea is to leverage solutions by grouping people with common characteristics, wants, and needs. Talent segmentation provides the same benefit, but it also helps define what capabilities exist and may need to be developed. Examples of talent segments at Children's Healthcare are people leaders, business operations managers, first-year nurses, and all nurses. Talent segmentation thus serves as another filter that guides the type and degree of investment in any given segment of our population.

Perhaps our most important guiding filter is the voice of our employees. Our Employee Promise was developed with input from employees, who identified specific aspects of the Children's Healthcare environment that would be necessary to create the ideal workplace. Our listening process uncovered four central themes: mutual respect, learning, work-life success, and total rewards. Our Employee Promise thus forms a filter that guides our organizational commitment to employees and, in turn, the commitment the organization asks of employees to pursue excellence in all we do.

Planning for the future, segmenting our talent, and listening to our employees are vital for all our strategies. To bring to life the desire for learning expressed in our Employee Promise, Children's Healthcare has developed a strong development culture. New knowledge is absolutely exploding in all aspects of health care delivery, and our organization realizes that learning and performance improvement must be a continuous process. Delivering on this promise is accomplished through our Develop-and-Perform Strategy, which organizes and focuses our efforts to effectively serve the needs of our different talent segments and the organization.

The Develop-and-Perform Strategy

The Develop-and-Perform Strategy of Children's Healthcare focuses on several areas. The first focus of our development is on demonstrating foundational skills. These are skills essential to delivering safe and effective care. Our second focus is on building strategic capabilities. We define these as capabilities that require significant change and propel us toward the future. Our goal is always the same. We strive to convert learning and development into improved performance. Achieving this goal requires a continuous commitment from the organization to understand that development goes far beyond the delivery of training events.

People leaders are one of our most important talent segments, and our organization has made a significant investment in their development. Over the past several years, we have developed and begun implementing an integrated approach to leadership development. Through this approach, the organization has gained significant traction in improving the effectiveness of leaders in their current roles, readying leaders for the future, and delivering tangible impact along the way.

Leadership Development as a Business Improvement Process

In late 2004, a central challenge was recognized by the Children's Healthcare Executive Team and Board of Directors. With the explosive growth of the Atlanta metropolitan area and the corresponding growth of Children's Healthcare, a leadership gap was emerging. Analysis of hiring trends showed that for every open position for manager or above, we hired internally less than 40 percent of the time. With a hiring rate of more than 100 leaders a year, representing almost 30 percent of our entire leadership core, the sheer number of externally sourced leaders would need to be very high. Though hiring externally is not necessarily bad, we worried that the large numbers could send a message to internal talent that leadership opportunities are slim. Also, would the unique Children's Healthcare culture be put at risk?

The quality of the Children's Healthcare leadership was also in question. Our senior leadership realized that the leader of the future would be different from the leader of the present. The growth of health care needs and the increasing complexity of the process for delivering care would require new capabilities. Acting strategically, demonstrating business acumen, leading change, and managing complex relationships would become much more important. The days of purely managing the current operation well were quickly coming to an end. We would need leaders capable of both leading us into the future and managing the day-to-day realities of the one of the country's largest pediatric health care systems.

In response to these realities, the Children's Healthcare Center for Leadership (CFL) was formed and officially launched in 2005. The CFL's goals were to

- ♦ develop a robust pipeline of internal leaders so that our internal hiring rate could reach 70 percent
- ♦ build the brand of Children's Healthcare as a great place to be a leader to retain and attract the best leadership talent available
- ♦ deliver direct business value through the leadership development process itself.

This third goal was the cornerstone of our entire philosophy and approach. The CFL could not be seen as a training program. Closing the quantity and quality gap required a comprehensive approach, spanning every level of leadership, with an architecture designed to ensure that learning is applied in ways that create impact. Figure 6-2 shows the CFL core processes and business logic at a high level.

Leadership Talent Planning

Leadership talent planning is a process performed annually, through which Children's Healthcare analyzes both our projected demand for leadership positions and our current supply of leadership talent. Our

Figure 6-2. Core Process and Business Logic of the Center for Leadership

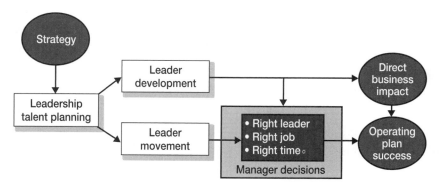

leadership supply is analyzed in two basic ways: through nine-box mapping and succession planning. We map all our leaders in the positions of manager and above across the organization. Our nine-box axes are based on performance and potential factors. We have created a standard definition for each box so that we can achieve greater levels of consistency from group to group. Initial mapping is done by individual leaders, followed by successive rounds of talent reviews aimed at calibrating the analysis. Strengths, development areas, and movement opportunities are captured for use in subsequent steps of the overall process. These reviews play an important role in helping leaders to learn more about the talent with whom they are not familiar.

Although each box in our nine-box map has its own meaning, three aggregate pools emerge. The first pool is our top talent. These are leaders with high potential and performance. The second pool is referred to as the leverage talent pool. These leaders are new to their role, solid contributors, or well-placed high-performing individuals with little desire for promotion. The third pool is the performance pool, which comprises leaders who may have performed well in the past but are currently struggling, leaders who have reached their limit in terms of advancement, and leaders who do not belong in leadership positions.

This three-pool segmentation of our leadership talent provides guidance for individual leaders working to develop or improve the performance of their leadership talent. To make this a practical reality, we have defined specific development and performance improvement approaches for each box of our nine-box map. The entire nine-box mapping approach and the tools required to maximize the return-on-development is taught to leaders as a core part of their CFL development experience. This analysis also has enormous strategic value. The distribution of talent across the nine boxes provides incredibly useful insights into the state of our leadership core.

Information from our nine-box talent map is used to create succession plans for key senior leadership positions. These plans consist of both named successors and pools of individuals who have the potential to fill key positions in the future. This approach creates a good balance between a fairly rigid replacement planning approach and a more flexible acceleration pool approach.

Analysis in and of itself is not worth much unless it leads to action, which takes us to the next steps in our process. In simple terms, the nine-box talent map leads to actions that are either primarily development focused or primarily movement focused.

Developing Leaders

All development is grounded and guided by a set of leadership competencies. These competencies, defined by our senior leadership team, are tailored to each level of our leadership hierarchy. They work together so that what is required to progress in the organization is clear. Each of our eight competencies is described by a summary statement, eight high-performing behaviors, and eight low-performing behaviors.

Figure 6-3 shows the four distinct segments to which leader development is delivered through four main experiences within an architecture designed to drive application and impact. As shown at the bottom of the figure, our Supervisor Certification and Management Certification programs are foundational. They provide new leaders with the skills and tools they need to manage effectively at the unit or department level. Content is tailored from tried-and-true management fundamentals programs.

As shown at the top of figure 6-3, the Management Acceleration Experience and the Executive Experience are designed to develop more

Figure 6-3. Leader Development Architecture

Senior executive and manager engagement

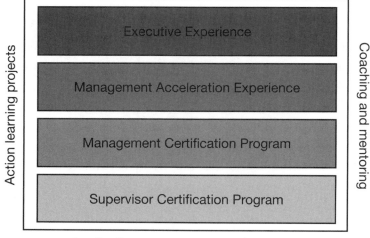

Application management and support

strategic leadership capabilities. For these programs, it was important to create a language of leadership and set of methods and tools that would be used as the standard leadership practices across the organization. This idea was central to CFL becoming persistent in the organization. If new methods are learned in a workshop but never seen in the day-to-day workings of the organization, content soon becomes "shelfware." Working with functional leaders across the organization, we developed Children's Healthcare models for strategic planning, leading change, and building capability. These models, along with an introspective component called Personal Mastery, and a healthy dose of more advanced business management concepts, form the core of these learning experiences.

At the time of this writing, more than 490 leaders are enrolled or have graduated from one of these programs or experiences. A total of 110 people have either graduated from or are enrolled in the Executive and Management Acceleration experiences. Just over 100 participants have graduated from the Management Certification and Supervisor Certification programs, and more than 270 participants are currently enrolled.

This level of involvement encompasses a substantial percentage of our leadership core.

An analysis of our leadership transitions data highlighted a troubling situation. Too many managers were struggling after being promoted to director positions. As we dug deeper into the issue, we came to the conclusion that the transition from manager to director was perhaps the most challenging to make successfully at Children's Healthcare. Making this transition requires a completely different orientation and set of skills. The primary orientation for most managers is to focus down and in. They need to make sure their operation runs smoothly and efficiently. Director-level positions require a much stronger system orientation and the ability to look up and across, so to speak. Directors must tackle a wide variety of complex issues that requires them to lead change and exert influence through a complex web of stakeholders. Our Management Acceleration Experience was designed specifically to improve our manager-to-director success rate. Through our talent planning process, cohorts of 12 to 15 top talent managers are selected to participate in the experience, which lasts about one full year.

Our Executive Experience brings together cohorts of administrative, clinical, and physician leaders for an 18-month journey. One of the less tangible, but no less important, aspects of this approach is the relationship building that takes place. As the organization grows, it is important that our ability to collaborate grows, so that our increasing size becomes a benefit and not a risk. The Executive Experience serves as a platform for leaders to come together in a unique way. They hear each other's perspectives, learn together, and make positive changes. With all the content being delivered by Children's Healthcare executives, a healthy dialogue is created, which leads to new insights for everyone and practical solutions to leadership challenges. The Executive Experience journey is shown in figure 6-4.

All our experiences use the same architecture, including assessment, workshops, coaching/mentoring, follow-through support, and action learning. The Management Acceleration and Executive experiences utilize the most advanced implementation of this architecture. They involve multidimensional assessments used to create robust talent profiles and customized workshops. Assessments and workshops are necessary, but not sufficient, to ensure application and impact, our primary goal. The key is to surround the learner with support systems and application opportunities at every turn.

Learning, Application, Impact

The available research on learning transfer points squarely to the role of the direct manager as perhaps the most vital link in the transfer chain. Though highly motivated people will generally find a way to apply their learning, more people create more impact when their managers are actively involved in the learning process. Before any leader starts a CFL development experience, his or her manager is briefed on the specifics of the experience and the expectations for the manager's role in maximizing the experience's effectiveness. The manager and participant meet to discuss mutual expectations and opportunities for impact. The delivery of workshops over time provides a rhythm whereby managers are engaged with participants to discuss what is being learned and how it can be applied in their local context.

The application of learning is, first and foremost, about not forgetting what you have learned; and, second, using what you have learned to

Figure 6-4. Executive Experience for the Center for Leadership

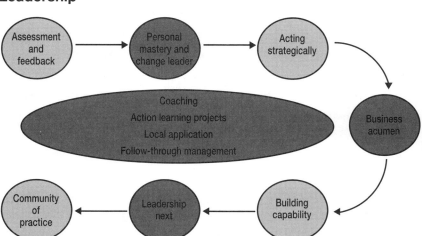

do your job more effectively. We all know that developing new skills takes practice. Because the skills are new and we may not be all that good at them, trying to use them can end up at the bottom of our to-do list. This is where application management and action learning, along with coaching and mentoring, come in. In each of our workshops, reflection time and coaching are used to help participants define specific development goals that they feel will have tangible impact. Their goals are loaded into an online system set up to provide regular reminders of what they have committed to accomplish. The tool asks participants questions about what they are learning and tracks their progress. In addition, it gives them the opportunity to request online counseling from people they have identified to support their development. Aggregate information from across our different cohorts helps the CFL core team understand which competencies our participants are focusing on and how they are progressing through the experience.

Action learning is a well-known technique. However, delivering projects that have an equal balance of learning and business benefit is much easier said than done. Though our success rate is less than 100 percent, we always strive to achieve this balance and add real value to the operation. Our definition of "done" is that the project has been implemented or the conditions for implementation have been established. Projects are required in all our experiences. Projects for the Supervisor Certification and Management Certification programs are scoped at the department level and led by individuals. Management Acceleration projects are led by individuals and are scoped to achieve multidepartmental impact. The Executive Experience projects are performed in teams and are designed to align with organization-wide strategic challenges.

Staffing our cardiac care intensive care unit was one such challenge. With a historical retention rate of 74 percent and vacancy rate of 30 percent, our difficulty in finding and keeping qualified nurses in this unit had been a key risk for the organization for many years. Our action learning team composed of physician, clinical, and HR leaders tackled this challenge using the full suite of CFL methods and tools—with stunning results. Retention has improved to 91 percent and vacancy to 0 percent. The unit achieved a net gain of 28 nurses, up from a five-year average of zero. Even more impressive is that by using CFL principles for leading change, the team has transformed the nature of nurse-physician relationships in the unit. Nurse retention is now seen as everyone's issue, not just a nursing issue, and an overall culture of improved collegiality has taken hold.

The accomplishments of other action learning teams include reductions in medical supply costs, improved care coordination, and developing a decision model that helps guide the geographic distribution of our services. Members of our organization effectiveness group work with these action learning teams to reinforce CFL concepts and stimulate personal reflection. All our projects provide a fertile practice ground for individual learning and, in the aggregate, help build skills in project management, leading change, and financial analysis.

Coaching and mentoring provides a powerful lever for impact. Participants in our Supervisor Certification and Management Certification programs primarily rely on their direct leader for coaching related to leadership development. The "leader as coach" is a core theme that runs through all CFL experiences, with skill building built into each. The Executive Experience utilizes a pool of Children's Healthcare–qualified executive coaches for about 30 percent of the participants. All coaching is developmental. Participants are offered external coaching based on four key criteria:

- They must demonstrate a desire to make the required time available.
- Their development area must be "coachable."
- The improvements they seek to make should generate tangible impact.
- The employee's direct manager needs to commit to actively supporting the process.

This is a high bar and has served us well in maximizing the return for the dollars we spend. Participants who are not selected for external coaching or are not interested in it have a broad array of internal resources available.

Once a participant and his or her manager agree to external coaching, we go through a disciplined coach-matching and goal-setting process to ensure that all parties are aligned. Our coaches are a vital link in the application chain. We keep the pool small and have a mix of coaches that have expertise in each of our competency areas. We train all our coaches in our core models and tools so that they are prepared to help reinforce previous learning, where appropriate. We learn a lot about ourselves from our coaches. By bringing them together to discuss what they see during their coaching engagements, we gain valuable insights into the CFL and the organization, in general. One successful integration point we have implemented is having Executive Experience graduates act as mentors and coaches for Management Acceleration Experience participants. This approach has amplified everyone's learning and provided essential role models for our up-and-coming leaders.

The Rest of the Process

Referring again to figure 6-2, let's look at the rest of our CFL process model. As discussed above, talent planning can lead to development or movement actions. One of our goals is to become more proactive in moving leaders into roles that fit them well. A valuable deliverable obtained from our CFL assessment system is what we call "leadership orientation," which describes the combination of business situations where a leader excels. Used wisely, along with other key factors, this information can help raise the probability of a good match between positional needs and leadership talent.

In the end, development and movement actions must come together to get the right leader into the right job at the right time. The strength of this match has a direct effect on our ability to achieve our operating plan. However, the goal of increased internal leadership hiring can only be achieved if hiring manager decisions are aligned with this goal. One of the lessons we've learned is that hiring managers are people, too. They are just trying to figure how to accomplish aggressive goals in a complex environment. If one of your leadership positions became available and you could choose between an external candidate who seems to have "been there and done that" and an internal candidate who seems to have all the right stuff but will require coaching to develop in the role, who would you select? This is an important, and common, dilemma faced in all organizations that does not have a simple answer. We communicate to hiring managers that they must make the right decisions for their specific situations and that taking risks on internal talent can pay off in ways that go beyond that one hiring decision. At the same time, CFL experiences are helping leaders feel equipped to take that risk.

Toward a Comprehensive Measurement System and Results

A comprehensive solution such as the CFL at Children's Healthcare requires a comprehensive measurement system. Ours is based on several guiding principles. The first is that the measurement system must prove and improve the CFL's impact. The second principle is that the system must demonstrate value in both rational and emotional terms. In practical terms, the CFL competes for funding with other important organizational initiatives. To understand its true impact, the logic of the CFL's results must both make sense and be quantifiable. It's equally important, however, to capture the spirit of the human journey of growth that our leaders experience. If the numbers make sense but CFL sponsors don't hear and see the progress in their people and others, the value equation is put in serious question. The converse is also true. The measurement framework we established is shown in figure 6-5.

As shown in figure 6-5, the first area we assess is the CFL's impact on each individual. Preprogram and postprogram 360-degree feedback is used to gauge competency improvements. Promotions are tracked, and nine-box grid movement is used to determine improved readiness to lead at higher levels. Our results show strong competency improvement in participants' areas of focus. Feedback consistently points to leaders feeling a sense of increased confidence and a broader view of the organization. They are grateful for the investment in them, and many say the experience helped them realize for the first time that the organization's future is in their hands.

Figure 6-5. Impact Measurement Framework for the Center for Leadership

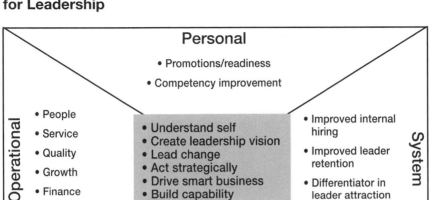

The second area is system leadership impact. Since the CFL's inception, our internal hiring rate has improved from less than 40 percent to over 60 percent, which puts us well on our way to meeting one of our primary goals. In a recent restructuring, leaders were needed for new pivotal positions at the center of our clinical delivery system. All these positions were filled internally. Leader retention has improved from the under 88 percent in 2004 to over 91 percent at the end of 2008. This improvement represents both more leader stability and the avoidance of unnecessary hiring costs. Our cardiac service line is one good example of the CFL's attraction power. Our chief of service, a CFL graduate, uses the CFL as a recruiting tool to help hire new physicians interested in expanding their horizons beyond pure clinical care.

The third area is where the rubber really hits the road with regard to direct operational impact. This area explores the connection between what participants have learned and what they have applied, along with the impact both of these have created in their local operation. Operational impact is categorized into the areas of people, service, quality, growth, and finance. This schema is important, because these categories define our core business operating model. All organizational goals, initiatives, measures, and results are tied to these categories. Aligning the CFL's results this way reinforces the idea that the CFL has a direct impact on our business outcomes.

The primary technique we use to understand the types, degree, and consistency of operational impact is the Success Case Method pioneered by Robert Brinkerhoff (2003). A detailed discussion of this method is beyond the scope of this chapter. However, the important points are that through surveys and structured interviews, success threads that weave from learning to impact can be discovered. The reasons behind why people achieve different levels of impact can be diagnosed and used to guide improvement efforts. Finally, both rich data and stories can be gathered. The key to ensuring a credible analysis is to include only those improvements that are directly attributable to the development experience. In our organization, we have interviewed every CFL Executive Experience graduate, and their stories and results are inspiring. All success threads that pass the credibility test are captured and verified in a database that currently contains more than 225 distinct impact items—including new staffing models, better leadership teams, improved customer service scores, safer care, expanded partnerships, and the launching of new services. Thus the progression: stories, data, impact.

Financial impact is the final area we evaluate. Though not every operational improvement is intended to create a financial benefit, our participants have implemented many changes that have achieved strong financial results. To stay aligned with our financial system, CFL results are classified as cost savings, cost avoidance, increased revenue, and increased extramural funding. Financial impact candidates are identified directly through the success case interviews. One of the interesting lessons we have learned is that people have a difficult time connecting the dots between what they have learned and applied and the impact generated. The success case interview itself seems to solidify the connection in participants' minds and serves to reinforce the success they've experienced. This insight has led us to use "success case thinking" during the development planning phase of a participant's CFL experience, because it helps him or her articulate tangible outcomes. Another lesson is that our participants have a difficult time converting from operational to financial impact. We learned that we need to provide concrete examples and keep asking questions. Let's listen in on a typical interview:

Interviewer: You said that you really applied the methods around delegating for development and got positive results. What happened?

Participant: I delegated in this new way to one of my direct reports, and she stepped up in new ways, took on new responsibilities, and started delegating for development with her team.

Interviewer: What did that lead to?

Participant: We found we could redistribute the work in new ways. Originally, we thought we needed two managers to handle all the work, but since we started doing this, we realized that we will not need to hire the second manager.

Interviewer: What impact has this had on your operation?

Participant: People feel more valued and are growing in new areas. We are executing well as a team, and I am more focused on what I need to be doing.

Interviewer: Do you think there is any benefit financially?

Participant: I'm not sure.

Interviewer: Was the second manager position budgeted, and have you definitely decided not to hire someone new?

Participant: Ahh . . . I see where you're going. Yes, the position is budgeted, and no, we will not fill it, so we are going to avoid that fully loaded cost this year.

Through conversations like this, along with subsequent analysis and verification of the financial results, we have captured more than $5 million in cost savings and avoidance, as well as more than $3 million in increased revenue and extramural funding. The biggest payoff, however, has been the ability to make improvements that matter. Targeted changes to participant selection criteria, assessment techniques, workshop designs, and action learning approaches continue to help us to improve the impact on participants and the organization.

As I stated above, converting learning and development into improved performance requires an organizational commitment to development that extends far beyond the delivery of training events themselves. This is perhaps the greatest lesson of our journey. HR leaders must provide the business logic for how employee and leader development initiatives will create tangible business results. We must actively engage the organization in the process, clearly defining roles and expectations. We must hold ourselves to a high standard of demonstrating impact and be transparent about what is working and what is not. We must balance principles with practicalities so that we do it "with" the organization and not "to" the organization. In my experience at Children's Healthcare, as we do our part, the organization responds by providing the time, energy, and attention required to take advantage of the investment being made.

A foundational part of our Develop-and-Perform Strategy is performance management. The phases and activities of performance management define some of the most basic and important aspects of the relationship between a leader and an employee. A strong, ongoing process leads to increased goal clarity, robust development, and higher performance. Though managing performance is good, imagine what could happen if each employee achieved his or her personal best. Our goal is to drive excellence, and our approach is based on several key beliefs.

From Performance Management to Performance Excellence

At Children's Healthcare, we believe that people deeply desire to contribute their skills and abilities to a worthwhile cause. We further believe that everyone has something to contribute and wants to know how he or she fits into the bigger picture. We believe that each employee is ultimately accountable for his or her performance. At the same time, we believe that the employees' environment has an effect on whether they deliver at the highest level and realize their potential. We believe that what someone does and how he or she does it are equal factors in the performance equation. Finally, we believe that a strong partnership between the employee, manager, and organization is essential to stimulating and supporting higher levels of performance.

This does not mean that poor performance does not exist and does not need to be handled fairly and swiftly. It does, and we do handle it this way. It only means that building our system with an emphasis on telling people what they are not doing well runs counter to our overall cultural underpinnings. Our philosophy is executed through the high-level process shown in figure 6-6.

Performance Planning

Children's Healthcare has established a long-range vision and strategic plan that we call Vision 2018. Each year, we analyze our results and develop a system-level annual operating plan. This plan defines goals that are critical to maintain ongoing operational excellence and initiatives that propel us toward Vision 2018. Goals and initiatives are aligned with our operating model categories—people, service, quality, growth, and financial. Specific measures and targets are set so that performance will be stretched in selected areas and will be maintained in others.

Once the system plan is established, we go through a process of setting goals and initiatives for our leadership core. Working with their

Figure 6-6. The Performance Excellence Process of Children's Healthcare

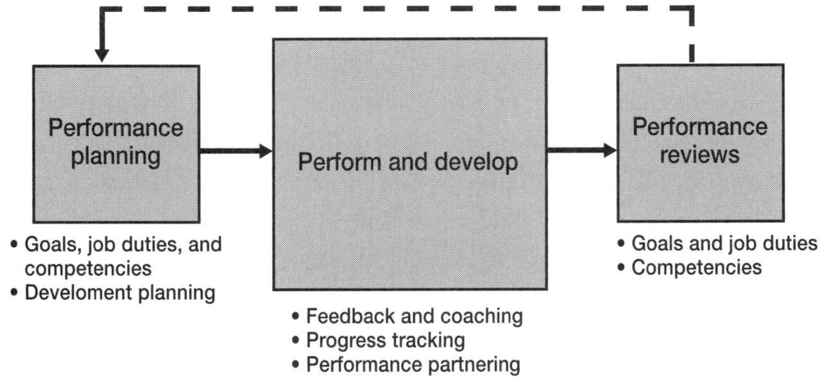

teams, our senior leaders establish a set of five core goals that align with our system plan for each leader at the director level and above. These goals are articulated specifically, with quantified targets and a range that defines what it means to meet, exceed, or not meet the goal. Initiatives are assigned, and the process continues by cascading goals to our manager population. All goals and initiatives are loaded into our technology platform, where progress can be updated and tracked. Staff-level expectations are defined through job duties, and our Children's Healthcare competencies are written specifically for our staff population.

We feel that development planning is an important part of performance planning. In our experience, both managers and their employees struggle to establish truly powerful development plans. We see two main issues. First, development goals are either direct copies of business goals or completely disconnected from them. Through the CFL and other avenues, we are working to educate leaders on how to set development goals so that the skills being developed are strongly linked to higher levels of achievement toward core goals. The second issue is that most people restrict themselves to a fairly limited set of development actions. Again, through the CFL, we are working to educate leaders about how development happens in the real world and how to expand their repertoire of tactics.

Perform and Develop

As you will notice in figure 6-6, the box for "perform and develop" is larger than the other two. This is because it's where all the action is and where a large part of our philosophy must play out. It is well known that one of the keys to stimulating high performance is frequent and actionable feedback and coaching. It's very important that leaders learn these skills early in their tenure, which is why they are the core focus of our CFL Supervisor Certification and Management Certification programs. Tracking progress and getting relevant feedback always seems to be an issue, given the hectic schedules most leaders keep. This is an area where technology can provide great value. Our platform allows managers to easily capture communication and documentation associated with their employees' performance and development. Online social networks can be used to receive feedback on any aspect of an employee's overall plan.

Information such as this, captured during the year, provides the substance needed for successful coaching sessions. It also makes the preparation of annual reviews much easier.

Performance Reviews

In line with our performance philosophy, our annual review process assesses both goal accomplishment and the behaviors demonstrated for every person in the company. The process starts with self-assessment, so that everyone can reflect and provide comments on his or her own performance. For positions at the director level and above, all goals are scored as to whether the goal was exceeded, met, or not met. This is where the work put into the performance planning process to set specific quantified performance ranges really pays off. Leadership competencies are assessed on a scale of exemplary, frequently exceeds, meets, and needs improvement, using our behavioral definitions as the basis for the assessment. Training and tools are provided to help leaders make more objective judgments.

After an initial assessment by their direct manager, each leader's competency assessment goes into calibration sessions. During these sessions, rating consistency is improved, and comments are captured in our technology platform. These calibration notes will eventually be discussed with the leader during his or her annual performance discussion, because they represent important input from multiple perspectives. The attention paid to the process of leadership calibration, along with the fact that leadership competency performance is equally weighted with goal performance, sends a strong message that we take leadership behavior seriously.

A new approach we are currently implementing for leaders at the director level and above addresses the issue of assigning an overall performance rating. What do you call someone who gets results but does it in the wrong way? Instead of trying to formulate an overall label that confuses the issue, each leader will now receive a separate rating for goals and for leadership. Our hypothesis is that this will lead to more honest assessments and clearer conversations about past accomplishments and areas for future focus.

Performance review discussions represent the moment of truth in the minds of many employees. The tone and substance of the discussion defines how well the company's performance philosophy is truly understood. In many companies, performance management is equated with the performance review. We are definitely not perfect, but we strive to make performance excellence an ongoing process. If the first two steps have been executed well, disconnects between the messages sent and received during the review discussion can generally be avoided.

We have recently implemented the performance module of our new technology platform. If I could dispense only one piece of advice, it would be to use technology implementations as a way to clarify your organization's performance philosophy and then figure out ways to embed it in your tools. We did just this as part of our recent implementation. We refreshed rating standards, communicated our beliefs, and engaged the organization in the process. With the aid of technology, our goal for performance reviews is to efficiently bring together employees' and managers' perspectives to enable productive dialogue and improved performance partnering. To make this goal actionable, we added a section in our online review that allows employees to comment on areas of development. It also enables them to identify the support and tools they feel they need to be successful. This small addition helps direct review discussions into areas that drive increased engagement.

Finally, although pay is absolutely connected to performance, we have learned that introducing pay into the performance review discussion makes it the central focus. For this reason, we separate these conversations.

People Informatics and Technology

In the previous section, I highlighted some of the ways technology supports the execution of our process at Children's Healthcare. However, the larger theme of integration guides our efforts to develop the technology infrastructure needed to support our People Strategy. The movement toward a platform approach that serves multiple talent needs with a central data repository is one that we like and are currently implementing.

One major benefit of this approach is that it will allow us to more easily weave information from one context into another. For example, the information obtained during the hiring process can be made available for development planning. Process automation is certainly a goal and is important to drive efficiency. The big payoff, however, will come from the ability to analyze currently disparate data sets to gain new insights and support smarter decisions.

If talent management is about supply and demand, then making smarter talent decisions requires up-to-date, reliable, and comprehensive information about positions and people. As part of our multiyear plan to implement a fully integrated talent system, we have begun development of the core position and talent profiles that live at the heart of the system.

Our people scorecard reports the data we gather monthly to track our progress in key areas such as candidate flow, retention, vacancy, and internal leader hiring. Our goal is to extend this capability so that these kinds of data can be easily brought together, based on different views of the organization. This will enable managers to see the talent in their organization through a new set of lenses and feel more equipped to make smart decisions. Ultimately, it will allow us to ask questions we didn't even know we needed to ask.

Back to the Future

The world I imagined at the beginning of this chapter is fast becoming a reality. At Children's Healthcare, our People Strategy is providing a road map to the future, and the practices I have outlined here are only a part of our overall approach. Important innovations in attraction, selection, engagement, and retention strategies have proved equally helpful in moving us forward. As we connect our strategies through the lens of our talent segments, we truly see the whole becoming greater than the sum of its parts.

Moving to the future in a sustainable way is a journey that requires organization-wide effort. The first, and most important, decision to make when embarking on this journey is not which strategy or program to implement. It is to recognize and accept that managing talent in a purposeful way is among an organization's top priorities. Like Children's Healthcare, many organizations have recognized that the key to sustained positive results lies in their people. For these companies, HR leaders are tasked with providing solutions to talent challenges that are more prescriptive, proven, and predictive. In turn, operational leaders must make talent solutions work by focusing more and more on the management of talent.

At Children's Healthcare of Atlanta, we have made great progress on the journey defined by our People Strategy. We are not perfect, by any means, but our healthy dissatisfaction with the way things are propels us forward. Everything we do at Children's Healthcare is for our kids and their families. We understand that there is a direct link between how well we manage our talent and moving toward fulfilling our mission of providing the highest quality of care. Think about your company. How do you make the link between talent and mission? Imagine. . . .

Acknowledgments

I would like to sincerely thank Linda Matzigkeit, Gail Klein, Michelle Reid, Tim Whitehead, and Liz Wysong for all their ideas, support, and encouragement in the writing of this chapter.

Talent Management beyond Boundaries at Ciena

Jim Caprara, Vice President, Global Human Resources Development

What's in this chapter?

- The challenges of talent management
- How Ciena developed its talent management philosophy
- Keys to talent management success

In today's economic environment, perhaps more than ever before, the definition of talent management must remain fluid, based on the needs of the business unit or function being served. As a learning industry, our desire to define talent management and neatly package it should never overshadow our most basic goal. The role of talent management in any business unit or function is to bear the responsibility for the readiness of the organization to perform. Accepting this responsibility means understanding that the definition of organizational readiness can vary, depending on the characteristics of consumers of talent, their strategic goals, and the metrics used to determine a successful return-on-investment.

In each company for which I have worked, I found both key constants where talent management will always prove valuable, such as leadership development and succession planning, and those nontraditional interdependencies that, when leveraged, truly accelerate business connectivity and the effectiveness of talent management overall. Examples of nontraditional roles for talent management become most apparent with a learning organization's heightened awareness of where the development of human capital, organizational mechanics, and business targets and metrics converge.

In 1999, while working for Sears Roebuck, I founded the Sears Technological Institute. At that time, the institute was the first fully accredited corporate learning institution in the United States. Although the creation of a school with 122 satellite training locations was a true benefit to our development strategy overall, it was made practical by addressing core business challenges. Sears, which was supporting the world's largest and most-experienced technical repair fleet, was at a near standstill in recruiting high-quality technicians. Simultaneously, the long tenure of the existing staff presented huge staffing challenges because a large percentage of them was approaching retirement eligibility. Conversely, most potential candidates emerging from technical schools wanted to repair jet engines—not washers and dryers.

The creation of a fully accredited school allowed us to develop mutually beneficial partnerships with vocational organizations and with strategic vendor partners like Whirlpool and General Electric. It also enabled us to offer scholarships to technical school graduates who agreed to further their education while working for Sears. Existing technicians, many of whom lacked formal technical training, found that they could gain from participation as well.

The Challenges of Talent Management

The challenge often faced by those undertaking talent management efforts is that a traditional approach may address a problem head on, and be reactive or even proactive, but be limited to the challenge at hand. Here we may fall short of our greatest potential value. A talent management organization has the ability to influence and provide value at every point in both the employee and customer life cycles. Understanding that there is no barrier to where talent management does or does not play becomes a strength and allows a talent management organization the freedom to interface and influence at business levels more commonly left untouched.

While working at Nextel Communications, I found that a key challenge was the ongoing development of our internal and third-party partnered sales force. Specifically, with the accelerated introduction of new products and technologies, Nextel had as many as 400 projects in play at any given time. Frequently, new applications were being marketed to customers before appropriate sales teams had even been exposed to them. The nontraditional answer to this challenge was to shift resources associated with the creation of customer collateral from marketing to the learning organization. Embedded as part of the company's learning resource, this hybrid group would take on the responsibility for all new product and application test trials, documentation, training development, and customer-facing collateral. The result was the simultaneous creation of both marketing and training content from the same assets, at the earliest point in the product development cycle. This approach was acknowledged by the company as a strategic advantage, and the resulting connectivity both on the marketing front end and in training delivery created a more visible and accepted link between business goals and talent management. Often, existing resources used for a specific purpose will find that an organization's talent management strategy provides an avenue through which a nontraditional interdependency becomes mutually valuable.

Valuable Lessons Learned

NVR is one of the 10 largest homebuilders in the United States. Here, it was critical to have the ability to identify quality issues with product, process, sales professionals, and production personnel in real time. My solution to this problem was to shift the company's critical customer service function into the learning organization. With the learning organization monitoring all posted activity through service, managing incoming customer call activity, and facilitating the company's customer satisfaction survey program, we were able to identify valuable opportunities for improvement. As a result, we could uncover needs with broad impact, as well as identify specific developmental needs among field managers, the sales staff, and production employees. These opportunities could then be addressed, monitored, and measured in real time through our field training organization. In this example, the customer service function was better managed and utilized as part of the learning organization. The quality trending and analysis from a developmental perspective added significant value, and the speed with which resulting actions could be implemented was dramatically accelerated due to the merging of the customer service function into the learning organization. Metrics related to the company's level of customer satisfaction and field audits both indicate that this nontraditional approach, taken as part of the talent management strategy, clearly has improved the organization's readiness to perform.

NVR also provided an excellent opportunity to prove talent management's vital role in the predictive forecasting of business performance. In 2006, the home-building industry was fast approaching an anticipated downturn. At NVR, the learning organization provided key insights into predictive success metrics with great accuracy, well ahead of the impact. This was accomplished through a process leveraging two measures of the organization's readiness to perform: skills retention and skills utilization. In the fall of 2006, NVR's learning organization implemented proctored testing of the company's entire sales organization. Both sales representatives and managers were tested to determine their retained knowledge of the company's accepted selling skills and process. The first result of strategic skills readiness testing was a sales assessment that yielded a clear company profile of the current enterprise-wide state of skills retention. This assessment offered the learning organization the opportunity to accurately target program resources and begin to accelerate improvement in the sales organization's readiness to perform.

Companywide Effort

Immediately following the testing, the learning organization shifted the company's sales training resources geographically. More than 180 secret shops were conducted companywide in the following two-week period. Each secret shop was videotaped and followed carefully controlled scripting of the tester. Scripts were designed to mirror the content of the just-completed retention testing to accurately measure skills utilization. This second measure of strategic skills readiness demonstrated the utilization of retained skills by the sales organization. Correlating directly to the retention testing, this assessment provided the learning organization with the opportunity to accurately target needs related to the sales organization's practical application and readiness state.

By combining the readiness (retention) and utilization data, the learning organization was able to provide a validated assessment of NVR's go-to-market readiness as it related to the existing skills inventory and the ability of the sales organization to leverage and execute. Figure 7-1 depicts the model that was used as a basis for this assessment.

The diagnostics that followed identified specific strengths and weaknesses by division, companywide. The results clearly predicted dramatic anticipated shifts in performance if the housing market were to shift downward. Several of the sales teams historically demonstrating the highest sales performances were identified as at risk, while many of the company's lowest-performing sales teams were labeled as strengths. Organizations geographically placed in areas that for years had enjoyed strong economic growth scored low in both retained knowledge and utilization of skills, whereas organizations positioned in more challenging environments had for many years exercised skills and were therefore better prepared for a down market.

In early 2007, as home sales rapidly fell, NVR's learning organization, without exception, had already accurately predicted the strengths and weaknesses of the sales organization. Learning programs, customized by division, were in place to address the gaps in the company's skills. Control groups, along with ongoing testing and secret shops performed over the following 12 months, indicated significant performance improvements

Figure 7-1. Strategic Skills and Readiness Assessment

Using strategic skills readiness and utilization assessments: sample assumptions

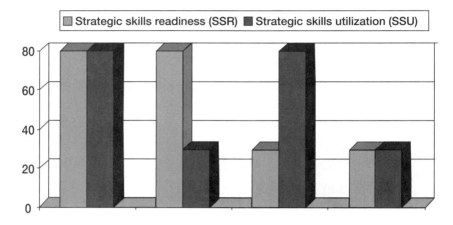

SSR = HIGH / SSU = HIGH	SSR = HIGH / SSU = LOW	SSR = LOW / SSU = HIGH	SSR = LOW / SSU = LOW
• Organization is operating at peak efficiency with skill sets introduced through training and supported by the field operation.	• Organization has high skills retention but is operating with underutilized skill sets. Indicates low post-demo day support and promotes a low quality–high volume sale environment.	• Organization has low skills retention but is using skills at hand. Indicates need to reintroduce skill sets, which are not being used.	• Organization has low skills retention and low utilization.
• Strong ability to respond to industry trends.			• Product of strong market and low need to exercise support.
	• Moderate ability to address industry trends.	• Product of strong market with limited need to exercise all skill sets. Those needed are being supported.	• Low ability to address industry trends.
Improvement opportunity	**Improvement opportunity**	• Moderate ability to address industry trends.	**Improvement opportunity**
• Address gaps by targeted exception and performance management criteria	• Targeted programs to ensure sales managers reinforce skills-resource available	**Improvement opportunity**	• Targeted programs to reintroduce skills
• Design and implement advanced skills program		• Targeted programs to reintroduce skills	• Sales manager support programs

as a result. In this example, waiting for a need to emerge from the organization would have yielded catastrophic results. The preemptive talent management approach demonstrated a clear and measurable value.

The lessons and knowledge described above, as well as many other past experiences, have been incorporated into the design of Ciena's talent management philosophy.

The Development of Ciena's Talent Management Philosophy

Ciena Corporation is a global player in communications networking equipment, software, and services that support the transport, switching, aggregation, and management of voice, video, and data traffic. In addition, the company provides consulting and support services, including network analysis, planning and design, network optimization and tuning, project management, staging, site preparation, installation activities, deployment services, and a suite of certification and training products. Ciena was founded in 1992 and is based in Linthicum, Maryland.

Ciena supports and maintains a comprehensive human resources development (HRD) model that is linked closely with the company's business strategies. Additionally, it addresses the individual characteristics of the company's various work environments and demonstrates its strong commitment to its greatest resource: its employees. From sales, engineering, product and policy training, to leadership, succession planning, and the leverage of diverse and high-potential talent, Ciena recognizes the value of investment in the development of its people and is positioned accordingly—including my position as part of the company's extended leadership team. The company's training function operates with a preemptive learning focus, allowing the learning function to identify requirements and be the driver/designer of the appropriate solution, as opposed to being asked to react to performance deficiencies after the fact.

Ciena Learning Solutions
To provide training representation and support through a direct business connection, Ciena's HRD function, Ciena Learning Solutions, represents

the centralization of all company functions and activities related to the development of human capital. The targeted goal for this learning organization is to provide a globally consistent learning experience to both our internal and external customers. This experience is delivered through high-quality professional delivery using scalable resources and with standards and guidelines that can be set globally and executed as close to the customer as possible.

With the full implementation of Ciena's HRD concept in 2008, resources previously dedicated to individual businesses and functions became a single, integrated organization, expanding the core capabilities of Ciena Learning Solutions and raising the bar on speed, efficiency, and the quality of program design, implementation, and return-on-investment. Linked closely with Ciena's business strategies, the learning function provides talent management by creating development solutions for all internal audiences while managing succession planning, providing leadership development, and simultaneously maintaining profit-and-loss responsibility for a customer-facing learning business.

Ciena Learning Solutions consists of a core management team representing functional disciplines, which include learning operations, learning delivery, documentation engineering, curriculum development, and program production. Learning managers are positioned geographically to provide global representation and hands-on management of local learning resources. Learning managers are also attached directly to business units in sales, IT, and engineering. Embedded within the businesses and functions is a network of learning professionals. Individuals on the learning team were carefully selected to act as single points of contact to facilitate connectivity between the business or function and the learning solutions teams. These individuals are designated as learning performance managers (LPMs).

Learning Performance Managers Defined

The LPM's designation is a function, not a specific position. The LPM's role is not defined by job, grade, or reporting relationship but rather by the strategic positioning of an individual to best leverage Ciena's learning resources to the benefit of the host business and, ultimately, the customer.

In short, the role of the LPM is to understand business metrics, act as the business's resident learning expert, and leverage all of Ciena's collective learning resources on behalf of the business. The result is a free-flowing needs assessment and engagement process that provides access to all learning resources with clear portfolio management through a single designated contact.

Operationally, to support Ciena's centralized learning model, all learning-related head counts and budgets, globally, are managed by Ciena Learning Solutions. All content for product engineering documentation, as well as learning programs, is created simultaneously from the same assets. Core content is multitemplated to allow for expanded audiences, who only receive content that is specific to their requirements. To facilitate this process, all company development resources are managed by the learning function. This includes both the design and development of learning programs and the creation of technical documentation.

Keys to Talent Management Success

The key to Ciena's go-to-market learning strategy was the shift in 2008 that connected the learning organization to the earliest point in the company's product life cycle. The learning function's documentation engineers and curriculum designers are now engaged at gate zero (that is, the end of the first major stage of product development) and are responsible for the creation of "first concept" learning documentation at the initial stage in the company's go-to-market process. This creates a level of awareness and connection to the company's business process and strategy seldom attained by learning organizations.

Documentation, development, production, and delivery resources leverage a common workflow tool within learning operations to coordinate learning resources, subject matter experts, and learning delivery, allowing for companywide management of the learning portfolio.

Today at Ciena, learning metrics are more critical than ever before. In many organizations, the talent management strategy is "reactive" to business requests. Filling the request successfully equates to success. At Ciena, the learning organization is positioned to be "preemptive," and it is the trusted expert addressing the design and implementation of the appropriate talent management strategy to address the business requirements in real time. This raises the learning organization's level of responsibility, and metrics become far more critical success factors.

Ciena measures standard operating metrics—including resource drain, expense, productivity, capacity, and revenue from learning—as well as the metrics attached to learning outcomes. Ciena performs level 1 and level 2 evaluations on all training. Internally, "readiness to perform" measurements are used to attach learning objectives to business results and provide a measure of return-on-investment. For customer training, Ciena collects feedback from all students and logs these results into its Learning Management System for analysis and reporting. Currently, additional metrics are being explored to attach learning utilization and retention directly to business results. Let's look more closely at some of Ciena's keys to talent management success.

Best Practices Are Not Enough

Ciena competes in an industry where emulating best practices is not acceptable. Only "being" the best practice and having the finest technology solution with the highest return-on-investment will yield results. Ciena consistently outperforms its industry rivals in a competitive environment where innovation and imagination are the key drivers to being first and best.

Taking its lead from the CEO, senior management encourages collaboration and celebrates innovation. Because Ciena is a technology leader, as opposed to a follower, unique aspects in the growth of human capital apply here. This amplifies the need to invest in the development of new talent and means that the development and retention of high-potential talent are critical.

Leadership Indicators

Ciena has introduced a set of 14 leadership indicators, each of which is supported by four to nine attributes. These support fluidity between our approach to line-level employee development and the approach we leverage to develop our executives and emerging leaders.

Annually, and largely separate from the company's performance appraisal process, managers are evaluated to gain companywide insight into Ciena's talent pool. The review is based on performance and potential. This is worked through a "nine-box" distribution and supported by manager input—the most current performance appraisal and an assessment against the company's 14 accepted leadership indicators. In conjunction with the review, high-potential candidates are identified, and both biographies and development plans are created for each candidate.

Two aspects of the process differ from most similar executions. First, the biographies are created to gather information regarding skills and experiences that are not clearly evident from looking at a candidate's current or recent-past assignments. For example, a high-potential sales executive may have, at sometime in his or her past, worked in marketing or finance. The prospective advantages this experience may have given the candidate receive special consideration as the viability of more challenging assignments are considered for this individual. The Ciena talent assessment process rolls up to senior management through a complete "report back" of the company's high-potential talent resource, as measured through performance, leadership assessment, experience, and manager input.

The second aspect of the process that differs from most is that the objective for the high-potential development plans is only to complete the needs assessment, and the manager is specifically instructed not to complete the plan at this initial stage. Instead, needs assessments for all employees with high potential are forwarded to the learning team. Trending of these requirements produces a targeted learning investment portfolio. The company's learning investment requirements and the resulting program are constructed, based on these validated needs, and a menu of learning options is released to managers to aid in the completion of individual development plans.

Succession Planning

The talent review process is also a data-gathering vehicle for succession planning. At the conclusion of the talent review process, HR representatives work with each business leader to review these data. They complete a succession planning document identifying mission-critical roles, "ready-now" candidates, and developmental candidates. The rollup of these business-level succession plans is compiled by the learning organization and reviewed in a C-level staff meeting, at which the senior staff in attendance has all the data items (leadership assessments, performance rankings, manager feedback, and biographies) for all the candidates being discussed.

As a result, Ciena's senior executives guide succession planning, career development at the senior executive level, and the identification and development of high-potential talent collectively. Viewing talent management cross-functionally and addressing Ciena's talent as a company asset ensures the selection of high-quality future leaders and that emerging leaders are prepared for promotional advancement.

More Than 200 Courses Online

Development opportunities include an online catalog of more than 200 business and product courses, a leadership seminar series enlisting C-level executives as adjunct faculty, 360-degree feedback, mentoring opportunities, and selected vendor programs. Additionally, action learning teams, coached through established business schools and addressing significant business challenges, are also available.

Ciena Learning Solutions' talent management resources, targeted to the development of frontline managers and teams in core businesses, extend beyond the delivery of training programs.

Ciena's sales organization is a product of careful recruitment of the finest technology sales professionals worldwide. Core selling skills and training centered on customer-relationship capabilities are a given. However, these sales professionals come from various companies, backgrounds, and experiences. Similar to any all-star team, when you are working with the best of the best, you cannot have your stars working out of different playbooks.

Sales Methodology Refined

In 2008, Ciena Learning Solutions partnered closely with its global sales teams to facilitate the design of a refined and standardized selling process that supported Ciena's sales methodology. This high-performance sales program is targeted to embed a consistent sales process throughout the company and clearly promote a "sales culture." Additionally, this program delivers important foundational skills along with training on standard processes and forms, and it ensures that practice executes on the sales process.

Ciena Learning Solutions is responsible for the management of all global learning resources: the centralized development of learning and technical documentation; global learning delivery; global resourcing, budgeting, and portfolio management; global training revenue strategy; technical training for employees, customers, and partners; predictive preemployment testing; 360-degree assessments; mentoring and coaching programs; and organizational talent review, succession planning, and leadership development. Interdependencies among resources, such as documentation and training development, create strong cost efficiencies and yield improved quality, consistency, and speed. This blending of the internally facing learning function with outwardly facing for-profit resources has allowed improved portfolio management, and the strategic construction of a higher-quality training product.

Leveraging Comprehensive Work

A significant advantage to Ciena's comprehensive approach to talent management is Ciena's Learning Solutions' profit-and-loss responsibility. By maintaining a global learning business presence and providing learning solutions, a suite of product courses, and technology certifications both through Ciena's services organization and to external customers directly, the Ciena learning organization is connected to the business, as a business. Cross-engineering of shared learning resources, content, and programs offers flexibility, cost efficiencies, and the higher investment in the level of quality learning product that is required to satisfy a for-profit function—all leveraged back into the internal learning offering.

A training product that is publicly marketed as having a technical certification must be of extremely high quality. Most internal training functions would find this standard cost-prohibitive. Ciena leverages a multitemplated development process, shown in figure 7-2, that allows for the simultaneous creation of a differentiated internal training product, without incremental cost. Shared delivery resources also ensure that both the external customer and internally facing functions maintain professional and scalable delivery resources on call. Here the linkage of the internal and external programs benefits both training functions and contributes to a cost-effective, high-performance companywide solution.

Talent management at Ciena is tied directly to Ciena's strategic business core. The learning organization's mission is to understand the individual characteristics that make each of our businesses successful in the markets where they compete. The learning organization's broad architecture allows us to deliver tailored learning solutions supporting corporate objectives, business needs, and high customer loyalty with speed and quality and in a cost-effective manner.

Figure 7-2. Ciena's Multitemplated Development Process

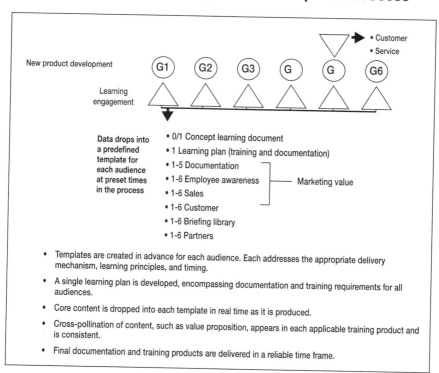

Summing Up

Having developed high-performance learning organizations for companies in the retail, services, construction, manufacturing, telecommunications, and network solutions fields, I have learned that the only consistent approach to a high-performance talent management model is understanding that there is no one single model. The learning organization simply carries the responsibility for the readiness of the organization to perform. The definition of talent management must be shaped by the needs of the business unit or function being served, and there will always be those nontraditional opportunities that will add value and be the differentiator in a high-performance talent strategy. A learning organization that grasps this concept and develops a talent management strategy that plays in concert with the business will be highly valued. In today's world, talent management plays a more important role than ever before, a role that will only increase with time.

Managing Talent at the Liberty Mutual Group

Larry Israelite, Vice President of Human Resource Development

What's in this chapter?

- The Liberty Mutual Group's approach to talent management
- Alignment via "this is who we are, this is what we do"
- How management development contributes to managing talent
- Developing a coordinated, consistent curriculum
- Evaluating success

◆ ◆ ◆

He walks through the door and takes a quick look around the room. He smiles, nods to the class, and then Edmund "Ted" Kelly, chairman and chief executive officer of the Liberty Mutual Group, shakes hands with each of the 50 frontline managers who have traveled to Boston from all over the country to attend their mandatory management training. Mr. Kelly spends an hour with this group of new managers, many of whom have neither been to the corporate headquarters before, nor had the opportunity to talk with the CEO of their company. Mr. Kelly discusses the insurance industry; Liberty Mutual's past, present, and future; his beliefs about management; and, perhaps most important, he answers every question he is asked. There are few topics that are off limits or subjects that are out of bounds. He answers honestly and directly, and at the end of the hour, everyone in the room understands at least one of the reasons why Liberty Mutual has been so successful under his leadership.

Mr. Kelly participates in as many as 35 management programs each year and has done so since 1996, when he and his predecessor, Gary Countryman, decided to strengthen management practices across the Liberty Mutual Group by investing in the development of managers from the time they move into their first management role and throughout their careers. And though management development is a significant part of Liberty Mutual's culture, it is but one part of a carefully planned, rigorously implemented, and relentlessly measured approach to the management of talent, much of which will be explained here.

There is no question that the effective management of its talent is absolutely critical to Liberty Mutual's ongoing success. In fact, Mr. Kelly often says that the company's single biggest investment walks in each day on two feet, so it needs to be well managed. However, the company has no "talent management" function; no one (well, maybe one person) whose title includes those words; and, with the exception of the semi-annual Talent Management Metrics Report, which will be explained in detail below, the term "talent management" isn't used as much as it might be in other companies. However, if anything is unequivocally clear to all managers, irrespective of where they work, what they do, or their level in the organization, it is that they are fully responsible and accountable for managing the workforce. Simply put, managing talent is what Liberty Mutual managers do. This chapter includes a description of three key factors that contribute to this intense focus on the management of talent:

- Alignment: a shared understanding of, agreement with, and application of the company's creed, principles, employee expectations, and what it takes to be successful in the organization.

- Management development: the structure and content of management development at Liberty Mutual.

- Measurement: the measures and metrics used to show the degree to which Liberty Mutual's key management processes are being used throughout the organization.

The challenge with this approach is it implies that each of these factors is separate and can be discussed independently of the others. In fact, the exact opposite is true. They are all intricately bound together, with the whole being greater than the sum of the parts. As a result, different sections of the chapter will address some or all of the factors simultaneously, which is, in the end, how they are experienced throughout the organization.

There is one more thing to consider as you begin reading about talent management at Liberty Mutual. What you will read here is neither remarkable nor all that unusual. There is probably nothing you haven't heard at a conference or read about in a journal. Perhaps you have even done some of the things yourself. But what is unusual, and maybe even extraordinary, is the impact of doing *everything* you will read about. It is the degree of focus on and commitment to doing what is required to manage the company's talent that makes this story interesting. And what it shows is that what may really matter is choosing a few things to do that make sense and doing them all very well.

The Liberty Mutual Group

Boston-based Liberty Mutual Group is a leading, global, multi-line group of insurance companies. With revenue of $28.9 billion, Liberty Mutual ranks 86th on the *Fortune* 500 list of the largest U.S. corporations based on 2008 revenue, and it is the fifth-largest property and casualty insurer in the United States based on 2008 direct written premiums. Liberty Mutual Group today employs more than 47,000 people in more than 900 offices throughout the world. The company operates four distinct business units: Personal Markets, Commercial Markets, Agency Markets, and Liberty International—each of which offers a wide range of products to its customers through a variety of distribution channels. Liberty Mutual Group is dedicated to our Customer Choice Model, allowing our customers to do business with us whatever way they want. They can access Liberty Mutual via a call center, website, agent or broker, or a network of regional independent agent companies.

Since the late 1990s, Liberty Mutual has grown significantly, through a combination of organic growth and strategic acquisitions, culminating with the acquisitions of Ohio Casualty in 2007 and Safeco in 2008. Its revenue has grown from just under $11 billion in 1998 to $28.9 billion in 2008. Its pretax operating income showed a similar increase during that period, going from $374 million in 1998 to $1.6 billion in 2008.

This represents a significant and, perhaps, remarkable turnaround from the late 1980s, when Liberty Mutual was on the brink of financial disaster. Liberty's near-death experience resulted in a significant number of changes. The company diversified, ending its reliance on workers' compensation for a majority of its revenue and divided into independent business units, each fully responsible and accountable for its own profit and loss. Liberty Mutual also began a process for changing the way it managed its talent, starting with who it put into senior management roles—traditionally, it had promoted from within—which is when Mr. Kelly began his tenure at the company. Much of what will be discussed in this chapter found its origins in the work that began at this time and continues today. It is important to note, however, that much more was done to effect the turnaround than will be described here. The turnaround of the Liberty Mutual Group is a longer, and perhaps more compelling, story—involving much more than managing talent, though talent was, and is to this day, a critical part of the company's success.

Alignment: This Is Who We Are, This Is What We Do

What sets the Liberty Mutual Group apart from other companies is a more than 90-year-old creed of "helping people live safer, more secure lives," and its employees' dedication to three clearly defined principles:

◆ We behave with integrity—we are in the business of trust. People build their lives on our promises and trust us to keep these promises, to our customers and to each other. Our most important promise is that we will strive to do the right thing, always.

◆ We treat people with dignity and respect—ours is a business relationship. We benefit, and our customers benefit, when the relationship is strong and long, and that means treating our customers well so that they will want to continue doing business with us. However, we can't be one thing to our customers and another to each other; we must treat everyone with dignity and respect.

◆ We aspire to provide consistently superior products and services at a fair price—we do business with those who value high quality and are willing to pay a little more for it. We aspire to provide consistently superior products and services at prices that are fair to our customers and allow us to make a reasonable profit.

It is this shared commitment to this creed and to these three principles that creates the culture of performance and growth that has been a critical part of Liberty Mutual's success.

Liberty Mutual is explicit about what employees can expect from the company. Further, it believes that its success is "inextricably linked to our employees' satisfaction and success; satisfaction that they work for an industry leader committed to improving safety, satisfaction that they work for a company that does the right thing, and satisfaction that the company will reward them for their contributions and provide opportunities for personal growth and success" (from the *This Is Who We Are; This Is What We Do* brochure, Liberty Mutual Group). Table 8-1 illustrates how the company's creed and principles come to life through employee expectations, which describe the commitments of the company, the responsibilities of managers, and the expectations of everyone.

The phrase "This is who we are, this is what we do" is well known throughout the company, and the concepts and content it represents are the cornerstone for a wide variety of communication and training efforts used in all parts of the organization, from the brochure we send to people who have chosen to work at Liberty (quoted above); to the posters

Table 8-1. Employee Expectations at the Liberty Mutual Group

Commitments of the Company	Responsibilities of Managers	Expectations of Us All
• Foster a work environment with equal opportunity for all, an environment that challenges, encourages, and helps employees grow and succeed. • Provide compensation and benefits that are very competitive. • Provide opportunity for participation in the company's superior financial performance. • Provide a performance management structure that clearly defines expectations, measures, results, and ties pay to performance. • Provide skill-building education and coaching that prepares employees to be successful. • Be a career-building organization; we always look to promote from within.	Managers have the responsibility for turning principles into actions; therefore, they are expected to adhere to the following: • fully understand the company's expectations • achieve objectives • treat everyone with dignity and respect • provide clear and explicit performance expectations • provide honest performance evaluations • coach constantly • make things better • be a champion for the company with your people • be a champion for your people with the company.	Each employee has a role to play in creating this supportive environment; it's not just up to managers. Here are the things we all share responsibility for doing: • do our jobs well; do what is asked of the job and hold ourselves accountable for results • learn constantly; develop the skills we need; push ourselves to succeed • take personal responsibility • take initiative and manage our careers; always participate actively • communicate—speak out when it's warranted and be willing to listen with an open mind • take responsibility for our own behavior; don't blame others.

on the walls of our conference rooms; to the "The Fundamentals," an e-learning program completed by every new employee during his or her first weeks on the job; and, finally, to the first morning of our required management programs, which are attended by practically every manager from all areas of the company. Employees and managers learn how the company's creed and operating principles, along with their commitments, responsibilities, and expectations, should inform their behavior and influence their interactions with each other, customers, suppliers, and anyone else with whom they interact on behalf of the company.

The Four Management Frameworks

Although the Liberty Mutual Group's creed and operating principles play a significant role in the organization, they do not describe, in precise and specific terms, what managers and employees must do to be successful in the organization. Because the company has more than 45,000 employees and more than 5,000 managers, additional information is required to create the level of alignment necessary for consistently achieving business goals. As a result, we developed four frameworks, each associated with one of the organization's talent segments: individual contributor, frontline manager, operations (middle) manager, and senior manager/executive. The frameworks describe the characteristics, capabilities, and capacity that are required for success in each of these employee segments.

Capabilities, sometimes referred to as competencies in other organizations, focus on the knowledge and skill required for success in the organization. They can change from time to time, as the needs of the company change, and usually can be learned. Table 8-2 contains a list of the capabilities used in the frameworks. As you will see, many capabilities are common to all four frameworks, while others are not.

As table 8-2 shows, there is a great deal of similarity among the capabilities for the four frameworks and across talent segments. However, this is not the entire story. Each capability has additional detail associated with it, referred to as dimensions, which describes in specific terms how the capability is demonstrated at each of the four levels of the organization. As you might imagine, the way one "communicates effectively" or "applies financial acumen" as an individual contributor or frontline

Table 8-2. Capabilities Used in the Management Frameworks at Liberty Mutual

Support or Create Alignment	Development	Execution	Long-Term Value
• Seeing the big picture • Communicating effectively • Working effectively with others • Influencing others (MGT)	• Developing capabilities (IC) • Building the team • Engaging and motivating people	• Planning and organizing work • Focusing on service • Analyzing and solving problems • Applying financial acumen • Executing well (IC) • Managing execution (MGT) • Achieving results	• Building relationships (IC) • Supporting innovation (IC) • Managing and improving process • Encouraging innovation • Practicing thought leadership

Note: The four frameworks are associated with these talent segments: individual contributor, frontline manager, operations (middle) manager, and senior manager/executive. MGT = management only; IC = individual contributor only.

manager might be entirely different from how one does the same things as a senior manager or executive. The dimensions are designed to reflect and document these differences. Though the capabilities are often the same for segments, the way these capabilities are demonstrated, as described in the dimensions, typically differs from one segment to the next.

Characteristics and capacity, which have been described by some senior executives as the Liberty Mutual DNA, tend to be more about who people are and much less about what they know or can do. Characteristics include values, traits, and personal style, whereas capacity focuses on stamina, adaptability, and motivation. As with capabilities, characteristics and capacity are further defined. Unlike capabilities, however, they are largely the same across all four frameworks.

With some exceptions, our belief is that characteristics and capacity cannot be trained. This is not to say that they can't be developed. Characteristics can evolve through the wisdom gained from experience, as managers learn how their actions affect others and begin to develop a style that helps them become successful. And capacity can develop as a result of the challenges associated with difficult assignments, through which employees discover reserves they often didn't know they had. As a general rule, we tend to hire for characteristics and capacity—but not exclusively.

Finally, each framework contains a description of the key work responsibilities of someone in that talent segment. Table 8-3 illustrates how this responsibility changes as one moves up in the organization, from an individual contributor to senior manager or executive.

Table 8-3. How Key Responsibilities Change as One Moves Up in the Organization

Organizational Level	Key Responsibility
Individual contributor	Getting work done with and for others
Frontline manager	Getting work done through others
Operations manager	Getting work done through managers, project teams, highly skilled individual contributors, and peers
Senior manager/executive	Identifying, defining, and directing the work required to meet company expectations

Additional information about how the key responsibilities listed in table 8-3 are operationalized appears on each of the frameworks. This information is organized into five categories—outcomes, process, talent, measurement, improvement—and contains detailed descriptions of the work required in each area for all talent segments. Once again, the goal is to create alignment regarding the work employees in each segment are expected to do and for which they will be held accountable.

The frameworks are ubiquitous. They are used to create job descriptions, interview guides, and developmental assessments. They form the foundation for management training, are a critical part of the performance management process, and are the basis for conversations about employee growth and development. And more important than any of this is the fact that they are exactly the same everywhere.

Although the frameworks are intended to promote consistency, alignment, and transparency across the organization, we recognize the importance of being clear about what they are and what they are not. This information is shown in table 8-4.

What this means is that managers have some flexibility in how they use the frameworks in their organizations. However, they do not have the flexibility to decide that the frameworks—or the creed, principles, and

Table 8-4. What the Management Frameworks Are and Are Not

The frameworks are	The frameworks are not
• flexible depending on business needs, role, and team composition • a common language that defines the parameters for success • the basis for developing tools and programs in support of selection, development, and performance management • aides to management judgment.	• psychological profiles • quantified formulae for executive success or performance evaluation • tools to develop personality homogeneity among management • a substitute for management judgment.

employee expectations, for that matter—are irrelevant in their organizations. In essence, managers have flexibility but not complete autonomy.

There has been an intense focus on alignment since the early 1990s. The core belief, which has been borne out by the company's success, is that the effective management of the organization's talent depends on a deep, shared understanding of who we are; what we do; and what characteristics, capabilities, and capacity we need for success. The creed, principles, employee expectations, and frameworks collectively help us to achieve this. But they are only the start. The next section describes how management development contributes to the management of talent at Liberty Mutual.

How Management Development Contributes to Managing Talent

Many companies offer some form of management training. Some provide a catalog from which managers choose programs. Others, like the Liberty Mutual Group, offer structured curricula, tied to management level, which are organized around competencies. But Liberty takes this one step further, because management development has become an important tool for implementing the company's business strategy and talent management agenda.

If you observed frontline management programs in 10 companies, it is likely that the content in most would be very similar. Upon reflection, this isn't surprising, because the issues facing most first-time managers as they transition into their new roles are remarkably similar, regardless of their employer. The same might be said for middle management programs. On the surface, Liberty Mutual appears to be no exception; the content of our programs is not particularly unusual. What is unusual, however, is the context in which our programs are planned and delivered.

First, managers are viewed as a corporate asset in a company comprising four wholly independent business units. So, although the customers, products, distribution strategies, and business systems may be different, the expectation is that the management practices and processes used in all business units will not be. Thus, a manager who moves from Commercial Markets to Agency Markets would be free to focus on acquiring the business knowledge needed to be successful in his or her new role, secure in the knowledge that the way he or she manages employees has not changed.

Second, Liberty's business units are held accountable for ensuring that all eligible frontline and operations managers attend their mandatory training within, respectively, 120 and 180 days of transitioning into their new roles. On a weekly basis, the human resources heads in business units receive a report listing the names of managers who either have not enrolled in required programs or who will complete their training after the attendance deadline. Participation in required management programs is measured in our semiannual "Talent Management Metrics Report," which is described later in this chapter. The expectation is that 95 percent of eligible managers will attend training within their designated compliance period. It is not unheard of for the manager of an employee who did not attend training on time to receive a phone call from the president of a business unit demanding an explanation. This isn't a phone call anyone wants to receive.

Third is the level of executive involvement in the delivery of management training. As was mentioned above, the CEO participates in almost every program, as do those who report directly to him. Their presentations vary somewhat, based on the audience and program content, but in every case they emphasize the significant role that managers and management play in the success of the company. Experienced line managers also participate. Though programs are designed and administered by a corporate management development group, line managers and technical experts are expected to deliver at least 60 percent of course content. This is another metric for which the management development group is held accountable.

Fourth and finally, though specific management skills are clearly a focus of core programs, a greater emphasis is placed on

♦ fostering a deep sense of identification with Liberty Mutual

♦ reinforcing managers' commitment to the creed, principles, and employee expectations

♦ developing an understanding of how managers are expected to do their jobs, as described in the management frameworks

♦ developing knowledge of the management processes and practices managers are expected to use as they go about their jobs.

Collectively, core programs create highly aligned and motivated managers, who practice their craft consistently in all parts of the company.

Liberty Mutual's recent acquisition of Safeco, in September 2008, provides an excellent illustration of the importance that Liberty places on alignment. Within eight weeks of the acquisition's close, almost every Safeco manager, including executives, had completed a modified version of our core Front-Line Management Program. The goals of this somewhat abbreviated program were identical to the longer version, which were listed above. In addition, the company's commitment to deliver this training sent a strong message to all Safeco employees that managers and management development matter at Liberty Mutual, as do the ways in which managers do their jobs.

The Curriculum Architecture

The Liberty Mutual Group takes a consistent approach to the development of managers at all levels of the organization. Figure 8-1 shows the key development activities that make up the curriculum for each level of management. In some cases, the content is the same for all managers. New employee orientation, for example, is a common experience intended for all recent hires. Individual contributors, frontline managers, and operations managers typically share professional and technical development programs. But role orientation, alignment, and advanced role development differ by management level.

Let's consider each of the key management development programs. The first is *new employee orientation*, known as Right*Start*, which consists of a yearlong experience intended to fully integrate new employees into Liberty Mutual. Right*Start* prescribes a series of discussions between new employees, their managers, and peers and the completion of several e-learning modules covering a wide range of topics. Not surprisingly, creating alignment is a key outcome of Right*Start*.

Figure 8-1. Key Management Development Activities

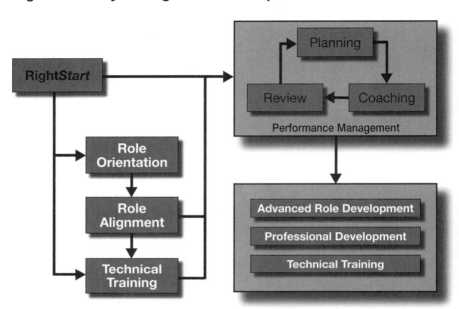

The second key management development program is Role Orientation, which can be viewed as a "survival kit" that helps managers as they transition into their new roles. In the case of frontline managers, the program introduces them to their responsibilities for

♦ managing their work units in a manner consistent with Liberty Mutual management philosophies and policies

♦ selecting new hires, managing and evaluating the performance of their teams, and creating development plans

♦ providing effective coaching and feedback

♦ explaining Liberty Mutual's compensation philosophy and its alignment with performance

♦ communicating effectively with their work units

♦ identifying and beginning to address the key management challenges faced by new frontline managers.

The program also introduces new managers to the variety of online tools and references they will use in their roles. The Role Orientation for Operations Managers Program is similar in structure but focuses on a more advanced content appropriate for people who manage managers.

The third key management development program is Role Alignment, the cornerstone for each management level, the structure of which was described above. As noted, all new frontline and operations managers are, respectively, expected to complete their role alignment programs within 120 or 180 days. The content of role alignment programs does not change frequently in an effort to maintain the consistency of the message and content from program to program and year to year.

The fourth category of key management development programs, titled Advanced Role Development, supports the development of advanced skills associated with specific business initiatives or processes. These programs are typically available to managers who have been in role for two to three years. Advanced role development programs are added from time to time to address strategic business issues, skill needs that have been identified by business leaders, or for other reasons that may emerge.

The fifth category of key management development programs, titled Professional Development, addresses the business skills and knowledge necessary for individual performance improvement and/or career development. Included in this category are internal classroom and e-learning programs, courses leading to professional designations, and college courses.

The sixth category of key management development programs, titled Technical Training, which is offered by the business units, includes technical programs that provide the job-specific skills required to manage technical professionals (sales, underwriting, and the like) and develop or maintain functional or industry knowledge.

The approach to management development explained here has been in place for more than 10 years. Certainly, improvements have been made, but the architecture has remained largely the same since its conception. And though it is difficult to reliably measure the real impact of the programs we deliver, there is evidence that it has yielded results.

As most people in the management development business will acknowledge, it is challenging, at best, to measure the impact of their work. It is no different at Liberty Mutual. However, there is evidence that the approach described above has yielded significant results. First, our programs are meaningful to participants. They greatly appreciate the opportunity to travel to Boston, to engage with the faculty and the content, and, of course, to spend time and interact with senior executives. More significantly, they recognize and take seriously the investment the company is making in them.

Second, managers often refer to the programs when describing the techniques they use when managing their teams. This is especially evident when experienced managers are invited to speak to their less-experienced colleagues, at which time they go out of their way to emphasize how frequently they utilize what they learned in the training and to refer to the materials they received.

Third, there is evidence that managers apply what they learn, as measured by the annual employee opinion survey and the "Talent Management Metrics Report," which is described in the next section.

Fourth, and most important, Liberty Mutual has a sustained record of business growth and success that started just before the management development initiative. Though no one would claim that the management curriculum has been responsible for this success, most would acknowledge its contributions. Liberty Mutual's ability to execute its strategy has been enhanced because it has developed an aligned management team that possesses the requisite characteristics, capabilities, and capacity.

What Gets Measured Gets Done

The title of this section is something most of us have heard (or said) before. We know, or believe, that it's true—that what gets measured gets done. At some point in our careers, we may have even tried to put in place a measurement system based on the idea this phrase expresses. The challenge, of course, is that an effective measurement system requires a shared understanding of goals and outcomes, which are often either poorly articulated or simply nonexistent; agreement on the metrics that will be used to make judgments; and a system for collecting, analyzing, and reporting data. Each of these is hard to do alone. Doing them all at the same time, and doing them all well, can be a significant challenge.

Human Resources and Talent Management

Throughout this chapter, I have tried to demonstrate that talent management is the responsibility of every Liberty Mutual Group manager. It is not something that is owned or mandated by human resources (HR). This is not to say, however, that HR is not involved. Rather, HR is responsible for providing an infrastructure—a strategy and then a set of policies, processes, and practices—that helps managers fulfill their talent management responsibilities effectively, consistently, and in a way that can successfully be measured.

HR's connection to talent management begins with the statement of a relatively simple strategy: "to select, develop, engage, and retain the people we need to enhance competitive advantage." Table 8-5 shows how the company does the first three of these things—select, develop, and engage—based on a belief that doing each of them well will increase the likelihood that our employees will choose to remain with the company.

It is important to note that this is not an HR strategy. Rather, it is a business strategy. And though HR may be responsible for providing an infrastructure that supports it, managers are fully accountable for making the strategy a reality. In the end, managers make final selection decisions, they choose to work with those who report directly to them to ensure that development occurs, and they endeavor to create an engaging work environment. Or they don't do these things. But these things are the managers' responsibilities; HR can only influence, drive, facilitate, and support.

What HR has done, however, is put in place a measurement system that provides information to managers about the degree to which the company is successfully implementing its people strategy. Are we really selecting the right people? Are employees, in fact, engaged in the appropriate development activities at the right times? Have we created a work environment that truly engages people? These are questions that the "Talent Management Metrics Report" is intended to answer.

Table 8-5. The Three Elements of the Liberty Mutual Group's People Strategy

We select the right people by
• being known as a successful, exciting, and growing company that offers challenging career opportunities
• developing recruiting strategies that yield people with the skills and talent we need
• tapping every pool of talent
• providing compensation and benefits that are competitive
• using clear selection criteria for each career path.
We develop the right people by
• welcoming them into our organization in a way that assures speedy assimilation
• providing clear and explicit performance expectations
• providing honest performance evaluations and ongoing coaching
• providing role-specific training and education
• embedding a training infrastructure for skill, technical, functional, and management development
• offering career-building options
• identifying high-potential employees and providing them with opportunities for continued growth.
We engage the right people by
• treating people with dignity and respect
• communicating clearly
• managing within a framework of clear policies and standards
• providing the tools and resources our people need to achieve superior levels of productivity, quality, and service
• ensuring a performance orientation by clearly defining expectations, measuring results, and aligning pay to performance
• ensuring our workplace is free from obstacles to doing a good job
• using common sense.

The "Talent Management Metrics Report"

The "Talent Management Metrics Report" (TMM Report) is created twice each year, covering the periods from January 1 to June 30 and from July 1 to December 31. It has three sections, each of which corresponds to one of the three elements of the people strategy, and it is used to identify and measure progress on the strategy's deployment. Each section of the report contains

- a series of goals associated with the particular element of the people strategy
- the target metric for each of the goals
- the actual metric achieved for each goal by the business units and corporate functions.

Detailed metrics information is available for subdivisions of the organizational structure.

The second section of the TMM Report, which focuses on employee development, serves as a good example. It includes measures of compliance with the mandatory training described in figure 8-1:

- the percentage of new employees who complete their orientation on time
- the percentage of managers who complete their training (role orientation and role alignment) on time
- the percentage of individual contributors who complete their required technical training on time.

In each case, we strive for a compliance rate of 95 percent.

Two other important indicators of effective employee development also are reported in this section of the report:

- the percentage of key management positions for which there is more than one qualified internal candidate
- the results on the annual employee opinion survey for questions related to growth and development.

Although the first three measures address the completion of development activities themselves, these measures focus more on the impact of development.

This approach of measuring both activity and impact is consistent for all parts of the TMM Report. When reporting on selection, for example, it gives measures of the selection process itself, the people we hire, and whether or not new hires remain with the company. Once again, both activity and impact are measured. The same is true for the report's third section, which addresses several aspects of creating an engaging work environment.

There are two other parts of the TMM reporting process that significantly increase its effectiveness—TMM data specifications and the visibility of the process throughout the organization. First, let's look at data specifications.

The TMM Report contains 31 unique measures, each of which has been carefully described in data specifications that are updated on a periodic basis. Table 8-6 shows an abridged version of the data specifications for measuring completion of the management training. The specifications comprise a detailed description of data elements, definitions, exclusions, data sources, and directions about how various data items are to be treated when calculating the metric.

Changes and updates to these data specifications are discussed with and agreed to by all key stakeholders. The value of the data specifications is that they greatly reduce the potential for any misunderstandings or disagreements about what is being measured and how. Helen Sayles, the HR senior vice president, described the reasons HR invested the effort to develop such detailed data specifications: "We really wanted discussions about the TMM Reports to focus on the results and not on the process we used to generate those results. Gaining agreement on the specifications helped us achieve that goal. John Kenneth Galbraith had it right when he said: 'Faced with the choice between changing one's mind and proving that there is no need to do so, almost everybody gets busy on the proof.' Changing managers' minds and their behavior is the purpose of the TMM Report. The data specifications eliminated the need to quibble about the proof."

Table 8-6. Abridged Data Specifications for Completion of the Management Training

Attribute	Completion of the Management Training
Formula	The number of eligible managers who have successfully completed Building the Capabilities for Success training within time guidelines/total number of program-eligible managers
Data definitions	Eligible managers: All active employees segmented as frontline manager or operations manager and who have direct reports in the human resource information systems (HRIS). Compliance is based on the date managers are segmented, not the date when direct reports are assigned in HRIS. Standard exclusions: • Prior completion of the required program or equivalent program • Co-op students • Corporate HR temporary students • Temporary employees and nonemployees • Inactive employees at time of report—including retirees • Employees rehired with previous completion of Building Capabilities for Success or an equivalent program • Managers exempted from the curriculum with proper approval • Managers in recently acquired companies
Internal data source	• Number of eligible managers: HRIS • Enrollment eligibility based on job segmentation and direct reports
Employment status	Full-time regular and part-time regular
Fair Labor Standards Act status	Exempt and nonexempt
Time period	• Frontline manager: Date of hire or promotion into job between (start date/end date) • Operations manager: Date of hire or promotion into job between (start date/end date)
Transfers within/ between market	Organization the employee was in at the end of reporting period
Contact for further information	HR development training administration manager

Finally, it almost goes without saying that reports only matter if people read, understand, and believe them—and, even more important, act on them. All are true at Liberty Mutual. Each edition of the TMM Report is provided to senior managers throughout the organization and is presented to and discussed with the CEO and those who report directly to him. Individuals who are accountable for each of the metrics are required to explain variances and are expected to present plans describing what actions will be taken to address process deficiencies. The bottom line is that everyone involved takes the TMM Report and all that it represents seriously. It is, in the end, a well-respected indicator of the state of the management of talent, which is provided by HR, but owned by managers at all levels throughout the organization.

Conclusion

In many organizations, the term "talent management" describes an organization or, perhaps, one of many responsibilities that HR or those concerned with management development are assigned as part of their jobs. But at the Liberty Mutual Group, the term describes the single most important responsibility of every manager and comprises much of the work they do each and every day. And it is one of the strategies that have helped Liberty Mutual achieve the continued success it has experienced for more than a decade.

Managers at Liberty Mutual can draw on a variety of tools, systems, job aids, and support as they endeavor to get the most from their employees. The same is true for managers at most companies. But managers at Liberty Mutual have something else as well. They are aligned—meaning that they have a shared understanding of, agreement with, and application of the company's creed, principles, employee expectations, and what it takes to be successful in the organization. They are well trained, meaning that they participate in a comprehensive development process that provides them with the tools they need to manage effectively. And they are provided with detailed measures and metrics, which help them understand what they are doing well and the areas where they need to improve.

Above, I said the following about talent management at Liberty Mutual:

> What you will read here is neither remarkable nor all that unusual. There is probably nothing you haven't heard at a conference or read about in a journal. Perhaps you have even done some of the things yourself. But what is unusual, and maybe even extraordinary, is the impact of doing *everything* you will read about. It is the degree of focus on and commitment to doing what is required to manage the company's talent that makes this story interesting. And what it shows is that what may really matter is choosing a few things to do that make sense and doing them all very well.

We have chosen those few things to do, and we work hard every day to do them well. And though we may be pleased with our progress, we are not satisfied. We continue to explore ways to do better. Our customers and our employees expect and deserve nothing less. So, in closing:

> Mr. Kelly answers the last question and walks toward the door. He glances over his shoulder, sees the faces of the class, and then heads off to his next meeting. In the hallway, he stops for a moment to comment on the quality of the questions these frontline managers asked, pleased, but not surprised, by the insight they have shown into the business we are in, the work they have to do, and the impact they can have on the success of the company by managing in accordance with our creed and our principles. Though no other words are spoken, it is clear that he believes the past hour was time well spent.

Author's Note

Although most of the words here were written by the author, the thinking and hard work that created the story they tell was done by many others. In particular, at the Liberty Mutual Group, I would like to acknowledge Helen E.R. Sayles, the senior vice president of human resources and administration, under whose direction and guidance all that is described here occurred; Richard A. Dapra, the former vice president of human resource development, who was responsible for the creation of the management development process and curriculum; and the many others whose hard work, clear thinking, and commitment contribute to Liberty Mutual's continued success.

Talent Management: The Elephant in the Room

Nigel Paine, Managing Director, nigelpaine.com

What's in this chapter?

- The five key shifts in the employer-employee relationship
- Findings from a U.K. study of talent and leadership
- Tips for moving toward a talent-driven culture

ASTD is running an online seminar called "Talent Management: The Key to Success in the Knowledge Economy." A new magazine has popped up from the CLO stable called simply *Talent Management,* and there are numerous senior corporate roles in both the public and private sectors with the word "talent" in the title. These include head of talent, head of talent management, and even head of talent planning! You cannot work successfully now in the human resources (HR) area without understanding some of the issues concerning talent—or, indeed, what talent is.

This was heralded in October 2006 by a prescient 20-page feature in *The Economist,* "A Survey of Talent," which seemed to open the

floodgates. *The Economist*'s insight can be summed up in its own conclud-
ing words:

> The success of advanced economies is increasingly dependent
> not on their physical capital but on their capacity to mobil-
> ise their citizen's brainpower. . . . [This will lead to] all sorts
> of benefits, from higher growth in productivity to faster scien-
> tific progress. It can boost social mobility and allow all sorts of
> weird and wonderful talents to bloom. (*The Economist* 2006, 20)

In some ways, this journey from *The Economist* supplement to the
ASTD webinar over nearly two and a half years takes us full circle. This
is the journey from the genesis of an idea to its extrapolation as a practical call to action.

Another Elephant in the Room

If you had been anywhere near Piccadilly in London on Saturday, May
6, 2006—at the point when *The Economist* was commissioning its supplement—an incredible and bizarre sight would have greeted you. About
a quarter of a million people thronged to a usually traffic-packed grand
London thoroughfare to witness something they had never seen before
and would never see again: a mechanical elephant over 45 feet tall and
weighing 42 tons walking down Piccadilly toward Piccadilly Circus, occu-
pying both carriageways (that is, all four lanes of a wide thoroughfare)
and dwarfing the street's grand facades. And when I say walk, I do not
mean being dragged on wheels, I mean walk! Each huge hydraulic, tree-
trunk-sized leg would raise up and stomp down, as the next one lifted,
and slowly, painfully slowly, the elephant would inch its way down the
street as the musicians played, and the dancers danced on the wide stage
on top of the elephant.

Above this scene, the sultan who owned this elephant wandered out
onto his side balcony and waved at the crowd or sat and sipped tea. This
was indeed his elephant. Meanwhile, the elephant's head turned, ears
flapped, eyes blinked and revealed lashes about eight inches long, and
trunk contorted in a prehensile way, up and down and sideways until, at

the height of its trajectory, it would disgorge gallons of water onto the unsuspecting (and remarkably good-natured) crowd.

This had been presaged two days previously by the arrival of a large (15 feet high) wooden barrel that simply appeared that morning in Whitehall, breaking up the ground where it "landed." This is narrative told on a grand scale!

In reality, this was the largest piece of open air theater ever seen in London, the creation of a French Theater Group called Royal de Luxe, which celebrated its 30th anniversary in 2009. The elephant has performed all over Europe, but nothing could take away the impact, amazement, and incongruity of this London spectacular.

The event told a story loosely based on a Jules Verne short story, "The Sultan's Elephant," and was commissioned to mark the 100th anniversary of Verne's death. But the elephant was big business, and if you needed to draw a massive crowd, this was the guaranteed way to do it. And for this reason alone, event organizers of various sorts were prepared to dig deep to secure this elephant.

But what makes the elephant even more interesting are some facts about its inception and creation. It had taken more than two years to design and build, and more than 1,000 people had been involved at one time or another in the construction process. It was the embodiment of the vision of the Royal de Luxe's director—Jean Luc Courcoult—but to make this vision a reality had required a team of skilled engineers, materials scientists, artists, puppeteers, actors, painters, logistics experts, and many more.

This team worked in multidisciplinary groups charged with executing their parts of the design. There were no models to copy, no blueprints, no benchmarks. No one, anywhere in the world, had ever done this before. The groups worked entirely in unknown areas. Every step was the creation of a new reality and the solution to numerous logistic, mechanical, electronic, and aesthetic problems that took small steps toward solving the bigger issue: how to bring Courcoult's vision to life. And as with many visionary companies before them, only with the delivery of the product did anyone begin to understand what it was all about.

There were three key characteristics of each and every one of the groups forming the elephant-construction team: massive diversity (they were multiskilled, multiethnic, and multiage), mutual respect for these various differences, and a belief that they could achieve their goal on time. For many of the team members who were interviewed, this was the best job they had ever had, and yet it was the most demanding and the most likely to fail. This project embodied the spirit of *The Economist*'s view that by mobilizing citizens' brainpower, it would be possible to achieve the impossible.

The elephant was neither a work of art nor an elaborate machine. It meant nothing and everything. And it was certainly not something that evoked lukewarm reactions from those who saw it. Like Ken Blanchard's call to create "raving customers," it evoked strong emotions (see Blanchard and Bowles 1993). People were astonished by what they saw. Most people there on the third day had been urged to participate by onlookers from days one and two; hence the exponential growth in the crowds.

There was also the massive logistical job of getting the crowds and the elephant from point A to point B and preventing any unwanted collisions between elephant and human beings. But this worked, both at the level of vision and the level of detail. The total experience was positive and delightful.

In many ways, "The Sultan's Elephant" extravaganza embodies the future of work. Most industrial economies will have extraordinary numbers of people working in areas that involve breakthroughs, are breathtaking, and are astonishing. Hundreds of thousands of employees will be working on projects that have no precedent and that, in their own small way, will change the world. And the only way that this will be possible will be to mobilize the brainpower employed and to understand talent, thoroughly and completely. The concept of talent is not a restatement of existing HR procedures that have existed up to now, but, rather, a reconceptualization of the relationship between employer and employee to build a talent-driven organization.

The Changing Relationship between Employer and Employee

There are five key shifts in the relationship between employer and employee that trace the trajectory from perceiving an employee as an entity to be corralled, controlled, and directed to seeing that same person as talent to be developed, encouraged, and, in a sense, set free. These five shifts are

- ◆ from doing a job to inventing a role
- ◆ from being skilled to being talented
- ◆ from development as a privilege to development as a right
- ◆ from knowledge hoarded to knowledge shared
- ◆ from individual performance to team achievement.

Each shift needs a certain amount of elaboration and explanation.

From Doing a Job to Inventing a Role

Clearly there are jobs to be done! A range of competencies fit each role. But in a talent-oriented organization, the individual grows into his or her wider role and therefore builds and constantly changes the actual role played. If you look at companies as diverse as WL Gore and Google, what links them is a more flexible attitude to the role of the employee.

At WL Gore, project leaders are chosen for their fit with a specific project and, when they finish, they may return to being a participant in someone else's project. An employee is an associate, and that is the only information on their business card. Job titles are ephemeral, roles change, and the individual grows with the company. Likewise, Google allows employees to focus on their own projects for 20 percent of the workweek. They can freely associate with self-directed and self-sustaining teams to get this work done, and therefore they increase their own competence and creativity for the company as a whole, not just for a particular role or a specific project. Every member of the staff is therefore expected to have ideas and be prepared to articulate them. And ideas transcend hierarchy.

Consider the treatment of the character Frank Wheeler by his boss and boss's boss in the film (or, indeed, the novel) *Revolutionary Road* (Yates 1961). The story, which is set in New York during the 1950s, illustrates just how little has changed over the intervening half century in employer-employee relations, whereas every other aspect of society has changed radically. Wheeler feels essentially alienated from the work process, and he moves seamlessly from being perceived as a difficult, and not very satisfactory, employee in the eyes of his dull, unimaginative boss to being seen as a special talent selected from the run-of-the-mill majority. This shift occurs because he designs a different sort of brochure for the Tacoma Regional Office concerning a machine he only begins to recognize later is a computer. He describes it to his wife as a big adding machine, and she could not be less interested.

Even Wheeler's special selection and promotion are poorly handled, and he never contributes a fraction of what he is capable of in his new (or old) role. This development of work roles that are as unfulfilling as they are futile is a norm, still expected by many employees. When employees the world over are questioned about their level of motivation, "unchallenging" is still their dominant description of their work. There is much evidence for this, from surveys of various kinds, but the YouGov survey quoted by Stefan Stern in a *Financial Times* article on May 14, 2007, is illustrative. YouGov questioned more than 40,000 employees, at all levels and in all sectors, and it found that

> only half (51 percent) feel fully engaged by the company they work for. Less than two thirds (63 percent) say they feel loyal to their employer and an even smaller proportion (51 percent) believes their employer deserves any loyalty.

From Being Skilled to Being Talented

Most governments of industrial countries have skill development policies. In Britain, the most recent report on these policies, by Lord Sandy Leitch, *UK Skills: Prosperity for All in the Global Economy—World Class Skills*, was published at the end of 2006. It makes the assumption that formal, recognized qualifications to standardized levels will improve, in themselves, the overall prosperity of a company or the nation. In the foreword to the report, written by the author, he argues,

> [i]n the 21st century, our natural resource is our people—and their potential is both untapped and vast. Skills will unlock that potential. The prize for our country will be enormous— higher productivity, the creation of wealth and social justice. (Leitch 2006, 1)

In other words, untapped human potential can be released by skills development. The reality is more complex, and it takes us away from the simple correlation that because training is good, therefore the more training the better for the individual—and the more a company invests in training, the better the company will perform. In short, more skills equal increased productivity.

One of the report's key recommendations is that companies make a pledge to fund, voluntarily, the upgrading of the vocational qualifications of their workforce up to a defined minimum level (called level 2). The weakness of this argument is that skills development alone is rarely enough. And in the current climate, spending training funds on skills development, with no clear idea of how or if payback will occur, is to tread on very thin ice indeed. The wreckage of corporate training departments around the industrial world—especially in the United States—attests to this.

Two companies with similarly skilled workforces can perform very differently in the marketplace. The difference reflects how work is organized, the quality of the processes in place, and the way the workforce is managed and positioned. Attitudes toward talent and a talent culture are therefore as significant for performance as the delivery of skills and qualifications. With such a culture in place, organizations naturally begin to evolve measurable outcomes and clear business benchmarks for success.

From Development as a Privilege to Development as a Right

Development as a right does not imply that individuals can take on any portfolio of learning they want, at any time that suits them. Rather, it implies a culture of learning in an organization. Learning and development are the expected norms of behavior. This is coupled with an attitude where questioning decisions, curiosity, and innovation are dominant. This is not the general experience of most employees, and this culture is by no means the dominant culture. The book *Organizational Learning and the Learning Organization* (Easterby-Smith, Aráujo, and Burgoyne 1999) makes this abundantly clear.

In *The Future of Management* (Hamel and Breen 2007), Gary Hamel describes Google as being more like a research university than a large multibillion-dollar company in terms of its attitudes and behaviors. Debate, brainstorming, and the free exchange of ideas are a dominant part of the culture. And in this economic downturn, it has posted increased profits and is still recruiting, though not at its former rate. Contrast Microsoft; the company announced 5,000 redundancies and abandoned profit projections for the later part of 2009. Both firms have smart, highly skilled workforces and function in the same sector. But their attitudes toward ideas, workforce innovation, and talent are different. Some of the answer to the success of one and the relative decline of the other must lie in this area.

Learning organizations tend to amplify the impact of informal learning and to create pathways for this to happen more regularly. They also encourage the sharing of knowledge, so success or problem solving in one part of the organization can be quickly replicated in other parts. IBM, for example, builds in a knowledge-sharing element to every project it runs, so that any staff member can access IBM's global position on any aspect of its work and trace the key people in any area almost instantly. And this is for a workforce of more than 250,000. Therefore, what IBM has learned about almost any situation is rapidly available across its networks to almost all employees.

At the third-largest supermarket chain in the United Kingdom, ASDA—now owned by Walmart—the then–chief executive, Archie Norman, inherited what many told him was a basket case of a company and the worst-performing supermarket chain in the United Kingdom. He set about rebuilding the company and transforming its performance, investing time and energy in the existing staff by

- Rewarding good ideas and implementing staff suggestions in as many cases as possible.

- Offering the loan of a Jaguar car for a month (formerly the exclusive property of senior executives) to the highest-performing shop-based team.

- Writing personally to every staff member who made an exceptional contribution to the company or made a suggestion on how to improve the place.

♦ Building loyal teams and a proud staff. (Each morning before the stores opened, the staff would huddle in teams and shout what was called the "ASDA Cheer": "Give me an A, S, D, A. . . . What does that spell? . . .")

No idea was overlooked, and every contribution was recognized. The massive learning culture that he instituted was largely informal and largely workplace based. Without paying any more than the supermarket norm, he built an exceptional workforce that changed the quality of the shopping experience for customers and bred loyalty and trust that continue to this day.

From Knowledge Hoarded to Knowledge Shared

The 16th-century British philosopher, scientist, and political pundit Francis Bacon (1561–1626) coined the phrase "knowledge is power." And the ramifications of this extend into the 21st century. A culture of hanging onto and hoarding knowledge exists in many workplaces. Your position can be related to how much you know and with whom you choose to share knowledge. This was perhaps more prevalent in Europe than in the United States, but it dominated structures and distorted organization charts and hierarchies. In one large British company, the general mythology was that it took eight years to work out with whom to talk to circumvent the bureaucracy and get things done. Conversely, you had to work out whom to avoid, for they would never help, almost on principle, and would disrupt any project in which they became involved.

In a climate where we rarely have eight months to get to peak performance, let alone eight years, a new culture is required that rewards the movement of information and the sharing of knowledge. Status accrues to the person who transmits knowledge rather than to the one who stores it.

One could argue that the large consulting firms are massive knowledge-sharing hubs. They can quickly assimilate what the organization knows about a given subject and "sell" it back to a new client. Talent and potential are associated with expert knowledge shared. The wider the net is cast, the more valuable the contribution.

One of Toyota's greatest contributions to auto manufacturing was the introduction of the idea that every person was responsible for the quality of the product, not just the quality control people at the end of the line. Therefore, any single individual or team on the production line had the right and responsibility to stop the line and fix a problem before the line moved on. This was diametrically opposed to the then-prevalent best practice that made it a punishable offense to impede the line—it kept running 24 hours a day unless it broke down. Any problem was simply passed down the line to, ultimately, the quality assurance person, who had to fail the car and fix it off the line or run it through the line again.

In one large car plant in Britain in the 1970s, the managers sat in a glass box in the center of the factory and managed their role remotely, speeding up the line whenever they thought they could get away with it and stopping it when there was a major problem. The workers on the floor were totally disempowered. One section, famously, had a sign attached to the workspace saying "Don't Feed the Monkeys."

Toyota, conversely, made its employees feel valued and rewarded for their contribution. Astonishingly, in a former GM plant in California, the former GM workers, now rebranded as the Toyota workforce, contributed an average of 50 suggestions a year each to the company and received compensation ranging from a few dollars to thousands of dollars, depending on the nature of the idea and its intrinsic value to the company. There were plaques all over the factory acknowledging the really great ideas that had emerged from the line, naming the individual who had made the suggestion, and building that person into a corporate hero.

Toyota saw its workforce as talent to be developed, whereas the other manufacturer saw the workforce as replaceable cogs in a machine. These are stark contrasts in the treatment of individuals that led to even starker contrasts in performance. But you will find analogies to this situation in every sector of every economy all around the world. The principle of treating the workforce as hard-to-replace talent will make a difference wherever and whenever it is applied.

Although it is naive to see the demise of General Motors in its pre-bankruptcy form as purely a talent issue, the issues of GM's failure to respond fast enough to market trends and reliance on a compliant U.S. consumer market buying the same cars year after year have knowledge sharing at their core. GM was not in touch with the consumption patterns of its own staff, let alone the rest of the world. Its failure was a long time coming, not merely a reaction to the current economic climate. It has been more than 10 years since another car manufacturer took over the worst-performing GM assembly plant near San Francisco and, using the same workforce, made it into one of the most efficient auto plants in the United States. The lessons were clearly written a long time ago.

From Individual Performance to Team Achievement

If we go back to that Toyota production line, every employee believed that he or she was building a perfect vehicle. Every car rolled off the line flawless. And there were no quality assurance teams to monitor the work. The members of each team on the line believed that they had a role to ensure that their element, whatever it might be, was a perfect contribution to the whole. When changes occurred, they occurred to make the process better, faster, and simpler. And when someone else stopped the line, the teams came into their own. They would discuss production issues, exchange ideas on how to improve their piece of the vehicle, and make notes to exchange with other teams about how they, too, could improve. Rewards were at the levels of the whole plant, the team, and the individual. The success of the element was a direct contribution to the success of the whole.

Contrast this with a financial services organization that was trying to increase the birthrate of new financial products. Its staff could manage about two new products a year, and some of their more fleet-of-foot rivals managed two a week! The ensuing investigation revealed that the company had no skills deficit. Its people were as smart and well trained as those of the rival company. The issue was about reward. This company focused on individual targets and individual achievement. There was no real incentive to contribute to the company's success over and above the individual's performance, to the point where sales leads that were not appropriate for one section were rarely passed on to the relevant team elsewhere in the company. Teams were collections of individuals who rarely helped each other, even though they managed a portfolio of clients or products that contributed to the overall firm performance. And interest was rarely ever shown in contributing to another team's success or assisting when it encountered difficulty.

If you demanded better and faster ideas for new products, what was the incentive? Time on new ideas could either detract from performance today or generate revenue for some other team tomorrow. Most new ideas did not fit neatly into the current structure, and they could therefore threaten everyone's bonus.

Radical change only occurred when there were incentives for sharing. Bonuses were based on the team, not just the individual, and there were rewards for team-spanning and cross-company ideas. Also, new appointments were needed in key influencing roles.

If talent is seen only as what an individual possesses to a greater or lesser extent, then the organization will not benefit from a talent culture and it will not learn from within or from outside. Recognizing the range and diversity of talent in an organization is the key to leveraging its talent and helping it flourish as a whole.

Talent is, therefore, a way of looking at the workforce and building a culture that leverages it for the best possible outcomes. A much-used quotation from Henry Van Dyke, the 19th-century American writer and Presbyterian minister, captures this holistic view of talent: "Use what talents you possess: The woods would be very silent if no birds sang there except those that sang best."

Generally, an individual working for a talent-centric employer feels valued, developed, and stretched, and is seen as knowledgeable, informed, and committed. A talent-centric employer sees the workforce as hard to replace; as trusted, with some autonomy; as worth giving a voice to; and as highly committed to the organization's success. In tough times, a talent-centric employer will do everything to retain that talent. In an organization that thinks differently, employees will be the first cost to cut.

In a talent-centric workplace, there is a continuous focus on the future—on building and developing capabilities, on seeking out new opportunities, on taking counsel from employees and customers alike. There is a strong culture of innovation fed by both continuous improvement and radical transformation. Such an organization is an exciting place to work. And this does not mean, necessarily, that such an organization must be located in one of the "sexy" industries. The best employer in the Asia-Pacific region in 2007, according to a report by Hewitt Associates, was a flash memory manufacturer in China called Spansion—SalesForce; an Australian call center came in sixth. And this was out of 750 employers who signed up for the study and after analysis of the data supplied by the 160,000 employees who submitted questionnaires. The final endorsements came not from managers but from the employees themselves.

Talent and Leadership

In an excellent report by Momentum Executive Development (2007), *Talent and Leadership Practices 2007*, 16 large companies, from a wide range of sectors, with a U.K. base, were interviewed about their current leadership and talent practices, and the results were chilling. The survey found

- ♦ Many managers simply lack the skill or will to identify and nurture talent, yet they are the key to this process.
- ♦ There is not yet a convincing correlation between talent, leadership, and business success.

These results draw the unsurprising conclusion that "no one is satisfied with where they are in meeting these challenges right now."

These conclusions are based on research that was conducted in 16 leading-edge companies employing well more than a million people worldwide who are at the forefront of traditional models of leadership development. They all (except one) work with top business schools or provide executive programs for leadership development and have complex and comprehensive performance management processes in place to regularly review the impact of their leaders. Yet only two of the 16 directly link leadership behavior and impact with remuneration.

When you move four levels below the top team, fewer than half the companies have systems to review the quality of leadership or determine its impact. And in all but one, talent, management development, and recruitment are separate functions with limited communication among them.

Five critical issues were raised in the Momentum study:

- ◆ engagement, in terms of catching top management's attention to talent issues and relating it to bottom-line business

- ◆ capability: building and ensuring the best investment in this area

- ◆ organizational boundaries, such as the structure and geographical spread of companies and how to manage across boundaries in a meaningful way

- ◆ life and career stages, with meaningful engagement at critical points to ensure both retention and development

- ◆ talent processes and their alignment and effectiveness, and how they are related to business outcomes.

Good practices are emerging across these five areas from companies all over the world. The talent issue is not North American or European or confined to industrial countries. Some of the best solutions come from the least-expected locations and the most-surprising companies.

Engagement

There are several indicators of good practice here. The first is to create a senior management role that has oversight of the total talent process from recruitment to retirement. Under this function, the processes should align and the managers should be clearly aware of their responsibility to implement the processes. The manager's role is critical, and this should be acknowledged and rewarded not as a performance afterthought but as a core job element.

In one Brazilian company, the recognition of an individual as having high potential led to difficulties on the line. Managers had to be specifically trained so that their behaviors reinforced rather than detracted from the centrally established process. Ultimately, they were rewarded for the number of high-potential staff they managed—more meant increased remuneration.

One U.S. company keeps track of its key staff when they leave. An annual "reunion" dinner is held, at which former employees are invited to consider rejoining the company. Job opportunities are circulated, and up-to-date résumés are collected. This revolving door has resulted in key former employees returning to the company with wider experience and better skills. Similarly, newly retired staff are kept on retainers for a certain number of days each year. These contracts allow knowledge to be shared at appropriate times, mentoring, and even temporary reemployment, should the need arise. There have been instances of nominally retired employees maintaining key intranet sites, shaping the knowledge contained there, and entering into online dialogues as coordinators. These critical roles can sometimes best be managed by someone who has the time and will enjoy the connection with the company. The quid pro quo is sometimes as simple as leaving the company computer hooked up in the person's home and paying a modest per diem. This can maintain loyalty and occasionally ensure that knowledge is not shared with the competition!

Capability

The mythology that any development is good development—based on the old principle that only 50 percent of advertising works, but we cannot be sure which 50 percent—is slowly being discredited. Companies that review all capability development for the impact that ensues as a result can better target their investments. Learning and development departments that add programs for no other reason than to increase the size of their portfolio, incorrectly believing that more is better, are coming to be seen as wasteful and out of line.

There are, therefore, three trends coming together: Learning and development departments are being held accountable for business impact, experiencing a more complex focus on evaluating learning programs for both qualitative and quantitative returns to the company and developing increased clarity about the kinds of capabilities required for both the present and immediate future. Detailing capabilities in minute detail via long lists of competencies is also falling out of fashion. In the Momentum report, a significant number of companies had moved away from this model to one incorporating more emphasis on values and attitudes.

This complex mesh of skills, engagement, and attitude requires more complex programs of support and development, including action learning, coaching, development outside the normal work environment, and community involvement. These newer forms of development are growing at significant rates in organizations worldwide.

Organizational Boundaries

Even big organizations can feel claustrophobic because of their structure and culture. In many large companies, movement between divisions is difficult, and movement between different locations can be complex and bureaucratic. Even within one division, the team focus can make it difficult for an individual to change teams, even if it is in the best interests of the organization. In one media company, an individual recruit (at any level) was seen as a member of that team until he or she left the company. Anyone making an internal change was shunned by the previous team and talked about as disloyal.

It took change at the top to attack this philosophy and breed a culture of talent pooling and career development. For example, it was made known that no one would rise to the level of executive director having remained his or her whole career in only one division. This was in direct contradiction to the previous model, in which "divisional loyalty" appeared to be the only way of rising to the top. This was exemplified recently when the head of radio retired after a lifetime career with the organization in that one division, to be replaced by the director of marketing, who had had no previous radio experience.

In a model apparently borrowed from the English Premier Football League, some organizations are prepared to loan out executives to other (nondirectly competing) companies for only salary recovery, to give these individuals the opportunity to gain new experience and new skills that can be applied when they return—usually to a new role. The benefits of being exposed to a different culture and ways of doing things go far beyond a simple skills development matrix. The receiving company also has the benefit of a new approach and an injection of capability, with neither the cost of recruitment nor the cost of a continuing salary to worry about.

Many companies now see a woman on maternity leave as an employee to be cultivated, briefed, and developed during her absence—rather than as a nonemployee who has the right to become an employee once again and in whom no one has any interest until she walks back through the door. In a large company, several hundred women can be in this position, often with some time on their hands. This cadre can be mobilized to think through new ideas, comment on policy, or remotely coach or mentor staff. Not only does the company get the benefit of this group's intelligence and skills while they are on leave, but these employees are also able to get up to speed far more quickly when they return to work than others who have stayed out of contact for the duration of their leave. Also, such staff may be allowed to work part time for several years without jeopardizing their chances of promotion, and flexible working can be a norm, not a privilege. These are boundary-breaking ideas that actually work. But to make them work requires a different view of talent and reconceptualizing the nature of the workforce.

Life and Career Stages

There are significant difficulties when someone is promised a particular opportunity during the recruitment process that is not delivered when that person arrives in the company. Often, recruitment is outsourced, and the person in charge of recruiting is deemed to have achieved his or her objective when the individual arrives in the company or completes his or her first six months. A more holistic approach would include the future line manager agreeing to preemployment commitments and an orientation plan built into those discussions. Some companies now ask a potential new recruit to meet 15 or more staff members before being offered a job. This has nothing to do with his or her competence and everything to do with fit.

Successful recruitment is not getting someone to sign on the dotted line but the achievement of delivering a new person to the team who is, or can be, fully integrated into the workplace and its ethos, and who feels committed to the new employer. New employees who feel that they were lied to during the interview process will rarely stay long and rarely deliver all that they are capable of delivering.

In a recent case, a bright, new recruit, not long out of graduate school, was persuaded by the HR recruiting executive to take a job that was not the recruitee's first choice but had been a difficult-to-fill vacancy.

On arrival, the new employee felt that the role was inappropriate and that she had been misled when she was persuaded to take it. She lasted barely a year and never performed up to her potential. Meanwhile, the recruiter was doubly rewarded for hiring a talented employee and filling a challenging position.

Most organizations do not pay much attention to career stages unless an employee is joining or being promoted. In reality, the critical stages in a career are at other times. Focusing regularly on an individual's career can have a dramatic impact on attrition rates. And this can be massively cost-effective. The Center for High Performance in Chicago has completed research on the cost of replacing talent in organizations. Even for middle-ranking executives, it can cost as much as $250,000 to temporarily fill, recruit, hire, and finally train to the point where the person can do the job as well as the previous incumbent. It is obvious that a modest reduction in attrition rates can save millions of dollars. That investment to retain an employee is far less than the cost of finding someone to replace him or her by several orders of magnitude.

Many individuals grow overly familiar and bored with the jobs they do over a period of time. This can occur at different times in someone's career, depending on the job or the person. Intervening at a critical career moment can help maintain that person's sense of development and personal growth and can ensure continuing commitment to the organization.

During the final two years before retirement, much can be done to stop a "running down" of the role and commitment of the individual. In some organizations, key staff are taken off their job for part of the time to allow them to concentrate on mentoring junior colleagues, organizing their knowledge, and conducting pre-retirement knowledge-sharing sessions. This helps to maintain the interest and commitment of the retiring employee and allows the employer to capture and transfer the employee's knowledge and experience—a win for everyone involved.

Processes

All the ideas discussed above require appropriate processes to make them work. And an organization where the processes work against a new culture will find the new culture far more difficult to embed. The impact of processes on one's experience of an organization is often overlooked. At the same time, the number of process blockers that exist before something can be executed is directly proportional to its success. Companies that take this reality seriously can often significantly simplify processes. But this is laborious work, and there are vested interests in maintaining the status quo. Unfortunately, complex and unnecessary processes can hinder talent development far more effectively than other more overt challenges.

Tips on Moving toward a Talent-Driven Culture

Following from the analysis above, here are 10 tips for moving your organization toward more effectively developing talent and building a talent ethos.

The first tip is to take a holistic approach to talent in your organization. Each employee should be working toward the same organizational goals, and at least some of employees' individual goals should overlap so that they have to work together to succeed. The result will be that employees will hear the same message from each team they support and will experience consistency and integrity across the whole organization. In this type of environment, one person must understand and be accountable for the entire employee life cycle and should report to senior management regularly on this area.

Second, the term "talent" should be interpreted widely. All staff should be seen as having potential, and efforts should be made to develop this potential in appropriate ways. Trust is an important part of this environment. Most employees make decisions with the best of intentions, so all individuals should be seen as trustworthy until they prove otherwise—not the other way around.

Manifestations of this can be cheap and simple to implement. One company invited its managers to take the time to thank staff for what they had done. This small alteration to hitherto normal behavior increased productivity and lowered the attrition rate. Yet many organizations take most people for granted, most of the time. It is a bitter irony that many staff only discover just how much they were valued on the day they hand in their resignations.

There has to be some kind of measurement of leadership performance in this area. 3M, for example, makes team development a significant part of a leader's appraisal. In the Momentum study, three of the 16 companies also ranked and reward leadership and team empowerment.

Third, talent is a companywide asset, not the prerequisite of an individual manager. Moving staff to new sections should be a norm, if the organization is big enough to offer such choices. Too many appraisal discussions focus on what an employee can't do and what needs improvement. People tend to do their best work when doing the things they are best at. And appraisals work best when good work is recognized and rewarded and where staff are given the opportunity to excel in the areas they are good at.

To deliver these things requires a systematic review of an organization's overall HR strategy and its goals. This is tip four. Such an HR review may raise painfully basic questions. For example, the gap between the aspirations of HR (a key strategic role) and the reality in many workplaces (tactical and process based) led *Fast Company* magazine to publish its much-quoted critique of HR in a 2007 article titled "Why We Hate HR" (Hammonds 2007). The opening stated bluntly:

> In a knowledge economy, companies with the best talent win. And finding, nurturing and developing that talent should be one of the most important tasks in a corporation. So why does human resources do such a bad job—and how can we fix it?

Fifth, check your processes. Make sure that they are aligned with the purpose for which they were created and include personal development planning, the right kind of appraisal systems, and regular performance feedback and performance management. If these are coupled with real choices for the manager in terms of developing his or her team, and the employee is given access to temporary transfers and placements within the organization, the processes move from routine impositions that add little to vibrant tools for engagement.

Sixth, get your organization's board or senior management directly involved. Have a standing agenda item on people issues that gets beyond recruitment and retention statistics. And make sure that the discussion of talent is not the one agenda item that can be dropped to make way for more pressing issues.

The seventh tip concerns knowledge sharing. No learning is possible if key people cannot share, will not share, or are discouraged from sharing their knowledge. If knowledge sharing as an ethos can be built, then knowledge will flow throughout an organization. Simple mechanisms can be developed to help achieve that goal. For instance, in the current economic climate, a mattress retailer issued cheap video cameras to its stores and invited managers to share their tips and techniques for making sales in difficult times. These could be quickly shot all around the company, so that what worked in one place could be made to work in another without the bureaucracy and controls that usually accompany the distribution of training materials.

Eighth, explore social networking in your organization. Bloggers have valuable insights, wikis allow many more people to co-create content, and podcasts allow instant stories to be heard and shared. But you need an etiquette that establishes the ground rules for the use of such tools.

The value of this is that the organization tracks reality rather than clinging to myths and incorrect perceptions about how they are doing at any particular point. This can be about employees' attitudes and perceptions, the impact of products and services in the marketplace, and the overall well-being of the company.

Ninth, make sure that all leaders up to and including the CEO know how to listen as well as talk, ask questions as well as give answers, and admit mistakes as well as champion successes. If you can build this kind of environment, there is a chance that employees will—in a phrase going back at least to the 18th-century Quakers—"speak truth to power," and reality is always the best base from which to operate.

Tenth, leverage the data you gather, so that at least some of the indicators you use track the points that we have been discussing above. Over time, an annual survey of staff opinions and feelings can track the staff's perceptions of the organization. Such questionnaires and surveys must be anonymous and fairly administered. Gathering data from most staff on 15 key questions can be illuminating and challenging. So not only must the organization face up to the nature of the emerging messages, it also has to be brave enough to do something about the results. The raw data can reveal problems that are like a cancer in the organization. So if you find something out, you have to have processes in place for dealing with it. These processes must be transparent, and action has to be seen to be happening.

Conclusion

Talent is a worldwide issue. And the emerging long-term shortage of talent will be a continuing trend, despite the current temporary staff surpluses in industrial countries. Employees with high potential will be sought out all over the world, regardless of their country of origin. This will mean that the right people will be able to pick not just their preferred employer but also the country where they wish to live. No company or, indeed, country is immune from this pressure, despite the short-term disruption of this trend.

There are signs that, in some organizations at least, real progress has been made in monitoring, developing, and supporting the workforce—with surprising and spectacular results in terms of innovation and performance.

The future will be more about building giant elephants that have never existed before than copying current best practices. The main instruments that you will need to accomplish this are freely available, such as creativity, knowledge sharing, and diverse teams. These have the potential to make work more stimulating, challenging, and infinitely more enjoyable. These seeds for successful 21st-century companies could well generate shoots that will aid the world economy in growing and thus resuming its upward trajectory.

Talent Management Software and Systems

Adam Miller, Chief Executive, Cornerstone OnDemand

What's in this chapter?

- A brief history of talent management software, including the rise of niche talent management solutions
- How software can help, and its limitations
- The current state of software development
- A look into the future
- Opportunities for building an integrated, software-based talent management system

◆ ◆ ◆

Clearly, talent management has become top of mind for most corporate executives and organizational leaders. Talent management—or components thereof—has been one of the most popular cover stories for trade and business publications, recently from the *Harvard Business Review* to the eponymous *Talent Management* magazine. It appears that these new concepts are all the rage.

But the reality is that most of what seems "new" about talent management has been around for quite some time. Many of the theories and processes that drive most corporate talent management discussions today were well documented long ago. Just pick up a copy of the classic business book *Execution* by Larry Bossidy and Ram Charan (2002), and you'll notice that much of what they describe as best practices in management during the 1980s and 1990s is really the stuff of what we today call talent management fundamentals.

So what is all the hype about?

I believe it is about the technology. The systems that exist today don't make enterprise talent management better; they make it possible. Talent management systems *enable* the management of people in accordance with best practices. In other words, it is today's systems that make talent management concepts a reality.

To truly understand the interplay between talent management theory and technology, it is helpful to walk through a brief history of talent management technology and what has been enabled by each step.

A Brief History of Talent Management Systems

Technology to support human resources (HR) has been around for years. In some cases, one might even argue that it performed some early talent management functions, though they may not have been described as such. But technology evolves, and the depth and breadth of features and functions that support modern talent management practices and processes have dramatically increased. In this section, I trace the evolution of the software systems in use today.

The Early Years: Human Resource Information Systems

With the advent of enterprise software applications in the 1970s, it became possible to track all things corporate. Soon financials, inventories, supply chains, and customer relationships were trackable. So, too, were people. The rise of human resource information systems—known as "HRIS systems" (yes, the "S" is redundant)—created a revolution in corporations around the world. Corporate HR departments spent millions to deploy a "system of record" for all employees.

Theoretically, all employee information would be available at the click of a button. The reality was, however, that most of these HRIS systems simply became a repository for administrative information for employees, including

- hiring information: hire date, referral source, compensation
- personal data: name, birth date, contact information
- organizational data: the employee's location, division, position, pay grade, cost center, and manager.

The HRIS systems would be used to manage the acquisition of new employees—including provisioning benefits, making access available to the information network and building, and recording organizational data—as well as the disbursement of employee-related information to payroll providers, pension administrators, and the like.

HRIS systems became central to the orderly administration of people. As a result, over time, these systems came to be considered a required cost of doing business.

However, the dream of cost reduction and operational efficiency was challenged by the complexity of managing these HRIS systems. With each installation customized to the needs of the specific organization, changes in processes and organizational structures became increasingly expensive. And because the systems needed to be maintained, rather than the technology creating efficiency and streamlining processes, HR departments actually needed to expand their staffs to support the technology. Many HR departments even created their own IT groups to manage the customizations required as organizational changes occurred. And soon, HR/IT organizations became their own fiefdoms, often in conflict with corporate IT functions, whose managers believed that they were accountable for the acquisition and management of all the firm's technology.

Global Company Complexity

The process became even more complex with consolidation and growth. Global conglomerates would find themselves with multiple, incompatible HRIS systems that would not communicate, further limiting the value of the systems for managing people. The "trough of disillusionment" became a reality.

Nonetheless, HRIS systems had become essential components of enterprise resource planning (ERP) systems. Once HRIS systems became "must-have" items, demand for them grew rapidly. As a result, competition in the human capital management software marketplace became intense, leading to commodification, consolidation, and, ultimately, the crowning of SAP and Oracle (following Oracle's acquisition of Peoplesoft) as the leaders in the field.

Because the focus of competitive ERP vendors was a broad range of enterprise applications and much time was spent integrating applications from acquired, smaller ERP vendors, a consequence of the ERP wars was the inability of HRIS systems to fully meet their potential and extend from HR-facing administrative systems to employee-facing talent management systems (the exception was the creation of employee self-service portals that allowed employees to update personal information). Although the ERP vendors built extensions to their HRIS modules to support other functions in the talent management continuum, they were unable to develop the depth of functionality required to fully meet the ever-evolving needs of their client base.

The Rise of Niche Talent Management Solutions

While the market penetration of HRIS systems dominated HR budgets and HR/IT mind share, the lack of end-to-end solutions for managing the entire employee life cycle opened the door for niche talent management solutions to meet the needs of executives and HR managers who wanted to more effectively develop and manage the workforce.

From 1991 to 2006, five separate talent management "subindustries" emerged, each dealing with a component of the talent management process that HRIS systems were not able to adequately address:

- learning
- performance
- succession planning
- recruitment
- enterprise social networking.

Learning Management

In the late 1970s, the advent of relational database systems enabled the creation of basic systems to track the learning that took place in the corporate environment. This basic record-keeping capability was deemed superior to paper-based records, especially as it related to regulatory training. The result was the invention of training administration systems that helped to automate the processes associated with managing classroom learning.

When e-learning first became popular in the 1990s, the concept of using learning management systems to catalog and track the training really took hold and became a requirement for all large enterprises—at least in the eyes of the companies that were selling them. By leveraging the Internet rather than the classroom or CD-ROMs to provide self-paced training to more people at lower costs, e-learning was seen as a great way to cut expenses. Learning management systems (LMSs) provided the means to deliver the e-learning.

Early learning management systems would allow companies to perform basic record-keeping tasks, in addition to providing the ability to browse, search, register for, and (for e-learning) launch training. Many vendors got into the game, including both entrepreneurial HRIS staff members, who would commercialize the basic systems they had built for their own training departments, and the broad range of e-learning vendors, who would package an LMS as part of their content sales, providing end users with access to their content.

Over the years, competition and consolidation in the learning management system space, which forced the remaining vendors to evolve their platforms, became a boon to chief learning officers and corporate training administrators alike. Today an enterprise-class learning management system offers a wide range of functionality related to onboarding, corporate training, and leadership and development programs.

In addition, learning management systems were no longer the sole domain of the training department. As corporations came under increasing levels of regulation, compliance departments formed, often with executive-level titles, such as chief compliance officers who reported directly to the CEO or the board. The use of e-learning for compliance training—combined with the capabilities of learning management systems for making training assignments, distributing notifications, and reporting—provided great efficiencies *and* improved compliance for these groups. And because of its place in the corporate hierarchy, compliance departments, in many cases, have taken precedence over HR or training departments in procuring and controlling assets like learning management systems.

Performance Management

Learning management was the first, but not the only, extension to HRIS systems. Performance management, particularly more automated means of conducting performance reviews, was another key component. As you might expect, employee performance management systems started simply enough. They were nothing more than automated versions of the standard performance review process, leveraging computer and Internet technology to simplify the distribution of paper-based forms. Many of these tools were created by IT and HR/IT departments, which required customization each time the review form was changed.

Today's performance management systems go far beyond the basic performance reviews, with some providing tools for managing

- goals
- reviews
- competencies
- development plans
- compensation.

Goal management is intended to improve overall organizational productivity by specifically aligning each employee's goals with those of his or her manager and business unit and those of corporate executives along the chain of command. This cascading ensures that even the objectives of lower-level individual contributors are tied to the stated objectives of the chairman or CEO. Theoretically, this means that all oars are rowing in the same direction, maximizing the speed and effectiveness with which the organization can accomplish its goals.

Because the goals can be tracked in real time, they transform performance management from its traditional reactive approach at the end of each year to a proactive process that enables managers to rectify problems as they are occurring, rather than when it is far too late. Further, by automatically tying each employee's individual goals directly into the performance review process, the employee performance management system makes management by objectives easy to implement for any manager, with complete transparency for the employee.

Enterprise performance management (EPM) systems also can track key performance indicators (KPIs). Each goal can contain specific targets that relate to the organization's KPIs. Because the goals are aligned from manager to subordinate, the KPIs can be consolidated. Viewed graphically as a dashboard, these tools allow executives to determine where in the company people are off track and thus enable executives to reallocate resources. In addition, some goal management systems support balanced scorecard methodologies, tracking organizational and individual objectives from a number of perspectives and automating data collection that could otherwise take weeks.

There are also *reviews*. The basic automated performance review has gotten a significant boost from today's EPM systems. Review forms now can be configured at will, allowing customization for different segments of the employee population. Also, because automation simplifies the process and raises the participation rate, it becomes much easier to do periodic, proactive reviews instead of being limited to annual, reactive reviews. Most important, some performance management systems can link reviews to goals, competency assessments, and compensation and development plans—providing a unique performance review for every employee.

Some organizations find performance reviews too subjective and/or too quantitative. Many organizational psychologists argue that the real way to make an employee more successful is to evaluate the person on the more qualitative aspects of a job. For example, an organization might believe executives should have strong leadership skills, business acumen, and decision-making ability to be successful and effective. To the extent that an executive has gaps in those competencies, development might be a worthwhile investment.

Because competency models typically are based on "softer" attributes, which are less easily measured than targets or key performance indicators, the ratings of the employee's manager usually don't tell the whole story. *Competency management tools* enable organizations to easily administer personalized 360-degree feedback processes, which choose the appropriate competency assessment for a particular employee and sends that assessment to the employee, his or her managers, and other qualified raters. By aggregating and weighting these multiple assessments, the ratings become considerably more objective.

Automation also enables a fair amount of sophistication in the administration of competency assessments. For example, results can be hidden from the employee to protect the anonymity of raters. And assessments can be sent to people outside the organization, enabling customers, suppliers, and partners to participate.

Most organizations do competency assessments to better develop their employees. Just as the competency assessments are personalized for the employee, EPM systems can automate the creation of an individualized *development plan* for each employee, based on his or her assessment results. These development plans serve as road maps for employees to develop the skills they need to be successful in their current roles or prepare for future roles.

Development actions, which can include traditional training, on-the-job activities, and stretch assignments, can be linked directly to employee objectives. When tied to a learning management system, development plans can be tracked, allowing organizations to measure the impact of development actions on employees' competence and performance.

With current and historical performance data now available to every manager, paying for performance across the enterprise becomes a possibility. Using a combination of organizational data, performance data, and corporate compensation models, EPM *compensation planning systems* provide managers with clear guidelines for making compensation decisions, including merit increases, bonuses, and equity awards.

The automation provided by EPM systems dramatically simplifies the compensation planning process:

- All the relevant information for a manager's direct reports is usually organized on a single screen, providing timely information and eliminating the need for data entry.

- Budgetary guidelines, eligibility rules, and approval workflows can be automatically enforced.

- Cascading budgets can be managed systematically, with executives allocating their budgets to senior managers, who then allocate their budgets to line managers.

- Prorations for employees who moved into a position midcycle can be automatically calculated.

In addition, enterprise-wide reporting helps ensure consistency and equity in compensation adjustments, as well as compliance with corporate standards.

Managing Succession Planning

Succession planning has long been the domain of public company boards and family businesses, dominated by a desire to smooth the transition to the next CEO. More progressive firms address the same challenge for all executive positions, identifying, as well, the next potential CFO, CTO, and COO. This process typically involves closed-door meetings at which detailed presentations on other senior managers are reviewed to determine the best candidates to fill potentially available executive slots.

Although the organizations following such processes have been better equipped to deal with unexpected changes at the top, the overall value of this type of succession planning for the entire organization is limited. Enter succession planning systems.

Succession planning systems automate many parts of the process, reducing the time managers spend on succession planning activities from weeks to days or hours. More important, these systems enable executives to quickly compare candidates at any time during the year, recall prior ratings, and provide reports for the enterprise.

As succession planning systems have made the process easier to implement, it has been taken to a whole new level. Rather than limiting the process to the organization's most senior executives, today's cutting-edge organizations are doing succession planning for *all* managers. This depth of succession planning—which for large organizations could include thousands of people rather than a handful of executives—can provide solid transition plans for staff at all levels. But it has a much more important effect: It helps identify high-potential employees throughout the entire organization.

Talent readiness has become the mantra of talent management professionals the world over. It is defined by an organization's ability to truly understand its "bench strength." Consider these questions for your organization:

♦ Do you have the right people in the right positions for today and tomorrow?

♦ Who are your young superstars who can be developed now to lead new business units in the future?

♦ Who has tremendous potential but is in the wrong job or is likely to walk out the door (that is, where is retention risk high)?

♦ What parts of the organization are vulnerable because there are no identified successors who could fill open positions (that is, where is readiness low)?

Because the succession management process typically includes evaluating employees across a broad array of metrics and because these systems can sort, filter, and report on results by any criteria, these questions can be quickly answered. And the graphical interfaces of enterprise-class systems allow the data to be displayed in four-box or nine-box grids, enable the computation of custom metrics, and may even allow interactive organizational charts.

Many companies now extend the process to include input of all types of employee attributes. As a result, managers and executives gain access to real-time talent profiles of their employees, which allows for even more effective succession planning decisions. The information that can be tracked might include

- education
- experience
- certifications
- skills
- career preferences (career goals, geographic preferences, and so on)
- competencies
- performance ratings
- potential
- readiness
- retention risk.

In combination, this information can be used for two purposes in addition to traditional succession planning: talent pooling and internal recruiting.

Talent pooling, which is now more popular with talent management circles in Europe than North America, focuses succession planning on critical positions rather than the management hierarchy. The organization identifies specific roles that are mission-critical to success and for which a prolonged vacancy could prove extremely detrimental. Then operational or HR managers identify employees who can fill those positions, resulting in a pool of available resources.

Similarly, talent pools can be created for certain attributes, most commonly for employees with high potential. By organizing these employees into a talent pool, management can more closely monitor their careers, track their leadership development, and keep an eye on their retention risk. Such a talent pool can then be a preferred candidate source for any open senior positions.

Perhaps the biggest value of automated succession management comes in the form of more effective internal recruiting. Because the systems track the attributes of all employees (or at least all those who have been reviewed during a succession planning or talent pooling process), tools are available to internal recruiters and/or hiring managers to immediately identify people who are the best fit for open positions. Some systems even allow managers to rank and compare candidates on a single page, showing, for example, that the candidate who may be the best match is not willing to relocate or is persuasive but not persistent.

An outgrowth of automated succession management gives power to the people through succession planning in reverse: career pathing. In much the same way that the more advanced systems can tell which employees would be the best fit for a given position, they can also tell which positions are the best fit for a given person. Essentially, the systems are calculating the compatibility of two sets of attributes—of the person and of the position—and can present them in any order. Thus career pathing, combined with development planning tools, allows employees to manage their own career paths—often resulting in higher employee engagement and retention.

Managing Recruitment

One of the most successful early uses of the web was for recruiting. Online job boards quickly proved superior to newspaper classified ads for job seekers and hiring managers alike.

The success of online recruiting produced the need for corporate recruiting departments to manage the influx of candidates from myriad sources. The result was the emergence of application tracking systems (ATSs), which provided powerful tools for recruiters everywhere.

Essentially, the ATSs supported the basic hiring process:

- opening a job requisition, including automating the approval workflow
- automatic posting of the job, initially on an internal corporate job board, but with some ATS platforms today, autoposting on multiple external job boards simultaneously
- automatic categorization and/or delivery of résumés from job applicants to recruiters and hiring managers
- tools to search, filter, and score applicants
- profile-based screening of applicants

♦ automated workflow management of the interview process

♦ tools to communicate with candidates throughout the process

♦ tools to process new hires.

Enterprise-class applicant tracking systems go beyond the basic recruiting workflow, offering an array of functionality related to the recruiting process. Some of the more interesting features include one-click background checks (typically done through an automated integration with a third-party background screener); automated résumé parsing, which enables résumé searching and comparison; campus recruiting tools; compliance reporting; and candidate relationship management tools.

These tools not only reduce costs and streamline the recruiting process, they can actually improve it. Different processes can be enforced for the hiring of hourly and salaried employees. Sourcing reports can be leveraged to provide enterprise-wide analytics on the most successful sources of candidates. And pre-hire assessments can be used to screen and select the most qualified candidates for open positions.

In addition, through the ATS, applicants can be routed directly to onboarding programs, which can be housed either in the ATS or in an integrated learning management system. Because the ATS has the pertinent new hire information, onboarding can begin even *before* the employee's first day on the job.

Managing Enterprise Social Networking

The most recent addition to the talent management continuum has been enterprise social networking systems. Originally described as collaboration tools, these systems are used to connect employees with one another, customers, partners, vendors, and, ultimately, timely information.

Enterprise social networking tools do not invent new processes; rather, they harness technology to account for the collaboration, communication, and informal knowledge networks present in every organization. This ongoing collaboration and the resulting user-generated content are typically organized through both a browsable taxonomy of topics and through the concept of virtual communities. Online communities might be established to bring together remote salespeople or partners, or as a way to connect corporate alumni with the company. These communities or affinity groups could be open to the public, or they may be invitation-only private communities sharing information, best practices, and case studies.

In many ways, enterprise social networking represents the next generation of knowledge management. Whereas knowledge management platforms were developed in an attempt to capture the tacit knowledge of employees in the organization, primarily through a document repository, social networking systems seek to share information in a more interactive way through the use of various online mechanisms, including

- ◆ Discussion forums: These have not changed much since the advent of the Internet, providing an online bulletin board for community members to share information. People can post their thoughts on a topic, and others can respond to that posting with a posting of their own, or start a new "thread."

- ◆ Blogs: These are now all the rage both in and out of the corporate environment. Blogs are similar to forums, except that the postings are typically from a single author on one or more subjects. Readers can comment on the blogger's postings or on another's comments. Readers also can subscribe to a blog so that they are notified every time the author posts a new entry.

- ◆ Wikis: These are community-contributed "articles" that allow all members of the community to update and edit over time. Wikipedia is the best-known example of a wiki.

- ◆ Podcasts and webcasts: These are recorded audio (podcasts) and web-based (webcasts) sessions that can be played back at any time. Often these are grouped into a series, such as a series of lectures or speeches from a specific person, to which you can subscribe.

- ◆ Documents and online resources: The social networking platform serves as a repository for documents and online links, including presentations, white papers, and other materials.

Any of the postings can usually be rated and commented upon by members of the community, with the enterprise social networking platforms typically providing access to the top-rated, most-commented-on, and most-recent postings.

But social networking is not just about documents and postings. Social networking also involves the concept of "friends" or connections, allowing members to connect directly with others. Because each member of the community typically has his or her own user-generated profile, often including photos, personal information, and his or her own postings, friends can keep tabs on that person. Some systems provide periodic updates on changes to profiles of your connections, including any postings they have authored or any connections they have made. In addition, friends can comment or "scrap" (as in scrapbooking) their connection's profiles, enabling constant communication through the system.

A number of free consumer-based social networking platforms are available with similar features and are heavily used by the under-30 crowd. However, enterprise social networking platforms provide the ability for organizations to manage the user-generated chaos in ways that popular, free services do not. Governance has become both a key differentiator and a key challenge for corporations adopting enterprise social networking systems.

In its short history, many use cases have emerged for enterprise social networking, ranging from customer self-service to partner enablement to community-based product innovation. Some uses directly relate to talent management, including onboarding, succession planning, informal learning, and employee engagement.

For geographically dispersed organizations, social networking provides an important benefit to the onboarding process by virtually connecting new employees with others in comparable positions to account for the socialization element often missing in routine orientations. For example, a new remote salesperson can immediately connect with other members of his or her sales team, sharing market intelligence, sales tools, and marketing materials and generally feeling like part of the team.

For succession planning and internal recruiting processes, social networking analytics and "social mapping" can provide important insights. HR managers and executives can gain a clear understanding of the informal organization chart (versus the static organization chart based on the formal management hierarchy) by showing the critical "connectors" on the team with the most connections. For example, there may be someone on the sales team who is the go-to person for advice on deals but who is not formally in the chain of command for any of those salespeople. That connector is a vital resource for sales success, but it may have gone unnoticed if attention had not been given to user-generated connections or the most popular authors in the social networking system.

It is often argued that the vast majority of training budgets is spent on formal training programs, despite the fact that the majority of what we learn in an organization is informal or social (for example, from a mentor, in a project team, around the water cooler). Enterprise social networking platforms also provide tools for managing informal training, or at least organizing resources for on-the-job training. Questions can be asked of experts for real-time answers, without knowing the appropriate experts in the company (which beats out emailing the whole organization and not getting any answer), and the answers become publicly available for future reference; bloggers can share their knowledge on specific topics that can be accessed for on-the-job performance support; and wikis, forums, documents, and online resources can be structured for easy search and retrieval. When tied to a learning management system, this creates a powerful tool for administering all forms of training within the organization.

Perhaps most important, enterprise social networking is becoming a corporate requirement for engaging younger employees in the workforce. For Generation Y and Millennials, who have grown up on the Internet using instant messaging more than the telephone and scrapping more than email, social networking is a way of life. They expect that the tools they have at work to be *at least as good* as the tools they have at home. Enterprise social networking platforms, especially those populated with vibrant online communities enabling dispersed employees to collaborate, provide a start.

Talent Management Today

The evolution of niche talent management tools has given way to the rise of talent management suites. These systems combine some or all of the functionality of niche talent management systems in a single application, often marketed as a suite of integrated modules.

Although the early niche vendors would argue that "best in class" was favorable to a human capital suite, some of those vendors have now become suite vendors and now argue for suites' superiority. Of course, "niche" and "suite" are matters of perspective, and today's talent management suites are still relatively specialized compared with the end-to-end ERP suites of the remaining HRIS providers.

The allure of the talent management suite is simple: All the tools used to manage someone are available in a single location. And because many of the functions are strengthened by one another, an integrated solution provides greater value—performance-driven development, onboarding supplemented by virtual communities, succession plans triggering leadership development programs, pay for performance, and recruiting tied to the competencies demonstrated by high-performing employees.

Deploying to the Extended Enterprise

The application of talent management systems is no longer limited to employees. Organizations increasingly see their corporate "ecosystem" as a key part of their business. For many corporations, indirect distribution channels are as important as direct sales teams. For many nonprofits, volunteers do more of the work than their internal employees. And with social networking tools transforming the way companies and customers interact, the lines among customers, partners, and employees continue to blur. In many cases, the talent management tools used for employees have equal applicability to customers, resellers, distributors, independent contractors, and other nonemployees.

Perhaps the most common way that organizations—from corporations to academic institutions to nonprofits—leverage extended enterprise functionality is through training-for-profit initiatives. Through the combined use of e-learning, e-commerce, and learning management technology, training previously reserved for employees or delivered on a limited basis in the classroom becomes broadly available to clients, partners, and even consumers at large. The training could even be restricted to certain populations or priced differently by client or category (for example, customer training could be discounted for top accounts). The result is that training becomes a new, or more meaningful, profit center.

Software as a Service

Deployments to the extended enterprise have recently benefited tremendously from the rise of software as a service, which makes deployments outside the corporate firewall relatively painless. One explanation for the recent dramatic rise in the use of talent management systems is the enterprise adoption of software as a service. As broadband connections became universal and use of the Internet became commonplace for all workers, it became feasible to deliver entire systems over the web. At its core, software as a service, or on-demand software, is software delivered over the Internet. Compared with the traditional model of on-premise, client-server-based enterprise software, software as a service marks the next evolution of software delivery.

The easiest way to understand the concept of on-demand software is to consider the difference between Microsoft's desktop products (like the Office suite) and Google's online applications (Google Docs). For example, with Microsoft, you need to install a specific version of the software to run on your computer, whereas with Google you are always using the current version and nothing needs to be installed locally. Also, your Microsoft Office configurations are limited to the computer on which it was installed, but Google Docs configurations are accessible from any computer, anywhere in the world.

At the enterprise level, legacy on-premise applications are like Microsoft and on-demand services are like Google. For example, traditional enterprise software installations can be complex and time consuming. By contrast, on-demand implementations tend to be less complicated and take less time. More important, whereas traditional software required each version to be maintained, configured, customized, and upgraded by the internal IT department or consulting firms, on-demand software is delivered as a service, which means that the service provider hosts and manages the software, making it essentially "version-less" for the enterprise.

Because the software is hosted by the service provider, equipment and maintenance costs are eliminated. So are the costs of upgrades. The on-demand software is typically purchased on a subscription model, paid for over time, which more closely aligns the service provider with the client's ongoing success. In addition, on-demand software can typically be configured rather than customized, further freeing IT departments for more strategic work and lowering the total cost of ownership. For example, administrators can configure their own email notifications and reminders using mail-merge-like functionality without the need to call the IT department or the vendor.

Nonetheless, software as a service had its early opponents, concerned about security, scalability, and control. As these concerns have been alleviated by successful, large-scale, on-demand software deployments by some of the world's leading companies, software as a service has become the fastest-growing segment of enterprise software.

Some argue that talent management is well suited for software as a service for two reasons: Configurability makes the systems easier to use, and, because it is not installed behind the firewall, it can be accessed by contractors, partners, and customers as needed.

I would argue that software as a service *enables* talent management. Despite the clear value offered to organizations in a service-oriented economy, where people are both the single biggest asset and expense, talent management tools were initially difficult to justify. Specifically, unlike inventory or financial data, people are constantly moving and evolving, so in the case where every organizational change required customizing the software, it was difficult to make the business case for systems. But today's on-demand talent management systems allow for configuration by business unit, real-time changes in workflow and organizational structure, personalization for employees as their roles and competencies change, and the ability to adopt increasing levels of functionality over time, as the organization's talent management needs evolve.

The Future of Talent Management

So what does the emergence of all these new systems and technologies mean for the future of talent management? Let's look at their main implications.

Niche Solutions Will Disappear

Niche talent management systems will become a thing of the past, as the interrelation between talent management "components" becomes a fundamental part of all talent management programs. In other words, looking holistically at organizational talent will become commonplace for managers and executives, in much the same way that they have come to expect summarized financials across disparate business units and real-time access to inventory and sales data. New managers won't just want things this way; they will expect it. As a result, vendors will need to move to meet the needs of the market. There will be product extensions and mergers and acquisitions as companies quickly shift from adding commodity-reinforcing nice-to-have incremental features to differentiating must-have feature sets.

Talent Management 2.0 Will Arrive

Just as the Internet has evolved from a one-way street to a multilane highway, so, too, will talent management. With "Internet 2.0" came the ability for the reader and publisher to simultaneously interact and the advent of user-generated content. No longer are websites simply static displays of content and pictures created by webmasters; rather, the web has become filled with user-created content, in the form of articles, blog postings, wiki contributions, comments, ratings, reviews, and podcasts (audio and video).

The result is a major change in the expectations of the end user. Rather than accept updates a few times a year, the new norm is sites that change continuously. Daily news updates are eclipsed by perpetual updates. Live sporting events, political debates, and financial conferences are blogged about *during* the event. Everything has become interactive; the raters even rate the raters.

Does this mean that talent management changes? Of course! Younger employees expect feedback constantly, not once a year. Geographical boundaries become irrelevant when team members communicate by instant messaging with the people next to them in the same way they interact with those 5,000 miles away. Trainers have to compete with (or leverage) subject matter experts in the field, who can weigh in on any issue for any co-worker at almost any time.

Managers will no longer be willing to wait for monthly reports on their teams. Managers will expect to see any information about their employees in real time, just as they can tap Google for the world's collective knowledge on almost any subject. And obviously, they will want it to be easy and intuitive to get that information.

At the same time, the capabilities of the tech-savvy "Internet elite" are expanding to the masses. As broadband connections have become ubiquitous and web browsing has become commonplace for young and old alike, standards have changed. Not only must there be tools to get this information and provide these services, but the tools must be accessible from anywhere in the style to which users have become accustomed. The DOS-based, administrator-only computer interfaces of the past have gone the way of the typewriter. It's got to be fast, easy, and look good— plus it needs to be available to the self-empowered managers of today when they want it, where they want it, and how they want it.

Corporate Walls Will Fall

Corporate walls become porous when people start viewing networks personally rather than institutionally. Contributions from customers, distributors, and vendors become as important as those from employees—and just as available when a person starts combining social networks from all phases of his or her life.

The rise in extended enterprise deployments of talent management solutions is one outcome of this trend. Employees and nonemployees alike are now often "managed" in comparable ways. Similarly, the use of enterprise social networks to manage relationships with customers, partners, and former employees blurs the line between what's "inside" and "outside" the company.

Productivity per Employee Is Becoming a Key Performance Indicator

A combination of economic pressures and improved employee performance management tools has made employee productivity a key measure of success. In much the same way that supply chain management systems allowed companies to optimize their inventory levels and customer relationship management systems helped companies optimize their service delivery, talent management systems enable organizations to optimize their most important asset: their people.

Arguably, the best metric for tracking success in this area is productivity per employee. Can you do more with the same number of people? If you can, and people represent your largest single expense—as they do in most organizations today—then you are more profitable. Increased productivity is enabled by more effective talent management in many ways.

True Talent Planning Is Becoming Possible

One dream common to talent management professionals and business management is the ability to accurately predict the need for talent, raising and lowering the head count in an optimal fashion, while simultaneously being able to maximize the productivity of all of those in place.

Succession management systems don't just track attributes for individual employees. Many already allow for analysis of talent readiness, including the identification of competency gaps, skill deficiencies, and leadership risks (especially where you can identify high retention risk and low readiness), by *organizational unit.*

In their next phase of evolution, these tools will provide the ability to conduct scenario planning for the workforce by automatically assessing the full impact of organizational changes throughout the organization. For example, if you plan to move a senior manager to an executive position, the system will be able to evaluate who will take his or her role from middle management and then who will take the middle manager's position.

As another example, if you make an acquisition and move people to manage the integration of the new business, the system could identify who can fill the gaps left in the existing organization and recommend development actions to help them to succeed. Organization charting, succession management, development planning, and analytical tools used in combination will provide the answers.

Workforce Analytics Is Becoming a Reality

The holy grail of talent management is workforce analytics. Imagine if you could quickly and accurately answer these questions:

- Who are the top employees in the organization? Why are they top employees?

- What is the correlation between competencies and performance? How can we accurately predict who will become a top performer when recruiting internally or externally? How can we develop someone into a top performer?

- Where are the weak links in the organization? Where do we need to reallocate resources? Should we build (develop) or buy (recruit)?

Truly integrated talent management systems are almost there. The more the systems are used, the more data that are capable of being mined become available.

Opportunities

So what does all this mean for you? When you consider implementing a talent management strategy, think big. The opportunity now exists to build an end-to-end talent management solution, from sourcing through promotion and retirement. Through the use of an integrated software solution, a company can now

1. Identify the talent required for an open position and then source candidates, internally and externally.
2. Assess potential candidates against the attributes necessary for success in the position, including competencies, skills, experience, and education. Or managers can compare candidates against the attributes of a top performer currently in that role.
3. Orient the employee to the position, irrespective of whether it is a new employee joining the organization or a current employee who is changing roles.
4. Connect the employee to others in similar positions, whether they are in the same office or geographically distributed.
5. Develop the employee against competency gaps for the particular position.

6. Set goals for the employee and ensure that his or her goals are aligned with the goals of his or her manager and business unit and the organization as a whole.

7. Periodically assess the employee against these goals and other measures of success for the organization. Rather than do reviews retrospectively, conduct periodic performance reviews that proactively identify and correct performance and/or competency gaps in relation to specific objectives.

8. Pay an employee based on his or her achievement of these objectives and calibrate against others in similar roles.

9. Develop employees throughout the year to ensure that they are best equipped to achieve their objectives. Provide tools for employees to get needed training, coaching, and/or performance support.

10. Empower employees to manage their own careers by clearly understanding traditional and nontraditional career paths, finding mentors for these paths, and understanding the development needed to become qualified for new positions.

Then, on an organizational level, you can:

1. Annually benchmark the potential and performance of team members to measure talent readiness and to ensure an appropriate level of bench strength is available, based on corporate growth plans and other considerations, such as historical employee retention rates and expected turnover.

2. Use succession planning to identify high-potential employees and put them into leadership development programs, tracking not only their progress but also their retention risk. Ensure that those ready for promotion are given ample opportunities for career mobility inside the organization before they seek employment elsewhere.

3. Ensure that compliance requirements are met and other types of regulatory training are completed in a timely manner, including ongoing certification and continuing education requirements.

4. Plan effectively for the future—understanding organizational strengths and weaknesses, comprehending the impact of develop-

ment programs and training expenditures, and learning when, how, and who to hire or promote.

These capabilities also extend beyond the enterprise. Resellers can be trained to perform as effectively as direct salespeople. Partners can be taken through self-paced certification programs. Volunteers can be identified and developed to fill the needs of nonprofits as they arise. Customers can be engaged to drive product innovation.

This is not a far-fetched dream. It is the state of the art for talent management today. When used effectively, it enables the creation of highly competitive, efficient, and productive organizations. It is not only how companies achieve unparalleled "execution." It is how they are "built to last."

Chapter 11

Talent Management at Work

Larry Israelite, Vice President of Human Resource Development, Liberty Mutual Group

What's in this chapter?

- The foundation for talent management success
- What works and what's been learned
- A way to begin managing talent

I set a relatively low bar when contemplating the primary goal for assembling this book: I wanted to provide some helpful information about the topic of talent management. "Helpful" was the key word in my goal, because I think a lot of information out there today isn't all that helpful. Specifically, I did not want to prescribe an approach, method, or process; nor did I want to make any promises about what results you might achieve if you implemented a talent management process or program in your organization. What I did hope to do was provide you with

- an overview of the subject
- some examples of talent management practices that have been

perceived as making meaningful contributions to the organizations in which they were used

◆ a point of view regarding how the changing nature of work and workers will influence how talent is managed in the future

◆ a description of the current state of talent management software.

I am reasonably confident that the information provided here can be helpful. I believe, or at least hope, that each chapter has made you aware of something you hadn't thought of before, confirmed something you already think or do, or, perhaps, simply given you an excuse and the time to reflect a little about how talent is (or isn't) managed in your organization and what you might do about it.

All of that said, I don't think it's enough. So in this chapter, I attempt to do two additional things. First, I identify what might be described as the "foundation of talent management process success." And second, I offer a structured way to get started—a series of steps you can complete if you want to begin to implement talent management practices in your organization. However, I first want to give you "Larry's Final Rule of Talent Management," which is that there are no rules or, perhaps, that each of you must make up your own rules. As a result, I want to be clear that any steps for getting started I might suggest are nothing more than one person's point of view. Your steps might be different (and better!), based on what you know about your organization, its culture, its leaders, and the people who work there.

The Foundation for Talent Management Success

One could argue that the six organizations whose approaches to talent management are described in this book are very different. They include high technology, consumer products, food service, insurance, and health care. One is quite large, three are of moderate size, and two are much smaller. But although we might agree that there are significant differences among these companies, it also is clear that there are important similarities when it comes to the reasons they have been successful with regard to talent management practices. It is these similarities that form the basis for the foundation of talent management success.

As you read each of the talent management case studies in chapters 3 through 8, you might have noticed that, in one way or another, most shared a common story. Specifically:

◆ The authors were able to describe, in reasonably concise terms, the outcome or outcomes they were trying to achieve or support through a structured talent management process.

◆ There was unequivocal executive support for the processes implemented in each organization.

◆ Each organization used a structured, multipart process for collecting, analyzing, and acting on talent data.

◆ Some form of measurement was in place to determine the degree to which the desired outcomes were being achieved.

In few cases were any of these exactly the same, but they were, at the very least, present. And though I would never claim that their presence guarantees success, I can say with some certainty that their absence will make it extremely difficult to succeed. So let's look at each of these four elements of the foundation for talent management success.

Clear Outcomes

As odd as it may seem, we sometimes tend to skip over the development of clear outcomes. This is true for much of what we do beyond talent management and it is, simply put, just plain dumb. I think, sometimes, that we fear commitment—perhaps this is a much larger issue than we have time to discuss here. By defining and communicating goals or outcomes, it means we that we are on the hook to achieve or deliver them. And that can be scary.

But if you think back to the goals of the talent management processes described earlier in the book, they gave purpose to the work. They were the stakes in the ground to which all processes were tethered, and they provided a yardstick against which all progress could be measured. And finally, although no one said this, they probably constituted the opening statement in any conversation about talent management, because if people believe in the outcomes, they are much more likely to listen to the rest of the story.

The importance of clear outcomes cannot be overstated, because they form the foundation on which everything else that follows is built. For example, it is difficult (an understatement) to enlist executive support without the existence of clear outcomes. Creating effective talent management practices and tools is challenging, to say the least, if they are not tied to specific outcomes. And, of course, it is almost impossible to measure something that one is unable to clearly describe. So if you don't have the time, interest, or, I suppose, the energy to get this right, save everyone a lot of effort and stop now. Simply put, you will not be successful if you have not identified and documented clear outcomes that the organization can get behind.

Executive Commitment

I have been lucky enough to work in organizations in which the support of talent management was a given. Others are not so lucky. When attempting to describe what executive commitment can look like, I have, in the past, used this hierarchy:

- ◆ *Level 0: no illusion of support*—The good thing about this one is you know where you stand, and while you might not like it, it can save you a whole lot of work.

- ◆ *Level 1: lip service*—In this scenario, executives express support but do little else. They provide no resources, no money, and perhaps more important than that, they do not provide themselves. The hard part about Level 1 support is that you often don't know what you have (or don't have) until *after* you have made commitments that require more than an executive is inclined to provide. And, as you well know, if executives aren't really in, it doesn't take long until everyone else figures that out and also chooses not to be in. (Another version of Level 1 is money, but little, or nothing, else. Although this may work for a little while, it doesn't take long for managers and employees to detect the lack of executive presence. And once that happens, you may as well not have money either.)

♦ *Level 2: support and presence*—Now we are making progress. In this case, executives express support (this can look a lot like lip service), but they also give you more. They may give you resources or allow you to redirect the work of existing resources. They will show up when you ask them to and say what you want them to say. To most employees, this may be all you need. But there is a downside, because the "leader watchers" will see the subtle signs of compliance—executives doing what they are asked—instead of evidence of commitment. And the latter is what you really want and need.

♦ *Level 3: deep commitment*—In this case, executives see the work as critical to their ability to achieve their own goals (or the organization's goals) and, therefore, their own success. They spontaneously talk about the topics you want them to support, and they make it clear that they expect the unequivocal support of the entire management team to do whatever is necessary to ensure success.

I am sure you recognize your own CEO or other senior executives with whom you work in the descriptions above. I also expect that the same executive might exhibit different characteristics based on the circumstances—the issue, the business climate, competing or conflicting issues, and so on. But irrespective of the circumstances, there will be a direct relationship between the level of executive support you receive for your talent management initiatives and the likelihood that they will succeed. And in each of the examples provided in the chapters, executives exhibited deep commitment to talent management.

Structured Processes

You have, I am sure, heard the phrase "To a man (or woman) with a hammer, everything looks like a nail." We typically say this when someone is trying to use a tool he or she knows to solve the wrong problem. The following statement, though not as elegant, is sometimes used in the same way: "To a designer, there is no problem that can't be solved with a clever design." When creating talent management processes, a designer is exactly what you need. Useful and meaningful talent management processes are not the result of random acts. Rather, they come about because of careful planning, design, and implementation based on the outcomes or goals you are trying to achieve, the context in which the processes will be deployed, and the people with whom they will be used. And though I might be a victim of my own rule, this sounds exactly like the start of any design.

In this particular design, there are several questions that must be considered, in light of the goals, context, and users:

- What talent decisions do you want to make?
- What data must be collected to make these decisions, and from whom do you want or need to collect the data?
- What methods will be used to effectively, efficiently, and, perhaps, confidentially collect this data?
- How will this data be collected, reduced, analyzed, and organized to inform the talent decisions identified in the first step?

Creating and implementing a talent management strategy is a process design problem, wrapped in a change management project, in the middle of a consulting engagement. It might be lots of things, but unplanned and haphazard it is not.

Measures and Metrics

Human resources (HR) initiatives often suffer from the perception that they are disconnected from the business because they add no visible, meaningful business value. Far too often, they seem like they are intended to achieve HR goals, not business goals. Talent management initiatives are no different, and, at the risk of being accused of overstating the case, they will fail if managers and executives do not believe that the results achieved are worth the work required to deliver them. And you can rest assured that doing this takes time and effort.

So, assuming you believe that measurement is important, the next question is, of course, What do you measure? Here are some suggestions:

- Measure the experience—expectations, clarity of instructions, ease of use, perceptions of quality, and the like. In this case, the goal is to collect what we might refer to as Level 1 evaluation data for training activities. Collecting this type of information is necessary, but it is certainly not sufficient.

- Measure the results—the outcomes you identified earlier. These can be short-term measures, focusing on whether or not you delivered what you expected to deliver. For example, if one of the things you created was an employee orientation program, you might measure the completion percentage. Or if you ran a succession planning process, you might be able to identify successors for each key position.

- Measure the impact—the material improvements in the quality of talent that can be directly or indirectly attributed to the talent management activities you implemented. We could be talking about something as simple to measure as an increase in the number of managers who are promoted from within (as opposed to being hired from the outside). However, we might look for increases in employee engagement scores or, even more complex, improved business results. Making direct links between talent management activities and these types of results can be challenging, but it is the Holy Grail we are all searching for, and it should always be the goal.

In this section, I have described the four key elements of the foundation for talent management success: clear outcomes, executive commitment, structured processes, and measurement. I cannot say definitively that a talent management initiative will fail if all are not present. But I can say with some confidence that the likelihood of success will be greatly diminished if you don't have all of them.

A Way to Proceed

So let's take stock of where we are. You have read some or all of the 10 chapters in this book about talent management. You have learned about how talent is managed at six companies, each different from the next. And in this chapter, you have been on the other end of a small lecture about the foundation you need to construct to be successful (again, in one person's opinion) if you try to improve your organization's talent management. So a reasonable question at this point is how to get started. Some ideas are provided below.

Before you start the next section, you should know that what you will read is not based on the big bang theory. Oddly, most, if not all, of the examples of effective talent management practices provided earlier in this book were associated with significant organizational initiatives (the big bang). In truth, it can be easier that way, because your work will then be part of a much larger effort that has institutional buy-in and support. In essence, someone else has already constructed the foundation you need to be successful. So if you do your work well, your ability to achieve your goals will increase significantly.

The message of the next section thus could be for you to simply search for a preexisting organizational initiative to which you can attach your work and go from there. And though this is a reasonable approach, it is important to realize that it represents nothing more than a good way to get started. A comprehensive approach to talent management comprises a broad range of processes and practices, which, in most cases, extends far beyond those that happen to support a set of goals that are linked to other work being done in the organization. I expect that each of the chapter authors could tell you other stories about talent management projects they have undertaken (some successful; some perhaps less so) without the advantage of being associated with a large organizational change project. So the real message here is to absolutely take advantage of the opportunities with which you are provided, but please also recognize the need to be able to do this on your own, which is what the steps outlined below are intended to help you do.

Choose a Place to Start

In chapter 1, I presented a simple definition of talent management: "the collection of things companies do that help employees do the best they can each and every day in support of their own and the company's goals and objectives." Choosing a place to begin involves two distinct steps:

1. Figuring out what might be included in this "collection of things."
2. Determining which of them has the greatest potential for helping employees do the best they can each and every day.

Here, the easy thing to do would be to try to land the big fish right away by going directly to succession planning or something equally complex. Though this might be the right answer, I would urge you not to make that decision for a little while. Improvements in recruiting, employee onboarding, development planning, and how you train managers can yield significant results.

You might want to consider these questions when selecting the talent management practices or processes you want to implement:

- What is currently being done in the organization that might fall under the banner of talent management?

- Is talent management viewed in the organization as something useful that helps to improve the quality of talent or, rather, as something that HR requires, but is of little value?

- Is there a well-known business issue or challenge that is the result of or influenced by the quality of talent in the organization?

- Can you identify any sponsors or advocates who would be supportive of new or improved talent management practices or processes?

Based on your answers to these questions and the various talent management practices you have heard or read about, choose a few things to do that seem to make sense.

Enlist Support

Another word for this step is socialization. Without investing an enormous amount of time in a detailed project plan, talk with your potential allies about what you are thinking. Be sure to focus on the business issue you identified in the previous step and how you could address it through improved talent management. Don't speak HR. I chose not to repeat this last sentence, but I considered it. Think back to the ASTD definition of talent management given in chapter 1—quite useful when talking with other HR professionals, but not so much when talking with almost anyone else. So use business language to describe what you are thinking about and what you might want to do.

The focus of your conversations should be on

- the issue you have identified

- the possible causes of this issue

- the potential contribution that better management of talent could play in addressing the issue

- the approach you want to take to improving talent management.

Please remember that you are just having a conversation; you are not selling. Your goals are to solicit input, determine interest, and, most important, create business allies.

There is one other somewhat contradictory issue to consider. If you work in a decentralized organization, your first stop might, in fact, be other HR professionals. Use the language you need to use to enlist their support. Remember that your success will be their success, so figure out, or ask them, how you can help them. After all, they may have direct accountability for talent management practices in the parts of the larger organization they support. They also may be the gatekeepers to others with whom you may want or need to talk. Finally, view your HR partners as collaborators. Talent management is a team sport, and the more people you have on your team, the better.

Get Started, but Start Small

If the meetings suggested above went well, you should have identified one or two things you could do that would have the support you need to be successful. But remember to think small, not big; simple, not complex;

easy, not hard; business, not HR. The goal here is success, and success can come in all shapes and sizes.

For the moment, let's go back to succession planning, which is a popular talent management practice that generates lots of discussion, because management bench strength continues to be a critical issue in most organizations. A comprehensive succession planning process might result in the identification of possible replacements for all key employees (or positions) in your enterprise (not just managers, because senior technical resources can be even harder to replace). In larger organizations, this can be a complex and time-consuming task. Doing the job well requires collecting a large amount of data from managers at all levels. These data must then be analyzed and prepared for presentation and discussion at a large number of meetings, potentially at many levels of the organization. You can imagine the amount of planning, process design, communication, and project management required to do this well—not to mention the number of resources it takes, even with supportive technology. I am in no way saying this isn't a worthwhile endeavor. But I am asking if it's necessary to do it all the first time out.

You might, for example, start in one organization or, perhaps, at one level in that organization. Rather than going all the way to succession planning, you might start much more simply, with a set of tools that enable robust, data-based discussions about the talent in that organization. Focus on making the process and the talent conversations go incredibly well, and make sure that they are perceived as incredibly helpful. Be happy with achieving a small victory, and use this as a basis for future expansion. The next time out, you can broaden the conversation in that organization and/or move on to another. I often use the phrase "do big things in small ways." It is appropriate here. You don't have to tackle every issue and solve all problems the first time out.

Learn from Your Mistakes

Implementing a talent management practice or process is a project. As such, you should use whatever project management methodology is expected in your organization. I have no interest in offering any advice on this subject, with one exception. Whenever you have finished the first iteration of whatever it is that you have chosen to do, conduct an after-action review or project postmortem. Talk with everyone who was involved to find out what went well, what didn't go well, and how you might improve the next time out. Listen carefully to what all of your stakeholders tell you, especially those who represent the business units you support. Above, I emphasized the importance of speaking with a voice that resonates with your business clients. You have to listen with ears that are sensitive to the same language. Think carefully about what you have heard, make adjustments and changes that make sense, and then start the process all over again.

Final Thoughts

Talent management isn't rocket science. It isn't some mysterious black art that requires special training, exotic spices, and secret chants. However, it is something that a lot of people appear to be interested in. A smaller number actually attempt to implement talent management practices and processes, which an even smaller number will do successfully. In this book, some of those who have been successful have told their stories.

ASTD (2009a) concludes its research study of talent management by saying,

> We see reason for optimism. Integrated talent management remains a relatively new phenomenon, and organizations seem to get better at it over time. New research, techniques, and technologies are emerging to improve the management of talent. Clearly, effective and integrated talent management is not easy to achieve. It is after all a complex system with many different parts. The sooner that organizations learn to set up and nurture these systems, however, the sooner they will be able to turn their organization's talent base into a genuine competitive advantage.

It's hard not to agree.

Appendix: The New Face of Talent Management

Note: The following is a slightly revised version of the Executive Summary of the ASTD white paper *The New Face of Talent Management: Making Sure that People Really Are Your Most Important Asset*, (2009b). To download a digital file of the complete paper, go to www.astd. org and type "talent management white paper" in the search box.

> For companies that are truly competitors in the knowledge economy, what was good enough performance yesterday is rarely good enough today—and will almost never be good enough tomorrow. For most organizations, the best way to meet this challenge is to become human-capital-centric, to focus on making talent their most important source of competitive advantage.
>
> —Edward E. Lawler III, author of *Talent: Making People Your Competitive Advantage*

As the knowledge economy has unfolded, the strategic management of talent for optimum performance has become indispensable for competitive advantage. But many current approaches to acquisition, retention, and development fail to produce the capability that organizations need to succeed today. And technology-based performance management systems can't compensate for a lack of a coordinated strategy.

A 1997 McKinsey Report, *The War for Talent*, alerted the business world to the importance of talent as a competitive advantage. More than 10 years later, there is still no common definition of talent management nor a leadership model for a comprehensive approach. Research by ASTD and the Institute for Corporate Productivity in 2008 revealed that only one in five organizations believes to a high degree that it manages talent effectively. To help address this situation, ASTD has created a definition of strategic talent management and identified some common components drawn from its research and the practices in leading companies. This definition and its corresponding model are given in figure A-1. ASTD plans regular updates to the definition and model as practices evolve.

Systemic Approach Required

The downfall of the energy giant Enron showed that it is not enough just to hire smart people. Their capabilities must be well understood by the organization and applied to specific performance goals with accountability for results. In a 2002 *New Yorker* article, "The Talent Myth," Malcolm Gladwell wrote: "If talent is defined as something separate from an employee's actual performance, what use is it, exactly? The broader failing . . . is the assumption that an organization's intelligence is simply a function of the intelligence of its employees."

In a Deloitte report *It's 2008: Do You Know Where Your Talent Is?*, analysts recommended a comprehensive approach to talent management. They noted that acquisition and retention strategies don't work without methods for engaging employees and continually developing the skill of those employees who drive the lion's share of a company's performance and generate higher-than-average value for customers and shareholders.

The Wharton School professor Peter Cappelli has also recommended changes in the approach to talent management. He notes that neither outside hiring nor internal development—the only ways companies "get" talent—are adequate on their own in uncertain business environments. Instead, he recommends adapting just-in-time supply-chain management practices because they address uncertainty and variability. He also recommends coordinating talent efforts across the organization to avoid duplication and to mitigate the effects of faulty predictions about talent requirements.

Figure A-1. Talent Management Defined

TALENT MANAGEMENT

is an organizational approach to leading people by building culture,
engagement, capability, and capacity through integrated talent acquisition,
development, and deployment processes that are aligned to business goals.

One company taking a comprehensive approach is Darden Restaurants, the parent company of such brands as Red Lobster, Olive Gar-
den, Longhorn Steakhouse, Bahama Breeze, Seasons 52, and the Capital
Grille. At Darden, a systemic framework addresses all facets of talent
management for the organization. This framework, which is based on
Darden's business strategy—to win financially and be a special place to
be—addresses culture, organization structure, objective alignment, and
leadership behaviors.

Success Factors

Analysis of the research by ASTD and the Institute for Corporate Productivity and input from the ASTD Talent Management Advisory Committee, made up of industry leaders in talent management, yielded these recommended factors for success:

- drive talent management from the top of the organization to ensure that it will have support from senior managers and not fall into silos
- ensure that talent management efforts support key organizational strategies
- align all components of talent management to support optimal performance
- manage talent with a long-range perspective but retain the ability to respond to changes
- manage talent actively and strategically, in good times and bad
- nurture talent-oriented corporate cultures
- use talent management metrics
- within the organization, cultivate the skills needed to manage talent effectively.

Leading Talent Management

Two powerful lessons of the economic downturn of 2009 are how important it is for organizations to anticipate change and yet how critical it is to have the right people in the right jobs at the right time. The economic crisis made it a practical necessity to operate as if people—human capital—are every organization's most important asset.

Susan Burnett, formerly a talent management executive with Deloitte and now with Yahoo, notes that "it is critical that as executive leaders are engaged in a strategy dialogue about the [firm's future], that they also consider what kind of capabilities the business will need to execute those strategies successfully. This essential input to the talent management process forms the basis of effective workplace plans, strategic development priorities, and succession strategies that build the leadership pipeline. Without this perspective, talent management will not be connected to, and enable, business growth and success."

Edward Lawler, of the University of Southern California's Marshall School of Business, asserts that organizations must be more human-capital-centric. He goes so far as to say that "business strategy should be determined by talent considerations and it in turn should drive human capital management practices."

Thus, an organization's expert resource on talent development should play a key role in strategy, organization design, and change, and have accountability for employees' effectiveness. Talent management leaders must be able not only to define and build capability but also employ business knowledge, communication skills, teamwork, and knowledge of learning technology to make talent management successful and effective across an organization.

Every company organizes talent management in the way that best suits its priorities, but many put a single person in charge of leading and coordinating the effort to help ensure a seamless approach. By integrating the talent management functions under one leader, companies are better able to overcome the vertical silo structures that have slowed progress in the past.

In a growing number of progressive organizations, leading talent management is the responsibility of the company's learning function and the top talent officer. Learning professionals with broad responsibilities often have expertise and experience with many of the levers of talent management. They are key players and leaders in companies that recognize that managing talent throughout the employment life cycle should be a centrally directed function that links workforce capability to specific strategic goals.

Action Plan for Leading Talent Management

Most talent management still focuses primarily on succession planning and executive development. Many contributing processes take place in silos throughout the organization and do not add up to a strategic approach. Many organizations do not know what capabilities they need to be successful or which ones exist in their workforces. And no single leader is responsible for enterprise-wide talent management. In short, talent management is not maximized because it is piecemeal, uncoordinated, and often directed at the wrong employees.

Managing talent successfully calls for a high level of integration of all the functions and processes that contribute to putting the right people in the right jobs at the right time. ASTD has created an action plan for a comprehensive approach to talent management:

1. Understand the organization's key strategies and key metrics.
2. Determine and prioritize the human capabilities needed to support key strategies and key metrics.
3. Define talent management throughout the life cycle of employees, from recruitment to retirement, and identify the key processes that constitute talent management for your organization.
4. Create an integrated model for managing talent across the whole organization. Align all the relevant systems and processes.
5. Enlist key stakeholders in implementing an action plan.
6. Measure results and communicate their impact.

This white paper was written under the auspices of the members of ASTD's Talent Management Advisory Committee:

Susan Burnett, senior vice president of talent and organization development, Yahoo!

Jim Caprara, vice president, global human resources development, Ciena; chair, ASTD Board of Directors, 2009

Mike Hansen, consultant

Jeanette Harrison, chair, vice president, CSBS Operations Planning, American Express

Rob Lauber, vice president, global training, Yum Brands

Edward E. Lawler III, director of the Center for Effective Organizations and professor, Marshall School of Business, University of Southern California

Daisy Ng, senior vice president for human resources, Darden Restaurants

Kevin Oakes, CEO, Institute for Corporate Productivity, Institute for Corporate Productivity

Deborah Wheelock, leader, Global Talent Management Center of Expertise, Mercer LLC

About the Contributors

Josh Bersin is president and CEO of Bersin & Associates, founded in 2001. During the last decade, he has worked with hundreds of companies to help them deliver high-impact employee learning, leadership development, and talent management. He has been quoted on the topic of enterprise learning and talent management in the *Wall Street Journal* and on National Public Radio and is a regular columnist for *Chief Learning Officer* magazine. In addition, he is often quoted and the firm's research is cited in *HR Executive, Workforce Management, Talent Management, Training* magazine, and many other industry publications. He is a frequent speaker at events including the annual ASTD International Conference & Expo and *HR Executive*'s HR Technology Conference & Expo. He is also the author of *The Training Measurement Book: Best Practices, Proven Methodologies, and Practical Approaches* (Pfeiffer, 2008) and *The Blended Learning Book: Best Practices, Proven Methodologies, and Lessons Learned* (Wylie/Pfeiffer, 2004). Earlier in his career, he spent 25 years in product development, product management, and the marketing and sales of e-learning and other enterprise technologies at companies including DigitalThink (now Convergys), Arista Knowledge Systems, Sybase, and IBM.

Jim Caprara is vice president of global human resources development for Ciena. He is charged with the enterprise-wide company strategy and implementation of human capital investment for both employees and customers worldwide. Before joining Ciena, he was chief learning officer for NVR, vice president of human resources development at Nextel Communications, and held director-level positions at Sears. He serves as chairman of ASTD's Board of Directors. He has spoken at Georgetown University, the Johns Hopkins University School of Business, the Robert H. Smith School of Business at the University of Maryland, the 2005 Learning Analytics Symposium, and ASTD International conferences.

Marc Effron is vice president, talent management, at Avon Products. His earlier experience includes starting and leading the global leadership consulting practice at Hewitt Associates, where he created the Top Companies for Leaders study. He was also senior vice president, leadership development, at Bank of America; director of organization effectiveness and learning at Oxford Health Plans; and a compensation consultant for a global consulting firm. He previously served as a political consultant and a congressional staff assistant. He is the author of *One Page Talent Management* (Harvard Business Press, forthcoming); coauthor of *Leading the Way* (with Robert P. Gandossy; John Wiley and Sons, 2003); coeditor of *Human Resources in the 21st Century* (with Robert P. Gandossy and Marshall Goldsmith; John Wiley and Sons, 2003); and has written chapters in eight management and leadership books. He received a BA in political science from the University of Washington and an MBA from the Yale School of Management. In 2007, he founded the New Talent Management Network (www.newtmn.com), a nonprofit networking and research organization that has grown to more than 1,000 talent management professionals.

Larry Israelite is the vice president of human resource development at Liberty Mutual Group, with responsibility for supporting the development of managers capable of functioning effectively in a changing, competitive environment and employees capable of sustaining a high level of performance. His other areas of responsibility include the development and management of processes and tools that support companywide human resources practices, management and professional development, training product design, and learning technology research and development. Before joining Liberty Mutual, he held learning management positions at Pitney Bowes, the Forum Corporation, John Hancock Financial Services, Oxford Health Plans, and the Digital Equipment Corporation. He has worked in all instructional media but has always focused on how technology can be used to enhance the effectiveness, efficiency, and impact of learning. He is the editor of *Lies about Learning* (ASTD Press, 2006), and he contributed chapters to *2009 eLearning Annual* (edited by Michael Allen; Pfeiffer, 2009); *Learning Rants, Raves, and Reflections: A Collection of Passionate and Professional Perspectives* (edited by Elliot Masie; Pfeiffer, 2005); and *The AMA Handbook of ELearning Effective Design, Implementation, and Technology Solutions* (AMACOM, 2003). He received a bachelor's degree from Washington College and an MA in instructional media and PhD in educational technology from Arizona State University.

Robert Kovach is the director of the Center for Collaborative Leadership at Cisco, where he also serves as the talent officer for European and emerging markets. He is internationally recognized for helping companies achieve their growth objectives by developing leadership talent. Before joining Cisco, he was managing director of the London office of RHR International; director of human resources for Central and Eastern Europe and Russia for PepsiAmericas, based in Warsaw; and a director of the Executive MBA Program and a member of the executive education faculty for both Ashridge Business School in England and the Central European University in Budapest. He started his career in human resources planning with Ameritech. He has provided expert commentary for many publications, including the *Financial Times* and *The Times* of London, and has written numerous articles and book chapters. He received his PhD in industrial and organizational psychology from Wayne State University.

Neal Kulick served as vice president, global talent management, at McDonald's, with responsibility for executive assessment, executive development, executive placement and movement, executive recruitment, and succession management and planning. He retired from McDonald's in July 2009 and is currently working on non-profit initiatives for which he has a strong interest and passion. Before joining McDonald's, he ran his own organizational consulting practice specializing in human resource effectiveness and leadership development. Before consulting, he spent more than 25 years at Ameritech Corporation, where, as vice president for corporate human resources, he helped lead the company's cultural transformation by developing the leadership talent needed to effectively manage in an environment of rapid change. He also spent seven years as a line operations manager at Michigan Bell Telephone Company. He received a BA in psychology from the University of Michigan and an MA and PhD in industrial and organizational psychology from Wayne State University. He teaches the course "Leadership and Organizational Change for the MBA" at the University of Windsor.

Adam Miller is founder, president, and CEO of Cornerstone OnDemand, which has achieved a leadership position in the fields of on-demand talent management and online education. Before founding OnDemand, he was an investment banker, with a focus on media and technology banking, with both Schroders (now part of Citigroup) and an international affiliate of Montgomery Securities (now part of Bank of America). Before that, he was a small business consultant with the Card Group and a small business owner. He holds a JD from the School of Law at the University of California, Los Angeles; an MBA from the Anderson School of Management at the University of California, Los Angeles; a BS in systems analysis from the Wharton School at the University of Pennsylvania; and a BA in European history from the University of Pennsylvania. He is the coauthor of *Business Capital for Women: An Essential Handbook for Entrepreneurs* (with Emily Card; Macmillan, 1996) and *Managing Your Inheritance: Getting It, Keeping It, Growing It—Making the Most of Any Size Inheritance* (with Emily Card; Random House, 1996).

Larry Mohl is vice president and chief learning officer at Children's Healthcare of Atlanta, where he is responsible for an integrated set of talent levers, including leadership and organization effectiveness, talent planning, and performance management. At Children's Healthcare, he is also responsible for clinical staff development, physicians' continuing education, and technology training, and he leads the development of human resources technology infrastructure. Before joining Children's Healthcare, he served as vice president and chief learning officer for American

Express. Earlier, he held senior positions in learning and organization development as well as in business operations at Motorola. He serves as vice president of programs for the Atlanta Human Resources Leadership Forum and as an adviser to the Human Capital Institute. He received an MS in electrical engineering from the University of Michigan and a BS in electrical engineering from the State University of New York at Buffalo. He holds three international patents in the field of telecommunications technology. He has been quoted in various publications, including *Training* magazine and *CIO* magazine. The story of the development of the Children's Healthcare Center for Leadership has been told in *Courageous Training*, by Robert Brinkerhoff and Tim Mooney (Berrett-Koehler, 2008).

Annmarie Neal is vice president of talent at Cisco, where she leads the Center for Collaborative Leadership, which provides succession management, executive assessment, and development and organization development for the firm's executives. Before joining Cisco, she served as the senior vice president, Global Talent Office, with First Data Corporation. Earlier, she served as a senior executive consultant for RHR International. She has provided expert commentary for many publications, including the *Wall Street Journal*, and has written numerous articles and book chapters. She also serves on the Advisory Board of the University of Colorado, Denver. She received her PsyD in clinical psychology from the California School of Professional Psychology. She serves as the co-chair of the Conference Board's Council for Talent Management Executives.

Nigel Paine, the managing director of nigelpaine.com, is a coach, mentor, writer, broadcaster, and keynote speaker of international acclaim. He is currently working in Europe, Brazil, the United States, and Australia on a variety of assignments that hinge on making work more creative, innovative, and aspirational, and making workplaces more conversational, team based, and knowledge sharing. His consultancy focuses on the use of learning technologies, organization development, leadership, innovation, creativity, and excellence, with a spotlight on maximizing human potential and performance in the workplace. Previously, he was head of people development at the BBC, where he built the training and development operation into one of the most successful learning and development operations in Britain—including an award-winning leadership program, state-of-the-art informal learning and knowledge sharing, and a highly successful intranet. He has published articles and white papers on diverse subjects, including "Creativity in the Workplace," "Building Corporate Heroes," and "Why Talent Walks Out of the Door." He was until recently a board member of Ealing Hammersmith and West London College, London's largest further education and higher education college. In 2006 and 2007, he was the part-time chief executive of the Broadcast Training & Skills Regulator, where he introduced media-sector training awards and produced a definitive state-of-training report for the industry. He has been a visiting professor at Napier University since 1998. He is a fellow of the Chartered Institute of Personnel Development and of the Royal Society of Arts.

References

ASTD (American Society for Training & Development). 2009a. *Talent Management Practices and Opportunities*. Alexandria, VA: ASTD. http:// www.i4cp.com/contact/download/media/talent-management-survey-findings/contact_download.

———. 2009b. *The New Face of Talent Management: Making Sure Your Employees Really Are Your Most Important Asset*. ASTD whitepaper. http:// www.astd.org/NR/rdonlyres/AC467C24=98B2=4613=8A95=10 86C7E3044D/0/010917TalentMgmtWP5.pdf.

Bersin, Josh. 2007a. *High-Impact Talent Management: Trends, Best Practices and Industry Solutions*. Oakland: Bersin & Associates.

———. 2007b. *The Role of Competencies in Driving Financial Performance*. Oakland: Bersin & Associates.

Blanchard, Ken, and Sheldon Bowles. 1993. *Raving Fans: A Revolutionary Approach to Customer Service*. New York: William Morrow.

Bossidy, Larry, and Ram Charan. 2002. *Execution: The Discipline of Getting Things Done*. New York: Random House.

Brinkerhoff, Robert O. 2003. *The Success Case Method: Find Out Quickly What's Working and What's Not*. San Francisco: Berrett-Koehler.

Cameron, Kim S., and Robert E. Quinn. 2005. *Diagnosing and Changing Organizational Culture: Based on the Competing Values Framework*. San Francisco: Jossey-Bass.

Easterby-Smith, Mark, Luís Aráujo, and John G. Burgoyne. 1999. *Organizational Learning and the Learning Organization: Developments in Theory and Practice*. London: Sage.

The Economist. 2006. A Survey of Talent. October 7.

Effron, Marc, Shelli Greenslade, and Michelle Salob. 2005. Growing Great Leaders: Does It Really Matter? *Human Resource Planning Journal* 28, no. 3 (September): 18–23.

Goldsmith, Marshall. 2006. Try Feedforward Instead of Feedback. In *Coaching for Leadership,* ed. M. Goldsmith and L. Lyons. San Francisco: Pfeiffer.

Hamel, Gary, and Bill Breen. 2007. *The Future of Management.* Boston: Harvard Business Press.

Hammonds, Keith H. 2007. Why We Hate HR. *Fast Company,* December 19. http://www.fastcompany.com/magazine/97/open_hr.html.

Hunter, J. E., F. L. Schmidt, and M. K. Judiesch. 1990. Individual Differences in Output Variability as a Function of Job Complexity. *Journal of Applied Psychology* 75, no. 1: 28–42.

Jones, C. 1986. *Programming Productivity.* New York: McGraw-Hill.

Lamoureux, Kim. 2009. *High-Impact Succession Management: Best Practices, Models, and Case Studies in Organizational Talent Mobility.* Oakland: Bersin & Associates.

Leitch, Lord Sandy. 2006. *UK Skills: Prosperity for All in the Global Economy— World Class Skills.* London: Her Majesty's Treasury. http://www.hm-treasury.gov.uk/d/leitch_finalreport051206.pdf.

Levensaler, Leighanne. 2008a. *The Essential Guide to Performance Management Practices, Part 1.* Oakland: Bersin & Associates.

———. 2008b. *The Essential Guide to Performance Management Practices, Part 2.* Oakland: Bersin & Associates.

———. 2008c. *Talent Management Suites: Market Realities, Implementation Experiences and Vendor Profiles.* Oakland: Bersin & Associates.

Momentum Executive Development. 2007. *Talent and Leadership Practices 2007.* Reading, U.K.: Business Momentum Ltd. http://www.businessmomentum.com/TalentandLeadership/69/DownloadtheMomentum.html.

O'Leonard, Karen. 2008. *2008 Talent Management Factbook: Global Trends, Facts and Strategies in Corporate Talent Management.* Oakland: Bersin & Associates.

Schein, Edgar H. 2004. *Organizational Culture and Leadership*. San Francisco: Jossey-Bass.

Stern, Stefan. 2007. Why Managers Need to Engage with Grumpy Employees. *Financial Times*. May 14.

Yates, Richard. 1961. *Revolutionary Road*. New York: Atlantic–Little, Brown.

Index

Note: *f* represents a figure and *t* represents a table